This is Bullshit, Not a Love Story

Nicole Kranz

Published by Norak Edition, 2025.

THIS IS BULLSHIT, NOT A LOVE STORY

First edition. March 21, 2025.

Copyright © 2025 Nicole Kranz.

ISBN: 979-8992581515

Written by Nicole Kranz.

Table of Contents

El Paseo:
Parade Into the Arena

The matador prepares in his dressing room...

He faces the mirror for one final check. Places his black hat carefully on his head, gives his vest a tug. Not a single wrinkle. The master of the arena is tall, thin and perfectly arranged. His body is snugly confined in the pink silk of his Suit of Lights. His slippers give him the flexibility of a ballet dancer and the arrogance of a boxer. Watching himself in the mirror, he erases his fear with a single movement of his hand. Watching himself in the mirror, he is surprised one last time by the blue of his eyes. He blinks, takes a deep breath. He holds his head tipped to the sky, chin out. He will enter his stage with confidence. Nothing will stop him, not the danger, not the regret. Has he ever felt so strong?

He knows the bulls he will fight. They are part of his family. He watched them grow like they were his own children. Until the day the beast is mature, until the day the animal is ready to be killed.

The matador enters first. As the trumpet sounds, he steps into the arena, the crowd applauds him, the crowd blesses him, the crowd adores him. Followed by a national hymn to the glory of the sacrificing priest and a prayer before the duel.

Next comes the bull – the bull-pen gates open for him, but this is not for chivalry. This is a gateway to the bull's imminent death. Head down, he enters the arena. With one swing of the cape, the matador judges his quality.

One May weekend, Cedric took me to see a bullfight in Torrelaguna, an out-of-the-way village about 20 minutes from Madrid. The medieval houses were rundown, neglected, and the earth was dry and desert-like. There was a sense of barrenness. It was easy to imagine this small town had lost all hope of becoming fertile again.

A bar was set back on one side of the square, in the shadow of the empty church. The front of the bar was covered in layers of weatherworn posters soaked by the winter rains and puckered dry by the summer heat. There were a few new ones, too, inviting the townspeople to the *corrida*.

The bullfighting arena stood on the outskirts of the village. Its bleachers wobbled on their worn-out scaffolding. This one couldn't compete against the arenas we'd seen in Madrid, but it was swept clean and freshly-painted – clearly the inhabitants of Torrelaguna were proud of it.

Cedric and I were on a romantic getaway in Spain. He had surprised me with the trip, saying we needed a break from Geneva, where we lived. We hadn't known each other for very long, and we both thought travelling together was a sure way to deepen our relationship. I liked Madrid. It was stylish, as a European capital should be, and when we arrived, we strolled through its old streets, enjoying the fresh green of spring and warm sunshine. The Spanish way of life with its slower rhythm was good for Cedric and me. On the second evening, we sat out on a restaurant terrace and I watched his face brighten in the setting sun, noticing how his breathing was calmer and his gaze softer.

"I want to take you to see a bullfight," he announced that evening. "Not in Madrid. I found one that's going to be held tomorrow out in the country, so I rented a car. You'll see, you'll love it."

I nodded, even though I never had any desire to see a bullfight. I respect traditions, but I didn't want to witness the massacre of some poor animals. I didn't dare tell him that, though. Things had been tense between us, probably because we were still getting used to living together, and I didn't want to make a ripple in our delicate peace.

Once he told me his plan, he couldn't talk about anything else. His eyes lost their sweetness, their candor. I didn't understand what was going on in his mind, but it was clear he wanted to experience a traditional corrida, the kind of event that celebrated the winner and served up the loser's testicles for the crowd to eat later.

"Can't you just imagine how cool that is? We get to eat the bull's nuts! His *cojones*!"

What a vulgar way to look at an ancient tradition, but I laughed along with him. His loud voice and exuberance were infectious. And anyway, he didn't give me a choice. I told myself it wasn't a big deal, that sometimes men are like little boys, and you just have to go along with them. I'd seen this with my own parents, how my mother never pushed back against my father. She always conceded, she always put aside her own self, her own wants and needs, and she did it with a smile. That was an era when most women filled a different role: the good spouse, the mother, and then the woman.

Cedric talked about the bullfight all the way back to the hotel, until I'd had more than enough of the subject. Before going up to our room, he reminded the concierge that he needed the rental car ready at 8 a.m.

"You get it? We don't want to miss the parade of the four bulls through the village. It's tradition! We can't miss any of it."

I rolled my eyes, but I didn't want to push it. I would have enjoyed making love that night, but he turned out the lights and turned his back to sleep. He wanted to save his energy for the next day. The alarm catapulted me out of bed at 7 a.m. Cedric was grinning, as excited as a child. He raced through his shower, then debated over which shirt to wear. I suggested his dark blue pinstripe – I knew people dressed up for the bullfight in Spain. He got ready, grabbed his wallet and the room key, then went out without even turning around.

"Hurry up, I'm going to get breakfast. I'll wait for you downstairs, but I'm leaving at exactly 8 a.m., with or without you."

He was barely seated behind the wheel of the rental car when he started getting annoyed. It took him several tries to get the car into reverse, and he complained that with his Avis loyalty card, he deserved a better class of car. But once we made it to the highway, he transformed back into the elegant man promising me a good time. He was calm again. He took my hand and placed it on his thigh, covered it with his own hand, and cupped it tightly, almost too tightly.

"I love you so much, sweetheart. I'm so lucky. Life is perfect, isn't it?"

He made sure to mention he knew how much I'd given up for him, my career and my life and New York, how much I missed. He agreed it wasn't easy for me living in Switzerland. "But you'll see, everything's going to be fine. I'm going to make you happy. I promise. And I'm sure you're going to love this bullfight. Besides, I'm doing this for you, too, as you're always so curious about things. You can write a fantastic article about it. Maybe for a Geneva paper?"

He let go of my hand and crossed his fingers. "I'm 'like this' with the editor of *News Mag*. I'll talk to him."

He winked at me, and we continued along the road to Torrelaguna. To the bullfight. A timeless tradition, and because of that, no condemnation of it was allowed. Cedric didn't want to miss anything. The fiesta had begun the night before, but we would be in time for the running of the four bulls into the arena. We parked just outside the village, then headed for the arena. As we approached, more and more people lined the roadside, hurrying and jostling for space, as excited as Cedric.

"Come on, come on, it's starting! We need a good place to see the bulls, right where they let them out!"

We found a spot, where I stood pressed up against a wall, clinging to him and observing the feverish crowd. Shouting and laughter echoed along the stone walls of the housefronts. It was 10 a.m. I heard hoofs beating against wood, then thudding on the ground, and suddenly the first bull leapt out of a gate ahead of us. It ran straight for me, a mass of muscles that raced like a lightning bolt. I hid myself in Cedric's arms. I was terrified, and yet I admired its spirit. What impressive size and power!

"Just imagine the strength of that brute!" Cedric shouted. "What if he's the one that's killed? And then we get to chomp its balls! I can't wait to see what they taste like."

I gazed at him, perplexed. I hadn't thought about the animal's death, or whether Cedric might make me stuff those garlic-sautéed gonads into my mouth. "No, no, Cedric." I wanted to accept this as an ancestral tradition, not simply a display of virility. His behavior felt improper, and it disturbed me for a second, but then he grabbed my hand and pulled me into the street, where he craned his neck to see what was going on, then we started trotting along with the younger people in the crowd. We just managed to see the bulls thunder into the arena and a pair of massive gates swing shut behind them.

The corrida wouldn't begin for several hours, so we decided to tour the Spanish countryside. As we drove, I sensed an air of melancholy in the region. The heat is humbling, and the land is imbued with a special kind of sadness, its joys more restrained, not like the feeling of *dolce vita* that characterizes Italy. It was difficult to be dazzled here in Spain, and as I couldn't enthuse over this landscape, so I kept silent.

Cedric, on the other hand, had a lot to say. "God, the Spanish countryside is so shitty. It's poor, it's ugly. There's nothing interesting to see. I'm glad we're staying in Madrid. I've never really liked Spain and I'm crappy at Spanish, so the culture is lost on me. But what matters is that we're together, right?"

He smiled and said, "Love you, sweetie... You're such a hottie."

He paused, then winked at me. "But maybe you could've worn something other than those jeans. I mean, it's true, right? Don't be mad. They don't flatter your amazing ass. You brought the Cavalli's I gave you, right?"

I knew I should've worn the Cavalli jeans. "Yes, I brought them. But these are my good luck jeans. My hippie flair! I love these jeans. I'll never stop wearing them."

He glanced at me, an eyebrow raised, his mouth set.

We returned to the village shortly before the corrida began. It felt like a small-town fiesta and also like a funeral. The smell of cotton candy turned my stomach and my apprehension of the looming spectacle of the bullfight made me smell something else beneath that artificial sweetness. A whiff of blood, of death. I wasn't looking forward to watching a bull being killed. I'd never witnessed an organized murder. Sure, I've seen cats smashed on the side of the road, little birds fallen from the nest, a spider drowned at the bottom of a bucket, but an organized murder, never.

Cedric pulled me from one *tapas* stand to another, complaining about the flies on our food, making fun of how people looked, far too common for his taste. I was vaguely aware that I was still getting to know him. After all, this was only our first weekend alone together since I moved to Switzerland to live with him. I was trying to adapt to his life as quickly as possible. I was in love, right? Didn't love mean leaving everything behind for a man? That's what my mother had done. And now it was my turn to make the leap.

"Shit! It's already 4:30. Hurry up or we'll miss the first bull!"

I jogged along beside him. He wasn't looking at me anymore, he let go of my hand, and didn't try to take it again. The arena was bursting with people. I felt the crowd's impatience, its eagerness to be close to the death match. Human perversion. I've heard that people quickly get used to the sight of blood, to the spectacle of a dead body.

"Come on, hurry up. They're getting everything ready for the slaughter!"

He was grinning. We found seats as it began. I tried to pay close attention. The parade into the arena, with the matadors, the mounted *picadors* and the *banderillos* with their equipment was polished and colorful, but a few minutes after the bullfight began in earnest, I had to turn my head away, using the people around me as a screen. I wasn't ready for this and didn't want to see any of it. I didn't want to understand it, either, but Cedric kept explaining every detail as it was happening – how the picadors shot home their lances, how the banderillos thrust their barbs and how the matador swirled his *muleta*, his bright cape. He had researched it enough to know the bullfight by heart. He seemed to relish the bloodshed.

"Look, Chloe!" he said, tugging my arm. "It's almost over, and you're missing it all. The matador looks ashamed because he messed up stabbing the bull. But he's young, it's fine. There, his assistants will finish the work."

I peeked with one eye. I saw the bull, still on its legs but weak and wavering, covered in his own blood, slowly dying. Two men slashed at him with knives, trying to kill him, hoping the next cut would be fatal. The bull fell to his knees, sank back on his right flank. He offered his last breath into the silence, then the crowd cheered. What horror. It was surreal. Hundreds of people were clapping but because the matador hadn't performed well, there were no shouts of "Olé!" According to tradition, though, he bowed to the crowd, then walked a lap around the arena, holding his head high and taking care not to trip over his fallen victim.

I couldn't cheer, which seemed to annoy Cedric. I could hardly move, and my eyes were glued to the grisly scene. To get ready for the next condemned animal, two magnificent horses drawing a sort of chariot entered the arena, and some men hooked up the bull's corpse. They dragged it out. Cedric told me they would bring it to a yard where the crowd could gaze upon it before it was brought to the butcher.

The large wooden doors closed, and several men took to their brooms to sweep the arena's ochre dirt floor smooth before the next fight. I would have to watch three more bulls die.

The audience began to discuss the first bullfight among themselves. They criticized the matador's false steps, his false moves at the wrong moments. His lack of perfection. But they were willing to forgive him because he was only 20. I felt like I was at a soccer game halftime and the supporters were grumbling at their own team, wondering how it would end.

"Well, since you didn't see anything, I can't explain to you what the matador should have done to kill the bull in one go. He doesn't want to make the bull suffer, you know. The winner is the man with the most direct sword thrust. One stab in just the right spot and bam! I hope you'll be able to see that in the next fight."

He caressed my hand, then turned my face to him so he could look me in the eyes. "So, do you like it? I'm so happy we could share this. I've wanted to do this for so long, and it feels perfect with you beside me. Now this time, watch carefully from beginning to end. It's just like a ballet."

Speaking of ballet, my mind was spinning and leaping. What was good? What was bad? I wasn't mad at him for bringing me to this barbaric event. At least I could say I went to a bullfight once in my life. I loved him, and that's the only thing that mattered to me.

I was 31 years old when we met, and I was a real New Yorker, a workaholic with a peaking career. But I knew I still had a long way to go to be fully happy. Cedric arrived at the right time. I'd been working too hard and felt like I needed a break. A clock was ticking inside me, too. Shouldn't I settle down and have a family? Isn't that what society sets us women up for? He seemed like a nice man who would offer me stability. Maybe I could become a mother, enjoy a comfortable life, the kind that many women hope for, even in these modern times. I didn't really think about what I was giving up. My freedom and maybe myself in the long run.

I left New York City only a few months after meeting him to live together in Geneva. He told me he would take care of me, that I wouldn't need to work, that I would have time to decide what I wanted to do in life. He convinced me this would make me happy.

I always loved working, and in my ten years as a travel writer, I'd been able to see the world. But I felt like I'd achieved my professional goals, and now it was time for me to build my personal life, and finally understand what it means to be a man's wife.

This vacation to Madrid helped me settle into my decision, and going back to Switzerland would be easier. Watching him leave every morning to go to the office would not leave me feeling empty and abandoned – don't all stay-at-home wives live like this? And I loved him, even if I was a bit outraged at his determined desire to witness a bullfight.

The crowd got impatient, growling and mumbling as they waited for the big gates to open again and let the second bull rush into the arena. The bullfighters were taking their sweet time, but suddenly the gate opened, the bull appeared and took a leap into the arena, then stopped short. Confused, he looked around him and saw only humans, everywhere. He took off, head lowered, and ran straight into the wooden barrier, which shuddered. He was far from me, yet I could hear his chuffing breath. The entire arena watched him, admiring his shining black coat, white horns and red nostrils. But then our attention snapped to another gate. The matador had strutted onto the scene, so beautiful and graceful in his suit, with his cape folded over his left arm. The crowd applauded. With one gesture, the president of the corrida signaled that the duel could begin.

I was struck by the studied gaze of the matador when faced with an animal moving by instinct, with lightning-fast reflexes. He never turned his back on the beast. Neither of them dropped their eyes from each other. A game of love and hate. A man dressed in such finery, ready to manipulate and win, looking for the animal's every weakness and tricking him into thinking it was the cape that wanted to harm him. Each of his movements was dramatic, exaggerated. Which of them was fighting for his life in the arena? The matador or the bull?

The bull's nostrils flared, and he pawed the ground with his hooves, angered by the cape, irritated by the man. I wanted to yell to the bull that the cape was nothing but a lure, that he should understand this. But it was too late, the bewitched bull wouldn't get out alive from that goddamn bright red cloth. I was transfixed, too, as I watched the two protagonists. The matador led the dance, his partner the bull just followed the steps. And this was only the prologue, a sweet song to get to know one another.

I knew now that bullfighting has its codes, and they are faithfully respected. After a few minutes, the matador disappeared, and the gates opened for two noble horsemen dressed in glossy embroidered suits and protective leggings. Their horses wore armored coverings to protect their flanks from the bull's horns. The first spears would be thrown by these men while the matador, king of the arena, waited behind one of the protective walls. The beast must be coaxed to create a more beautiful, more memorable dance. The matador's hands never get dirty.

The bull raced for one of the horses, his head lowered. He tried to gore it in the belly, but the picador's shield came between them. The barbed tip of his spear fell, and the first spray of blood wet the sand. The bull could do nothing but shake his shoulders and wait for his torturer to remove the lance from his shoulder.

Cedric was clapping along with everyone else. He nudged me with his elbow to do likewise. I brought my hands together so softly they didn't make a sound. I was filled with horror and my body trembled at the realization this man beside me was a stranger. It wasn't that he was aggressive with me, quite the opposite. He gave me so much attention, I felt spoiled. But now I was beginning to see who this man was, down deep.

My old friend David had introduced me to Cedric five months earlier, when I was on a business trip to Geneva. I'd stayed a few days extra to visit my parents, who lived in the suburbs. I still had some friends there, too. Visiting was fine, as I knew I was only passing through. My home was in New York City, a city I swore I'd never leave. Never say never.

I grew up in Geneva, but never felt particularly Swiss. Born Brazilian, with a multi-language and multi-cultural upbringing, I was lost as to my identity that way, plus I left Switzerland when I was 17 to go live in a Kibbutz. My mother's idea, to send me where I might feel I belonged. Since then, Judaism has become important for me as a way to discover my roots. I never felt I could breathe properly in Switzerland. It was too small. I was too much for that country and the close-minded mentality that reigned, so I decided I needed to see the world. Rootless as I was, I needed to explore the world and find my place where I could be myself and feel free. Totally free.

I'd remained friends with David, though, and always tried to meet when I was in Geneva. We had dinner together that night and caught up on our personal lives. He was married to a sweet girl he met in college. They seemed to have been made for marriage, for children, for a big house and the whole shebang, including headaches with in-laws and a dog to keep things fun. He seemed happy as he sat there trying to sell me his lifestyle. There was nothing better or more satisfying than living with your beloved spouse, experiencing the ups and downs of life together, for better or for worse. In his case, it all sounded "for better," I thought wistfully.

"And what about you, Chloe?" he finally asked. "Tell me about your exciting New York life. Have you met your Wall Street man yet? It's about time, isn't it?"

"Not yet, but I didn't spend so long in therapy to end up with the first comer, just because it's time to find a husband. I wouldn't mind having someone sometimes, or, you know, to be in love. I know what that feels like – you remember Paul. But he never left his wife, and I think I'd have left him by now anyway."

Paul, the love of my life. We met at a cocktail party, and immediately fell in love. Twenty-year age difference, but we never thought about it. We had so much in common. Career oriented, laughing at the same things, our naked bodies feeling at home when we made love. Paul. Yes, the love of my life, who never left his wife. I split after two years, tired of the same old shit: waiting for him to stop lying. He would never leave her and as far as I know, he never did.

"I don't get it, David said, breaking into my thoughts. "You're smart, beautiful, you've got a great career, and you still haven't found anyone?"

He then expounded on his usual feeble theory that even though I was all those things, I was too complicated, too difficult, for any man to put up with. Sure, I'd gone through a "hard time," but he didn't know why, or that I'd changed since then. And he'd forgotten our younger days, when we were both so carefree. We used to cut class to smoke pot in the fields, sneak out of our houses at night to go clubbing, steal one of our parent's cars to go for a joyride, the dancing, flirting, smoking cigarettes, drinking and waiting for the next weekend so we could start all over. Living adolescence to what we conceived as its fullest. Something I continued in my twenties, but he hadn't. To me, David had sold out, like everyone else I knew there, and his conformity made me sad and empty, and every time I returned to Switzerland, I felt it more strongly and felt more out of place. The norm made everyone comfortable, but I had never been interested in the norm.

Once again I thought, with relief, that New York was the place I could be wholly myself.

After dinner, we went to a hip new nightclub, where David recognized some of his buddies. He ushered me over to their table and proudly introduced me as his "friend from New York." Cedric was one of the men at the table. He looked me up and down, the way many Europeans do, and I felt like I'd just had an MRI, then he asked me to sit beside him. As if I'd passed the exam. I wasn't in the mood for small talk, so I said no thanks and headed to the dance floor instead. I've always loved music. I feel so free when I'm dancing, and I've never needed a partner. I love dancing by myself. But Cedric joined me. I felt obliged to open my eyes and step out of my bubble. Grace Jones's song "La Vie en Rose" was playing, which always made me think of Paul and our love story, the kind that lasts forever and feels the truest. That kind of story has no end. It was our song.

Paul was the only man I ever loved to dance with, but it wasn't the same with Cedric. He had no rhythm. He stepped right and then left, snapping his fingers like an idiot. Either you've got rhythm, or you don't. But he didn't take himself seriously, and I liked that.

Back at the table he bought me a vodka and tonic. He talked about the books he'd recently read, and I told him how I loved to write and to sculpt, to create, and that I considered myself an artist. I told him about my years in New York, my career, my friends, my apartment, my day-to-day life, my excitement at living in such a wonderful place and walking the crowded streets and feeling that endless Manhattan energy. My happiness at having finally found a home where I truly belonged.

I don't remember our first kiss. Was it in the club or in the elevator on our way up to my hotel room? This bothers me now, because every love story should start with a memorable first kiss. This is proof I didn't fall for him right away. For me, it was a one-night stand, and I left the next morning confident that a bit of cock wouldn't change my plans: getting back to my life in New York.

Plus, I'd had much better. Cedric couldn't seem to get it up unless I pinched his nipples and even then, I had to turn them clockwise. I felt like I was sleeping with a Rolex. "Harder!" he cried. I couldn't help laughing at him. But I knew how to give a man pleasure. I never left a man wanting more, and Cedric was no exception. Satisfied, he fell asleep snuggled up against my ass.

The morning light always brings clarity, and often, the attraction from the night before gives way to deception. This proved the case with Cedric, at least physically. He had love handles, and the stretch marks on his back showed he must have been fat once. His black hair was thin and receding, and there was a silvery gray fringe around his ears and temples, but his eyebrows were black, his thick eyelashes too. How old was he? 40, 50, 60? I couldn't really tell. He looked way older than me. Oh well. His less-than-appetizing physique meant I would have no regrets about not seeing him again, a superficial way of thinking, but one that helped me justify not getting serious.

THIS IS BULLSHIT, NOT A LOVE STORY

What had attracted me to him, enough to make me invite him to spend the night? I didn't drink so much that I would walk off with the first available penis. The night before in the club I'd felt good about him. He was tall, and I even thought he was handsome, with his beautiful green eyes that seemed to change hue depending on his mood. But in the daylight, he was a different man. I didn't blame him – I was the one who invited him up, after all. He seemed kind, and we had spent an enjoyable night together.

We left the hotel at the same time, and out on the sidewalk, I kissed him on the cheek and said goodbye, without adding anything about seeing him again, or giving him my telephone number "in case he ever came to New York." He was just another guy, and I jumped in a taxi and went on my way.

At the airport check-in desk, one of the flight staff had a surprise for me: a letter with my name on it. I didn't recognize the writing, and who other than David and my parents knew I was leaving Geneva that morning? As I read it, my heart started beating faster and my hands got warm and damp. I guessed Cedric must have written it, and when I saw his name at the bottom of the page, I smiled. As I read it over again, I could feel my cheeks reddening at the man's words:

"A night with you, just a single night, and already it isn't enough. I can still smell your skin and feel the intensity of your gaze. You're a rare creature. You are unique, Chloe. I've got our night on repeat in my mind. Your generosity is beautiful, and so innocent. But you're also a real woman... Should I chance fate to see you again? You've got the choice over there on your island of freedom.

15

Here's my number: 07 96 54 XX XX. I'm probably out of my mind, but it feels so good. Wishing you well, and hoping to see you again soon, Cedric."

His letter flattered me, kindled my interest and, I admit, my desire, but it bothered me, too. I felt a sudden dread it would pull me from my chosen path into an unknown adventure, one that might or might not turn out well. I tucked the note away, but by the time I boarded the plane, I'd resolved to at least consider the possibilities.

There were so many pros and cons. When I met Cedric, I was at peace with myself. I was happy living in New York, I loved my work, and I had a busy social life, joyous for the most part, as well as several lovers. Nothing serious, though. I didn't want to set myself up with the first decent man I found, like so many friends about my age, but the idea of love and all it entailed, like marriage and children, was entering my thoughts more and more often. But for me, "love" had to be based in a steady relationship, and so far, I hadn't managed to attain that. My earlier life hadn't been exactly propitious to it.

After I hit puberty, my emotions became intractable with a vengeance. My parents had to deal with me getting expelled from three high schools for the same reason: "Your daughter is different from the other students. She needs to see a psychologist." Which they finally agreed to do when they discovered I also had a drug problem. I tried everything – pot, psychedelics, cocaine, any kind of pill offered me, and often indulged in several at once. I myself felt I would not survive if I kept taking drugs. Underneath that tough-girl exterior, I was crying for help. I still hadn't told anybody about getting raped when I was 16, or about the anorexia following that trauma, or my absurd need to have sex with guys as some twisted kind of revenge. The risk of death for some reason gave me pleasure. When I started therapy, I discovered why I had zero respect for myself, and why I saw the world in black and white, high and low, good or bad: Borderline Personality Disorder. After the diagnosis, I worked hard to balance my shifting moods. I was tired of constantly pushing the limits and depending on that rush of adrenaline simply to feel alive.

Healing was a long journey, years long. I will never be completely cured, but I succeeded in conquering my demons. I could finally take pleasure in spending time in the marvelous world of happy people. People who seize the day. My anxiety subsided and made room for positive thoughts, I overcame my anorexia and was again able to experience food not as a mere requirement, but as a gift of life. My gaunt contours filled out, and when I looked in the mirror, I was glad at seeing a pretty young women. Having learned the reasons behind my compulsive behaviors, I disciplined my out-of-control sexuality, and my encounters with men became more about feelings and less about carnal desire. By the time I moved to New York City in my mid-20s, I was practically "normal," stable, and definitely on the good path. All was well with my little world.

And then I met Cedric Moreau. Maybe fate was telling me I was ready to find out what love truly meant, and how it would make me happier than my teen years of gleeful self-destruction had, or even the last five or six years of contentment. By the time I got off the plane, his letter had managed to set off my delicate emotional machinery. Suddenly, this was it, love! Nothing could stop me now; I was going to experience my ideal "one true love" and Cedric would be the man for me. Even if he wasn't exactly to my taste physically, I would learn to love him as he was, and see him as attractive and seductive. Besides, it's what's inside a person that counts, right? I felt a lightning bolt of love, or I made it up because I wanted it to hit me. I was at a critical age for a woman, and I suddenly longed to take on the role of housewife and throw myself into the mysterious universe of "Happyland." I would give up everything for a man! Just like in the movies. Exactly like my mother who, a week after meeting my father, left Rio De Janeiro to live with him in Geneva. In fact, I beat her record; I fell in love after only one night. I could also love and be loved! I deserved it, didn't I?

So I threw caution to the wind and sent him a text as soon as I got to my apartment in Manhattan. He replied instantly, and two weeks later, he flew across the Atlantic to spend the weekend with me. I did the same, spending Christmas and New Year's with him in Geneva. He introduced me to his two teenage daughters, Sarah and Ana, on Christmas day. Not exactly a congenial meeting. And Sarah, the older daughter, who was 14, made me especially apprehensive, but I believed Cedric when he told me later that both his daughters adored me and couldn't wait for me to come live with him.

A month later, I told my parents I was coming back to Geneva, moving in with Cedric, and that we would get married someday soon. My mother seemed thrilled I would be near her again, and my father seemed relieved that his daughter's troubles would be sorted out. My New York colleagues and friends were sad to lose me, but everyone wished me well, saying, "Go for it, Chloe, that's what love is all about!"

I sold my furniture, packed up the few things I couldn't leave behind and had it delivered to Switzerland. The day Cedric went to pick it all up from the shipper's warehouse, he called me, irritated. "You could have told me you had so much, I had to rent a van!" I'd warned him I was bringing my sofa and my favorite paintings, so I paid no attention to what he said, and calmed him down with a few jokes.

As my plane took off from JFK, I gazed out the window at the city that had helped me shed my anxieties, where I'd found hope for a happy life. My excitement about the future suddenly evaporated, sorrow and confusion overwhelmed me, and I started crying. I couldn't stop. The man next to me glanced at me several times, then moved to a different seat. I couldn't understand why I had decided to drop everything for Cedric, and that made it worse. Perhaps I didn't want to get to the truth, because deep down I was afraid I was making an irreversible mistake.

It was clear, even then, that our worlds were different. I never should have read that note he sent me at the airport in Geneva. And now I'd done it, left everything behind, including my freedom, in trade for an easy, conformist life with a banker. I was doing exactly what I'd accused David of. Cedric offered me a kind of holiday, a resting point in my busy life, a shoulder to rest my head on. Or maybe I just wanted to experience the kind of life my mother and so many other women had chosen, a conventional life, so seductive an option. But choosing it meant leaving an entire continent, a country, a city, a profession, a social life; it meant leaving behind my own self – that's the impulsive decision I couldn't figure out. I decided to blame it all on love, then I tucked it away, calmed down and numbly sat there for the rest of the long flight.

I arrived in the morning, and Cedric was waiting for me outside baggage claim. He had left work to pick me up.

"Nice flight? I'm sure it was, business class is always so great. Not so bad being partners with the guy with the Elite Flyer card, eh? You can thank me later. Come on, let's go home!"

A few days before I left New York, he'd had DHL send me an Elite Flyer card with my own name on it. The only way to travel, he'd said.

"Thank you, that's wonderful," I'd gushed over the phone. But I didn't care all that much if I flew economy, business, first class, whatever – all that mattered was getting off the ground and landing in one piece. But I knew men could be a bit childish, and I didn't want to spoil his delight.

Cedric lived in a post-war building in a quiet suburb near Geneva, dating from when architects focused on function and optimizing space. Still woozy from travel, I didn't yet realize those gray concrete walls would be my new home. He insisted on carrying both my suitcases to his third-floor apartment, where he opened the door for me and, smiling, waved me in. It had a large living room, one bedroom, and an office that doubled as a guest room when his daughters came for weekends. It had absolutely no charm. Then I saw my Turkish sofa in a corner of the living room, and I felt a sense of relief. I would be able to stretch out on a piece of furniture I was familiar with, and then I wouldn't feel so far away from my beloved New York.

Cedric broke into that thought. "It matches, doesn't it? Man, it was hard to get it up the stairs. But don't worry, I did it for you!"

"Thank you. It's perfect there. And my painting?"

"I put that...thing in the girls' bedroom. We'll discuss it later. Come and unpack your stuff in the bedroom." I was too tired to quibble about it, even though I loved that painting.

His closets were meticulously organized but full, so he'd set up a canvas hanging unit from IKEA in the office, saying, "If you don't have enough space there, there's room in the basement."

I was exhausted from my flight and jetlag, and everything seemed to be happening too fast. I figured Cedric had to be teasing me, another side of his personality I didn't yet know. I needed a shower, so I decided to unpack later. When I came out of the bathroom, he was waiting for me, lying naked on the bed and holding out a box. He gestured to me to sit down. Inside the box were the keys to the apartment. He'd selected a Fatma hand for a keychain, the sign of protection. His apartment would be protecting me?

"Welcome home! Now you can come and go as you please. I have something else for you too."

He handed me another box, an orange one. It was a gorgeous Hermès watch, the "H" model. Seeing my confused expression, he said, "You mentioned you'd love to wear one."

I must have told him I liked that collection, but I never said I wanted to own one. I don't wear a watch, but I'd make an exception to make him happy, and not disappoint him. It was the thought that counted, so I thanked him. He slipped it on my wrist, but the strap was too long.

"It's absolutely beautiful," I said. "I guess I've lost some weight recently, probably from the stress of moving. Anyway, I don't like it when the strap's too tight."

"Yes, I think you have lost weight. But don't worry – from now on, I'm going to take care of you like no one ever has."

He nuzzled me. "It's so nice to smell your perfume again. Now don't move, I have another surprise for you. Close your eyes and lay on your stomach, there you go. Guess what I'm putting on your ass."

I closed my eyes. He got up and padded away, then I heard some noise in the other room. He tiptoed back. I kept my eyes closed as he delicately placed something that felt a little like paper on my butt. It was neither heavy nor light, neither hot nor cold. There was no smell. I heard the click of a camera shutter, and then he walked out again. I lay there stretched out, alone, until he came back. I had no clue what he had placed on my body.

"You can open your eyes. Do you remember when you told me the price of a night with you would be $50,000? Well, here's what that looks like – the price of one night of love with you!"

He handed me a fat wad of bills. I didn't understand what he was talking about. And then I remembered a conversation we had on a walk in New York, and he asked me what I was worth for one night. I thought he was joking. Did other women fantasize about this sort of thing? I'd thrown out some random number sarcastically and we moved on to talk about something else.

"Well, what do you think? It was your idea. I thought you'd be tickled to see it for real..."

"I remember our conversation, but I thought you were playing around. Where did you get all this money?"

"It belongs to a client. He asked me to hold on to it until our next appointment. Anyway. I can tell you don't think it's funny. I'll make lunch."

I lay still as an awkward silence settled over the apartment. Again, the thought crept into my mind that I didn't know Cedric Moreau. I rolled over and stared at the ceiling, feeling empty, then pushed myself to get up and get dressed. I joined him in the kitchen. As if nothing weird had happened, he welcomed me with a wide smile. He was cooking Tom Kha Kai, a Thai soup he knew I loved.

"My daughters will be here tomorrow. They're going to spend the school holidays with us, a whole week. Won't it be great?"

Hmmm, not exactly, Cedric, that might not be "great." You could have warned me. I wanted to get to know his daughters better, but I was exhausted. I would have to get a solid night's sleep and be ready for them, and all I said was, "Sure, that's cool. But I don't think you told me about it?"

"Can't remember. Anyway, my girls are my number one priority. I don't have them here very often, you know. You'll see, they're the best."

And so passed my first day in Switzerland. I called my mother to tell her I'd arrived. She wanted to see me right away, but I diplomatically pushed our meeting to the following week. I thought I should spend some time with my future husband. I didn't tell her that his daughters were going to visit the next day. I didn't want to upset her. A typical Jewish mother, she would want to be the first to see me, before any daughters of his.

Cedric picked them up on his way home from work, and by the time they arrived, I was jittery. I didn't know these girls beyond having a few meals together in restaurants – would they like me in day-to-day life? A pre-teen and a teen, not exactly easy ages.

"Hi, sweetheart. We're here! Come say hello!"

I came into the room as jauntily as I could. I'd prepared. I wanted to pass myself off as a charming, young, and fun future stepmother. I had no idea what other role to play, and I wanted everything to go well. Cedric was happy to bring us together and I didn't want to ruin the moment.

"You remember Chloe, girls," Cedric said. We all said our hellos at once, then there was a awkward moment. Were we supposed to hug?

"Girls, go drop your stuff off in your room. I'll start making dinner."

Difficulty averted. When they came back out, Cedric insisted that I stay quietly with Ana in the living room. He brought me a glass of wine and went back into the kitchen with Sarah, his youngest, who was 12 years old.

Ana turned on the television. News hour. She was cold and distant, and I guessed she was marking her territory. I wasn't about to push my way in, as it was probably best to let things develop naturally. She didn't seem inclined to talk, but I could feel her watching me out of the corner of her eye. That made me uncomfortable, but Cedric and Sarah soon came back into the living room and relieved us.

"I'm so happy we have a whole week together," Cedric said. "I'm working until Wednesday, but I took the next two days off, so we can have a long weekend. What should we do? Any ideas?"

"Dunno," Sarah answered finally. "I want to see my friends, but everyone's skiing."

"Do you want to go skiing? We can do that. I'm sure Martine still has two rooms free in her chalet in Megève. How about it?"

I could see he was doing everything he could to make them happy. But who was this Martine? I wasn't jealous; I just wanted to know who was part of his life. I didn't have any close friends here, no work colleagues, no dreams, no ambitions here. The few people I knew in Switzerland lived in the city, and they were no longer part of my social life. They had their own lives now, and we didn't have enough in common to pursue relationships, and that even included David. I realized how difficult it was going to be to get used to my new situation.

I asked him about Martine.

"You know, Martine!" he said. "I've told you about her a million times. She's my best friend." He added in a sly tone, "We're just friends, even if deep down, she wants to sleep with me."

The girls giggled at their father's inappropriate remark. It was clear I wouldn't have a say in our plans because Cedric got up, grabbed his phone, and went into the bedroom. He came out a while later with the good news.

"Everything's set. We'll leave on Thursday morning for Megève! Martine can't wait to see us, and she's so looking forward to meeting you, sweetheart."

Neither of the girls showed any excitement at the news, no happiness or gratitude about it.

"When are we going to eat, Dad?" Sarah asked.

I went to help Cedric in the kitchen. I asked him if the girls ever helped to set the table.

"Never! I don't see them very often, so I just want to spoil them." Then he smiled broadly and handed me a stack of plates. "Here, take this, you can set the table."

THIS IS BULLSHIT, NOT A LOVE STORY

I knew nothing of how a bullfight unfolds. All I knew was that we were not even at Act One. This was the El Paseo. Paseo, meaning a walk. This walk, though, wouldn't be a peaceful stroll. The matador unfurls his cape. Pink on one side, red on the other. The magic object that would make the animal submit. First steps of the dance. And it's true. It is beautiful.

At first, my new life seemed perfect. A man was taking care of me, and together, we were going to create the perfect blended family. Finally, I was part of a real couple. And I was going to make this man happy. Isn't that an amazing ambition? There was no doubt in my heart or in my soul: I would accomplish this. There was no going back. "Happyland! Here I come!" I'd never yet had this opportunity, never had a proper boyfriend at school, the kind I could walk hand in hand with during breaks. I'd always seemed to bump into married men or one-night-stand kind of men. Now it was my turn to enjoy a conventional relationship, proper and secure. To be loved and never abandoned. And Cedric fulfilled his role, always looking at me as if I was the best thing that ever happened to him. I loved that feeling. It inspired me to play the role of my life: to be his perfect wife. And his kids' perfect stepmother, if possible.

Going to the mountains for a few days would be good for me. There's nothing like fresh air for building perspective. And I needed it to keep all these parts of my new life moving smoothly. I met Cedric's "Martine" for the first time, his very best friend. Martine had married a very wealthy man, Pierre-Yves, who granted her access to all a monied life had to offer, including a chalet for skiing vacations.

After settling into our rooms, we went downstairs and joined the other guests. Martine introduced us to her Parisian friends, including a famous writer, but I no longer knew much about Europe's celebrities, so I couldn't enthuse over her latest bestseller. There was a charming couple there, too, the woman a singer, and her husband a plastic surgeon.

Martine told Cedric that Pierre-Yves was in the kitchen, busy preparing couscous. "You know my husband, the recluse! He'll join us later. He considers his couscous a sacred task."

Finally, she turned to me and gushed, "It's so nice to meet you, Chloe. Cedric has told us so much about you. I feel I know you already!"

I could already tell how fake and hostile she was, but I smiled and acted polite. We instinctively disliked each other. She clearly wanted to meet me in order to evaluate a rival. I was only 31, and here I'd landed in the midst of some middle-aged first-class bobos – bourgeois bohemians. I get along well with people of all ages, but I'm easily bored with wealthy people who consider themselves "well-adjusted," who live complacently in their safe little world with their superfluous joys. As I observed the women around me that night, I wondered at what my own mother had impressed upon me: keep clean, keep calm, be dependent on a man. Even act a little stupid. She always told me it was better not to think too much, to just accept men as they were. Until that point, though, I'd managed my life by myself, and hadn't put her theories to the test. No man had ever taken care of me, and I'd never let my guard down. My 21st-century attitude was wearing thin, though. I liked the rush of working and living in New York, but I was tired. In the short time I'd been with Cedric, it had felt so good to take a break from it all, to be a little mindless and forget the daily grind. Why did it feel like I'd sacrificed something? It was for love, right? And for love, surely it was okay.

"Tell me, Chloe, what did you do in New York?" Matine asked.

"I'm a journalist. I worked for a magazine covering travel and luxury hotels."

"Oh, yes, I see." She drawled the last word out. "It's hard making a living as a journalist though, isn't it?"

"Depends on your salary, if you're on staff, of course. But I worked freelance, then launched a magazine called 'New World Mag' with two friends. Travel is really my passion."

Martine's eyes glazed over. She wasn't interested in my professional life; what she was looking for was a little morsel that would demean me in front of her guests. Our conversation was thankfully short, and she went to join her husband in the kitchen.

She had managed to make me feel uncomfortable. I drifted off into my own thoughts for a while, only half listening to the discussions going on around the room. Mentioning the name of my magazine to Martine had filled me with nostalgia for my years as a writer, my travels, the fascinating people I met, launching a successful business – I'd accomplished so many of my dreams. Once again it struck me how with all those things going for me, my sudden departure for Switzerland seemed incredibly impulsive.

And now I didn't even know when or if I would go back to work again. This was the first time since turning 18 that my life wouldn't be dictated by my striving after a career. It was perfectly normal that a woman at my age would begin to think of her personal life, I reasoned. Start a family? Make a man happy? Could Cedric really become my new passion and replace my career?

"Dinner's served!"

Cedric came over, wrapped his hands around my waist, and gave me a huge kiss in front of everyone. I was embarrassed, but I could only squirm, smile and move to the table. That show of public affection wasn't my style. His approach was a little uncouth, but I let him do it because I didn't want to make him uncomfortable or feel rejected. We all sat down and started to discuss the next day's weather, what the snow was like, and also Pierre-Yves's amazing couscous. We all went to bed early so we could get up at dawn and go skiing.

Unfortunately, the next day was a white-out, with a thick fog. No visibility. The snow was perfect, though. I was a veteran skier, as I'd learned very young. My parents had handed me over to a bevy of ski instructors for entire days at a time. I loved skiing. Cedric hated skiing, but he wanted to make his children happy, plus he would do anything to prove he was the perfect father. I waited for the three of them at the bottom of every run and watched them come down. They were terrible skiers, but I could tell they wouldn't appreciate any advice. The girls complained nonstop. The conditions were tough, granted, but they also griped about the smallest things. Their father reached the end of his rope after two hours, so we returned to the chalet. My body wasn't tired, but they had exhausted me in every other way.

Eventually the weekend came to an end. Back at the apartment in Geneva, Ana and Sarah raced inside without taking any of their baggage. I looked at Cedric questioningly, but he just started to unload the car in silence. I helped him, astonished they had not given us a hand, and I guess he noticed.

"They have school tomorrow," he said. "They're exhausted, and they need to get to bed. Don't you ever think of anyone else?"

I didn't mean to be selfish, so his attitude stung me. I just thought kids should help out more, a lot more. I realized his children would be a delicate subject between us, and I'd better learn to keep my mouth shut. Tomorrow, all three of them will be out of the house, I thought with a sense of relief. That immediately saddened me. Did I want to avoid my loved ones, already?

In the morning, Cedric came into the kitchen, where I was cleaning up the mess from our rushed breakfast.

"I'm off. The girls said to say goodbye – they're already in the car. Don't go shopping, I'll stop at the market on my way home. I can't wait for us to be alone tonight."

He gave me a deep kiss, running his hands up and down my back, then left. I closed the door behind him. What was I going to do all day? That question again, more and more ponderous as the first few months passed. I can't say whether they passed quickly or slowly, as I had lost all sense of time. That all began the same way every morning. I watched Cedric get dressed, a different suit, a tie with a different pattern, and then, his briefcase on his arm, a kiss on the mouth, with a "See you later, sweetheart." And then I had to find something to do all day.

During those first months, Cedric was devoted, tender, and loving. He worked a lot, but he always made it home before 7 p.m. He brought me flowers and cooked nice meals for me. Yes, he sometimes spoke crassly or was a bit snappy, but I wasn't worried about it. When his criticisms started to get harsher, I refused to consider them seriously, and made excuses for him every time. I realized this new life with a live-in girlfriend was a challenge for him. He wanted to make everyone happy, and so far, I was still first in line.

Despite all his efforts, I wasn't getting used to living full-time in Switzerland. The country paralyzed me. The quiet streets unsettled me, the lack of dynamism in our small town, in the air itself, sucked all the energy from me to the point I never wanted to go out. I didn't look for friends or a job, and felt too lazy to do any freelance writing or sculpting. Nothing shook me out of my torpor. I didn't want to bother Cedric with my moodiness. He didn't deserve it, I thought. He was doing his best, so I shouldn't reproach him for anything, especially my new life in the lap of luxury. I hid my melancholy. Before he came home every evening, I spent a long time getting ready. I wanted to be the perfect housewife who welcomed her man home from his hard day of work by looking pretty, made up and dressed to please. And because I still didn't know what to do with my days, I took baths, and more baths. Until then I'd never really enjoyed letting myself prune up in hot water. But my daily bath became a ritual. I started at 5 p.m., filling the tub with bubbles and exotic bath oils. I passed the time blowing clouds of suds from my hands, or staring at my toes, thinking a pedicure might not be a bad idea.

I tried in vain not to regret the life I'd left behind me. It seemed all I did now was wait for Cedric to come home. Sometimes, I was still in the bathtub when he arrived, and he would sit on the toilet and tell me about his day in lengthy detail. "My boss is a pain. Always asking for numbers, numbers, numbers." Or "One of my clients is inviting me on his boat in Saint-Tropez. And good news, I opened a new account today! Yay! How about we celebrate?"

I was proud of him, but I wished I had something exciting to share with him. My days dragged, and that's why he sometimes found me lagging in the tub.

But most often I was ready for him and made a big deal of his coming home. Isn't that what a good housewife does? I'd finish my bath and rub lotion over my entire body. I'd barely look at my face. Probably I was too reluctant to look in my eyes and see the truth. I developed a routine: swipe foundation on my skin, add color to my lips and shimmer powder to my cheeks to erase any signs of my sorrow, then dress in lacy underwear, black nylons and a slinky dress. High heels, of course, which meant I had to keep my shoulders back. Dressing like this put me into the role, gave me the strength to follow my chosen destiny and forget about the old me, the one I really cared about. Like this, I could pretend to prefer this other, fancier woman, the one who made Cedric happy. I would be desirable, no matter what. I would never let him down.

THIS IS BULLSHIT, NOT A LOVE STORY

We started to get to know each other better. We talked a lot. I had no trouble opening up to him, because at the time, I had the unfortunate habit of telling too much, too easily, plus I believed it would be healthy to share my difficult past with him, my adolescence full of alcohol, drugs, and sex, my mad drive for independence. I also shared my feelings of satisfaction with my recent past, my successful career in journalism, my travels, my emotional stability, my sex appeal. Everything that created the perfect woman in Cedric's eyes. He often told me he was proud of me. He even cried when I told him how I'd been raped at 16, the depression and anorexia that followed, and my fight to get past it all. I saw him as a protector, like my father had been to my mother. A man who took care of his woman.

I talked about my father, too, and how he rarely showed interest in me. Sometimes he'd been violent, but it was never gratuitous; I gave him plenty of reasons to be angry when I was a kid, and the only way he knew how to express himself was to give me a slap with cold deliberation, or tell me how much I disappointed my mother, or simply give me the cold shoulder for days. Born in a Jewish family living in Eastern Europe during WWII, he was from a generation set apart, raised to hide his feelings. "No explain, no complain," his parents always cautioned him, even after they made their escape to Brazil, and then the United States.

Cedric was only a decade older than me, but he reminded me of my father in some ways, like how he related to my mother, throwing himself into the role of savior, the one who could calm my passions and balance my moods, my extremes, my borderline tendencies. He told me he wanted only the best for me, and that I needn't worry about telling him everything, or ever feel ashamed.

It was my life, and I had nothing to hide from him. I was going to be his wife, and he needed to know the person he was marrying. So, I shared everything with him, without inhibition. In turn, he told me about his life. He didn't come from wealth, or from one of those

31

big bourgeois families with their portraits parading across the walls of some dusty manor. He had built himself up, even choosing his own religion. He converted to Judaism when he was nineteen. He was extremely zealous and learned all the prayers by heart. He even learned to speak fluent Hebrew. He told me how he would walk to the synagogue on every holy day. His obsessive devotion eventually enabled him to be accepted by what was usually a closed society in Geneva, the Jewish community, which could open doors to money and a new identity.

His religious quest brought him to reject his Christian roots. He became ashamed of his French family who, as European Catholics, had left the French protectorate of Morocco upon its independence. In fact, he confessed to me that he passed his mother off as a Moroccan Jew in his circle of friends, which meant he'd lied to my parents when he told them his mother Geraldine was Jewish. When I met her, I saw she was far from Jewish, even if she pretended to be one for him, and my parents may have thought the same thing. If so they had never mentioned it.

"Why not tell people the truth about your life?" I told Cedric then. "I'm proud of you. You chose your own religion and that's great. Don't deny your roots! You shouldn't reject your mother simply because she's Catholic."

But in his exaggerated way, he said his "greatest victory" was that his two daughters were born of a Jewish mother, and his "greatest disappointment" was his own mother and her fervent devotion to her rosary. She remained a thorn in the side of his orthodox Jewish in-laws, who, unlike my parents, knew her background.

His mother told me one day, with a little laugh, "Oh, it's fine, I don't mind, so long as I don't lose my son."

Pretending to be Jewish was the only way for her to stay in touch with her son and to watch her granddaughters grow up. I felt sorry for her. I tried to help her see Cedric as a man raised a Catholic but converted to the older religion. The difficult times were behind her, I hoped. The days when she visited from France and had to take her cross off before entering his house – she hid it in her purse when she was at the door. Her son had once made her throw away a chicken she cooked for them because she'd forgotten to buy it at the kosher butcher. Cedric made such a fuss of it because he was strictly kosher. At dinner, she could never remember which plate to use, the dairy one or the other one for the meat, which always made him roll his eyes.

It was so obvious she was not Jewish. There was nothing Jewish about her, or about Cedric either. Was his so-called conversion to Judaism only a way to get access to power? Was that Cedric's religion, riches and power? But I accepted the illusion he cultivated. Love was love, and love forgives all.

By the time we met, he'd already begun to let go of many of his rituals, even if he still ate kosher. He was living as a Jew, and celebrated certain holidays like Rosh Hoshana but he didn't keep the sabbath every Friday night. Our life together was carefully balanced, and he practically choreographed it, frequently inviting my parents, his mother, and his daughters as a way to bring his new family together. Never his father. He told me very little about his father, only that he'd abandoned the family when Cedric was 15, that he was a pathological liar who bragged he was bringing in all the money when he was actually spending it at the casino. He said it was a relief when his father left, but his emotions seemed confused whenever he spoke of him. He berated him in one breath and in the next, he would practically brag, saying something like, "At least I got his smarts and his Swiss nationality, with the right to enroll in a top business school in Lausanne."

He said his mother had worked long hours as a secretary to provide for Cedric and his sister. They grew up in Grenoble in France, and after high school, he crossed the border in search of a more comfortable future along the shores of Lake Geneva. I didn't see this side of him at first, or realize he was so hungry for power, for money. The cult of the golden calf had never been important to me. But this was not true for Cedric. I even wondered if he had recognized the social advantages my roots could provide him when he begged me to come live with him.

Cedric and I were complete opposites. He came from a monolithic world, his world of provincial France, whereas I was a multicultural mishmash, born in Geneva with European and Brazilian Jewish roots. I came from a multicultural universe, in fact, much wider and filled with possibilities than anything Cedric had ever envisioned. It didn't matter to me, though – a perfect union could work between people from different social classes. I was proud of his spirit in choosing his own religion, but he insisted I keep quiet about the fact he wasn't a pure-blooded Jew. Not a word, he said, not a single word. I accepted his request.

Cedric kept surprising me. In some ways, I found him touching, like how he came home with flowers, his insistence on cooking for me, and telling me how much he loved me. But I often found him ridiculous, like how he kept not only all his first-class plane tickets, but also his business-class menus, stationery boasting the logos of prestigious hotels, slippers and pajamas he got on first-class flights, bathrobes from fancy spas, like a shrine in his closet. He loved wearing t-shirts or polos with embroidered logos of luxury hotels from around the globe, and he kept a neat list of all the countries he'd visited. Knowing his background, I saw it as childish pride and a way to keep his poor childhood from catching up with him. It also showed his ambition was purely material. He wanted to travel in luxury, to own an expensive car and a beautiful house, and only these material things could signal his success.

To keep up this lifestyle, Cedric had incurred some debts, but they didn't seem keep him up at night. He called it "achieving his dreams." He said he didn't owe a lot, but for me, any debt was too much. My father had taught me not to spend more than I earned, and to know the value of money. Cedric saw it differently. His worst nightmare was to be sent back to the mediocrity of his upbringing, and debt was a small price to pay to avoid that.

I assured him I'd never spend his money irresponsibly. He was the one who spent it, spoiling me with gifts, which I accepted with profuse thanks, as I didn't want to make him angry, but inside, I considered it a waste of money. He wrapped me in fur coats and dressed me from head to foot in the most expensive high-fashion brands. He wanted to surround me in a bubble of luxury, saying that any girlfriend of his deserved only the best. He seemed desperate to make me smile, maybe because he knew how much I missed New York.

The days started to feel too long. I told him I wanted to start working again, but he didn't push me to look for any opportunities.

"You've got time, *chérie*. For once, let yourself be taken care of. It's my job. And besides, what would you do? After running your own business, could you be an employee? Not very glamorous..."

He was certainly right about that. After having tasted independence, I could not see myself kowtowing to a boss. In lieu of working a regular job, I became Cedric's greatest ambassador. I went with him on his business trips and built solid relationships with his clients. For the next year, we travelled the entire Middle East from the Persian Gulf to Southeast Asia, and in between these trips, we discovered new hidden places. At least we had this much in common: travelling and foreign languages. And we enjoyed them together, the long-haul flights around the world stretched out on our first-class seats, the five-star hotel suites, the gourmet meals.

I could easily have lost sight of reality, but I kept my feet on the ground, and tried to appreciate every moment humbly, as something special. Cedric savored this time, parading his success with more than a hint of pretentiousness. Maybe he didn't realize it. Reminding myself of his rejection of his background, this was enough for me to love him anyway.

I certainly had nothing to complain about all this time, especially the jet-setting and pampering, and yet I wasn't happy. What was missing in my life? I couldn't talk to Cedric about it, as he would see it as complaining. Besides, I had vowed to consider his happiness first and put mine to the side, so I convinced myself that by loving him, the feeling of loving myself and the resulting happiness would come naturally.

My mother had taught me the art of keeping your man happy. She never talked about love, only about charm. I probably confused love with seduction as a means of getting what I wanted. But more than that, as a skilled seducer I would never have to feel the sting of rejected love, and rejection became a taboo word. Even when very young, my aura was strongly sexual. And I knew how to use it. Caught in my own trap, I knew all the rules of a seducer and none of a woman in love, or even if there were any. Naively, I believed my future husband would teach me how to love, but Cedric reveled in my "charm," and said he was the luckiest man alive to have found the sexiest woman in the world. "My woman is so deliciously good," he often said, right in front of his friends. I took his comment as a compliment, even if it made me cringe, figuring he simply meant "I love you."

We had a normal sex life at this time but that started to change, step by step. I'd never had to set limits in this area, so I didn't see it coming. I'd slept with numerous men and had many one-night stands. I'd enjoyed a threesome once, and I'd lived for more than a year with a woman. It was a way for me to heal after being raped, and to get over my anorexia. I'd been in love once, hopelessly in love, with Paul. I never regretted it, because thanks to him, I discovered love.

In the beginning, Cedric never mentioned fantasies, and I didn't really have any of my own. If I masturbated it was while thinking of some man or another, and not to porn. But I eventually learned that sexuality for Cedric meant more than that – it made me look tame. He began telling me his sexual fantasies while we made love. I only half-listened, more focused on helping him come, but then he even returned to his ideas over a meal, or in the car. His persistence paid off.

One morning he asked me to wait for him at home, naked, wearing a pair of leather boots he'd given me for Christmas and a black wig I wore on my last Halloween in Manhattan. I was to put on dark red lipstick. I did it, thinking it might be fun. I was even a little excited. When he got home and found me like that, he said he wanted me to play the dominatrix, and he took on his role instantly.

"Chloe, I'm begging you. Make me submit. Make me do anything, I'll do it. Stick your heel in my ass and I'll lick it."

I felt frozen, no longer excited, but I did what he asked, and he licked my high-heeled boot. He ejaculated very hard, longer than when we made love in a loving way, and it took him several minutes to recover. I took off my wig, cleaned the boot, and took a shower. When I came into the kitchen, he was fixing dinner, talking cheerfully, like nothing was out of the ordinary.

That was the night I allowed the unallowable, and opened a door I wouldn't know how to close. Why had I agreed? I found reasons. I didn't want to upset him, I wanted to be the woman he dreamed of marrying, I was curious, I wanted to free my inhibitions. He immediately insisted on going further, forcing me into a salacious universe of hidden sexuality. He pushed me to tell him what fantasies excited me, but I kept them to myself. I had never shared such intimate secrets with anyone and I felt uncomfortable. I didn't need to ask him about his own fantasies; he let me in on everything in gritty detail, and our sex life definitely changed.

A new side of his nature also began to appear when we were alone. Behind his Mr. Elegant persona was an average guy who scratched his balls, who burped and farted. Nothing extraordinary there. But I noticed that as he let himself go, his language changed, too, becoming cruder and more provocative until it seemed like everything that came out of his mouth focused on sex.

Once I'd given that first permission – to dress with just a hint of the dominatrix – there came a flood of demands. The problem was, I couldn't say no. He said he detected a strong potential in me, and he expected me to transform his fantasies into reality. He asked for too much: to make me watch him lick his cum from the floor, to pee in his mouth. I had to drink liters of water before I could do that, but I did it, shuddering. I hid behind my costumes, playing the slut or the dominatrix or the virgin, hiding under my black wig, and somehow found a way to play the roles. Without realizing it, I handed him my soul. He kidnapped me, Chloe.

I didn't realize he was creating his own reality and had sucked me down into it. I had become the bull, convinced that the enemy was the red cape, not the matador. I couldn't imagine that the man I loved, who claimed to love me, wanted to hurt me. Cedric had convinced me I was the one and only goddess of his desires, trapping me inside the comfortable cocoon he created for me. And this was when I'd finally accepted it was time to conform to a conventional life. This was not conventional in any way!

He wouldn't have asked his ex-wife Rachel to play out these kinds of fantasies. The mother of his children, the sacred and pure mother – that would be blasphemy! But he had no problem when it came to me. He could dress me from sexy to trampy, paint me in the make-up of a whore leaving a hotel room, undress me without looking into my eyes, succumb to the darkest of fantasies. He made me his object, made me conform to his world.

As the months passed, my boredom left, and anxiety took its place. I paced the house, worried about what would happen when he came home. Would he ask me to kneel down and blow him on the doorstep in plain view of the neighbors, or something far worse? And yet, for all my apprehension and disgust, I was filled with love for him. Yes, I loved him. I was convinced this was what real love must be: the more sacrifices you made, the more you loved. I talked to girlfriends who were in enduring relationships about it in vague terms and they said things like, "It isn't always easy. Being a couple is hard work, each and every day. And women are good at accepting things, because we don't like conflict. You'll see you can accept it with Cedric, too."

And I did. It didn't require all that much effort on my part at first. After all, he was the one who worked hard and came home late, exhausted. He was the one who had to manage his ex-wife and subsidize his children's education. I felt I should be thanking him for this sumptuous lifestyle he was providing me, and the least I could do was to pretend I was happy and praise him before his family, his friends, his clients. Become his pillar. Yes, I finally knew what I was good at. Become the perfect woman, Chloe! Forget your independence, your intelligence, your logic, and dedicate yourself to who you wanted to become: a loving wife, ready to do anything to make her man happy. It was often a challenge.

One evening, Cedric came home in an awful mood. He slammed the front door and went straight to this room without greeting me. He made dinner quickly, banging the pots and pans. He drank several glasses of wine during the meal, and hardly spoke. I tried to make conversation.

"My friend Rose called today. She wants me to come visit her in New York. I do miss the energy of the city, you know. I wonder if a short stay might give me new inspiration. Maybe see some colleagues and arrange to do some work for them, but from here, of course, from Geneva."

Seemed innocuous to me, but he exploded.

"But why do you want so much to go back to work? I give you everything. Can't you see that you don't need to work? Enjoy this life, for fuck's sake! What I would give to be in your shoes!"

He got up and brought his plate to the sink and threw it in with a clatter.

"You're just never satisfied," he complained. "You have everything, yet you're still moping around. You need a psychiatrist! And please, stop yelling about your life in New York! It's getting on my nerves!"

I hadn't yelled. On the contrary, I had used a soft, sweet voice to calm his nerves and get him talking. But he was right. Maybe I didn't really appreciate my luck. For once in my life, I could count on someone, and that someone was Cedric.

I put my head in my hands. I figured I must not be done dealing with my old demons, that I hadn't buried them permanently, and they were coming back. I decided to book a few sessions with my old therapist, the one I saw when I was in the throes of adolescence here in Geneva. I'd gone through a huge life change, after all. I didn't think to question what I was doing here with him. Instead, I thought he might have touched some nerve of mine. A secret wound.

"You're right about my emotional state. I'll make an appointment with my therapist. That will help me settle in and deal with my anxiety."

I'd always been honest with myself. I understood now how I functioned – my deep need to push my limits further and further. I'd hit rock bottom and travelled the long road toward recovery. I'd finally learned to experience things without having to be completely in control, and I now knew how to seize upon the true moments of joy, to live in the moment. I had some real successes! And I managed to do all this right before meeting Cedric.

The next morning, I made an appointment with Dr. Thyssen, a psychiatrist I've known since adolescence. Lying on the familiar couch in her cozy office, I spilled my guts, then waited for her reply.

"Once again, Chloe, you leapt before you looked. You could have moved back here and gotten your own apartment, found a job, then gotten to know this man, but you threw everything aside for a relative stranger, and moved right in with him. I give you and Cedric five years, no more."

She wrote something on a prescription pad, then came over to the couch and patted my shoulder.

"You're a bit loopy, my dear. I know you too well. See you next week. And until then, here's something to help ease your anxiety. One a day."

I left, wondering if I made a mistake in coming to see her. After all, who was the guilty party, him or me?

That evening, Cedric asked me how it had gone with Dr. Thyssen.

"Very well. She gave me something to help me relax."

"You see, sweetheart? Listen to your doctor. You aren't completely healed. But it's going to get better."

He stroked my neck. I didn't think I was mentally unwell, so why was he talking to me like I'd just escaped from a psychiatric ward? Something about the tone of his voice was off.

Within a few days, the pills did their work. I was calmer. At the same time, my mother started acting worried about me. She called me to say, "Why aren't you ever happy? You're difficult to live with. Poor Cedric."

Over the next few months, my world began to get blurry. I was losing my memories of my younger self and settling into a routine. I took care of Cedric's daughters with a big smile, I set the table while Cedric made supper, I joined their conversations, and my sense of humor would often lighten the atmosphere, I urged him to do things with his daughters, and he made sure I came along. I didn't mind. I learned how to say yes to everything. I kept thinking of what a friend had said: "A 'yes' a day keeps the fights away."

I used this mantra many times. Especially when it became obvious that Cedric sometimes wanted to make me angry. He wouldn't listen. He always had to be right. I'd ask him to give me some space, saying I'd return to the discussion once I'd calmed down. Nothing worked. He was extremely stubborn, pushing at me until I snapped, and he seemed almost gleeful to see me so upset. I even suspected he was the one with mental problems, not me, with his yo-yo personality. Our fights always ended in some form of make-up sex, and he usually came in my mouth because he wanted the "comfort" of fellatio. Afterward he would roll over, saying, "Goodnight, darling. Sweet dreams."

I started to wonder if being around him was bringing back the emotional fragility I thought I had resolved. All that old mental anguish was pressing up, shaking me and worming its way into our relationship. It would only go quiet when I was sleeping. I realized I was far from healed, and I worried Cedric was going to push me to my limits. I didn't want to go there ever again. But then, he could be so kind, and he was most of the time. His "caring" blinded me, and I could not envision that my Cedric wanted to push me toward something so dark. I could not believe he could be a monster, when he could be such a gentleman. Here I was though, stuck in his story. I had left my life in New York, claiming to everyone he was the love of my life, and I'd vowed to follow through with my promises.

On New Year's Eve, we decided to turn over a new leaf. We made some promises: no more useless fighting; I could visit New York once a year; I would keep seeing my therapist; he would learn to listen to me and leave me alone when I needed time to myself. Then he announced he had a big surprise for me, to get the new year started right. "I left you some clothes on the bed! Go ahead, put them on."

He called those tiny pieces of cloth "clothes?" He was waiting for me in the hall, so I pulled off my elegant holiday dress, and put the so-called clothes on. The mini-dress was hideous, skin tight and cheap-looking. There was a garter belt, which was scratchy, and stockings that were so big they crumpled at the knees. Everything was uncomfortable. I strapped on the platform high heels he'd left at the foot of the bed, then looked in the mirror. I didn't recognize myself, even my face looked strange. Some big surprise, all right!

"I'm ready, honey, but where are you taking me dressed like this – a costume party?"

"Can't you guess? You can be so thick sometimes, sweetie. What do you think about going to a swinger's club? I found one just across the border in France, about an hour's drive. Let's check it out."

I had a hard time getting into the car, the dress was so short and tight. I had no desire to go to any swinger's club, but after all our resolutions and newfound peace, I didn't dare say anything. This would be a first for me, and for him, too, I thought.

"It's something I've wanted to do for a long time," he said. "But who could I go with? My ex-wife?"

The BodyX Club was in Amancy, a village in middle-of-nowhere France, the kind of village where the houses are all shuttered at dusk. There was a gravel parking lot outside the club, which made for a precarious walk to the door in my platforms. The manager welcomed us, conspicuous in a bright pink Hawaiian shirt. I left my coat in the cloakroom while Cedric paid our entrance fee.

"Mmnn, your wife is lovely, lovely... Won't she make them happy! Don't forget your two drink tickets."

Manager Vincent explained how the club worked. I kept intense eye contact with him, as I didn't want to miss a single detail. Fuck! Couldn't he see how stressed I was? He wouldn't save me! Him with his stupid shirt, no, it was too late. Cedric pulled me through the inner door, and pulsing music and lights hit me hard. The first floor was a disco. The DJ hadn't realized that music had changed a little since "Rock Me Amadeus." We settled down in a booth upholstered in black velvet. Its tiny round table almost touched the dance floor.

"I'll get us drinks and come back," Cedric said. "Check them out while you wait."

Check what out? Or who? Was he crazy? I certainly wasn't going to get off with any of these fat old men, and their wives were not more enticing. The human body can be so ugly. I saw no one better than mediocre-looking, people who'd found their kingdom at the goddamn Club BodyX.

Cedric returned carrying two plastic cups with the kind of paper umbrellas they stuck on ice cream when I was a kid. I had no idea these were still even made. The dance floor was surreal. Couples wearing '80s-style clothes – not the kind that was back in style – were gyrating under the colored lights. The only thing missing was a disco ball. I was laughing and crying inside.

Cedric was looking around appraisingly. He pointed out a middle-aged woman with large breasts. "See that girl over there? She's not so bad. I could see you with her."

Sure, man, in your dreams. I felt really uncomfortable. I was no prude, but the situation was making me feel sick. I grabbed the drink and took a gulp, thinking a little alcohol would help me relax and get through what faced me. I just wanted the night to be over with.

"Let's look around," I said. "I want to see what's downstairs. There aren't many people up here."

The real action was in the basement, it turned out. As we went down the stairs, various sounds accosted us: whispers, panting, bodies slapping, shouts of ecstasy. In the dim light, I could just make out lots of low couches and big pillows on the floor, all strewn with bodies. There were people standing against the walls too, doing things with their hands. My senses were on alert, and I was extremely uneasy. What was all this about? Did I have to join in this giant orgy?

"Don't be afraid, sweetheart," he whispered in my ear. "This is pure pleasure. It really turns me on, not you?"

No, Cedric, your games did not turn me on, and neither does this pile of flesh. I felt disgusted, and did not want to feel turned on, so I fought against the sexual urge, trying to will my body to numbness, to think of pure things like the sea, a meadow, round clouds in blue sky. I resented every twinge in my groin, resented Cedric for bringing me into this situation.

The slow song "True Colors" was playing as background to the primal sounds. What I would have given for this to be simply a slow dance right then. A girl passed by, checking me out, her eyes feral. She ran a hand over my ass, then, standing close enough to me for our skin to touch, she watched the whole scene: a woman on her hands and knees, being taken from behind while she sucked another guy's dick. The action seemed to end all at the same time, and everyone came. We moved into another room, and the girl followed us, then she stepped in front of us, making me face the invitation in her eyes.

"Cedric, I don't want—"

The woman moved on. Cedric grabbed my arm and interrupted me. "You're always saying you want to live life to the fullest. So, is that just bullshit? Besides, you've been with a woman before."

"But—"

"No 'buts,' sweetie. We're here, now, and we're going for it. She seemed ready for it."

He wanted to see me make out with another woman, obviously not yet ready to see me with another man, which could be due to jealousy or a threat to his virility. Or did he have an inferiority complex? I saw his eyes move around, then latch onto a likely-looking woman, younger than the others we'd seen so far.

"Do you like her? Go on and talk to her. I want to see you with her. I want her to lick you, to make you come. Let yourself go!"

He wouldn't let up, and he maneuvered me straight up to her. He whispered into her ear. She pulled me gently down onto a pillow, then started kissing me. I brought my sense of self to some inner place as I let it all happen, passive and not really there. I could feel people watching, and I watched my man jerk off like the other guys hunched around us. I stifled my body's responses, determined not to give in to brute sexual desire. She licked me, caressed me and sucked me until I pretended to have an orgasm. Yes, I faked it just to get the whole thing over with as quickly as possible.

As we left soon after, the doorman said with a leer, "Thanks for *coming*. Hope to see you again. We don't see a handsome couple like you every day."

Sure, Vincent. See you again. I would never see his ugly face again.

The first of many things I would get wrong. We became members of BodyX a few months later.

THIS IS BULLSHIT, NOT A LOVE STORY

I had permitted Cedric to discover some of my fantasies, which was a mistake, and to fulfill his own. From then on, nothing was off-limits. He believed I would say yes, so I didn't find a way to say no. He brought me into his way of life, and hardly a day passed without some new vice to try out. I thought it was all my fault, because I'd given him the right when I offered myself to him with a promise to do whatever it took to make him happy, like a good wife. Now he was free to tell me everything, show me everything. Like a child bursting with a secret that he could finally reveal. Woohoo! Victory to the matador!

Then I discovered Cedric had been hiding an even darker side. We were on a long drive when he told me he used to stop at a certain freeway rest area before going home to his wife and his kids.

"Really?" I asked naively. "Why?"

That seemed to be what he was waiting for. He told me he would show me, and I found out the hard way that highway rest areas had other uses than stretching your legs and using the bathroom. No need to wait for the dark of night to get off when these adult playgrounds were open day and night. We parked at the next one we came to. Cedric seemed familiar with it, and walked me to an area with bushes and trees.

"Don't make too much noise," he whispered. "Look at all those tissues on the ground. I think I hear something. Come on, it's that way."

I suddenly spied a middle-aged man, who to me, looked straight and married, but he was getting sucked off by a younger man. Cedric watched them, eyes intense. He started rubbing his crotch, and then he motioned for me to get down on my knees.

Nothing would ever be the same after that. Nothing would ever be simple again. "Making love" became a romantic euphemism for obscene deviant sex. I seemed to be that rare bird, a universal object of lust, an absolute fantasy for all men, and I soon became his trophy.

I think I visited every highway rest area in Switzerland, and in every season. It was easier in summer, of course, because in winter, I froze, to carry out Cedric's favorite fantasy: I had to open my heavy coat to show off my naked body to strangers hidden in the bushes while their car engines purred in the parking lot. These sessions of drive-by porno chic were short, fortunately, and the voyeurs never touched me. They watched, their pants down, their ejaculations well-timed.

"Bravo, darling! You were marvelous. Did you see how you mesmerized those guys? It's incredible. You must be freezing. Come on, let's go home."

He was so proud of me he told his swinger entourage that thanks to me he'd achieved the highest level of his perverse sexuality.

Cedric was extremely ambitious for power and success in his career, and he insisted I take an interest. He wanted me to love his money-distorted world. But I wasn't built that way. I liked being comfortable, naturally, but expensive clothes or cars or surroundings didn't interest me because of their price tags. What interested me was truth, authenticity, beauty, which seemed lost forever. He took it from me, spoiled it, and he was corrupting my senses and values, slowly but surely. I only began to realize this one night as we drove home in his BMW from a party with his friends. He shamed me that evening. I'd been having so much fun, dancing and laughing with the others. I noticed he started looking disgruntled, as if he didn't like me enjoying myself with anyone other than him.

Suddenly, he walked across the room to where I was dancing with several people, jerked my arm and said in a loud voice, "Come on, we're going home. Right now!" My face burned in front of all those questioning faces, amid the sudden lull in the fun, as Cedric marched me out. We didn't even say goodbye to our host.

Cedric knew how much I loved dancing, and before I moved in with, he'd promised to take me out whenever I wanted. He broke this promise. I felt sad about it, as if I were losing sight of my youth.

We stopped going out dancing altogether, and eventually stopped doing any normal activities people do for fun, like going to a movie or concert or play, or walking in the woods. Our social circle grew smaller, too, until it consisted only of that "best friend" of his, Martine, and a few of his college friends, all married couples with children, all wealthy and flaunting it with luxurious lifestyles, between their ski chalets and beach houses. I had to accompany him constantly to parties or trips with these people, even though I had almost nothing in common with them and would have preferred getting back to sculpture and writing. He kept up a pretense of supporting my individuality and my freedom, but in reality, he'd trapped me in a dangerous little cage.

Around this time, Cedric swiveled to a new focus.

"Don't you want to buy a house? Look at James and Laura, or Bertrand and Anne-Laure. They're so successful. You've seen their houses? I can't even invite my clients to this plebian apartment."

"Sure, why not?" I said. "That's a good way to start our new life together – a fresh slate, clean walls. Do you have some money put aside?"

"Of course I do, my retirement fund. It'll take a hit, but not too bad. And you're absolutely right, sweetie, a house would help us get settled the right way."

The decision was made. I finally had a project that would benefit from my creativity. We found my dream home, a charming village house with a beautiful garden and an exquisite view of a vineyard. I convinced Cedric it was perfect, so he made a deal with the owner. He'd slip him 100,000 Swiss francs under the table, then meet with the notary to finalize the sale. Everything went very quickly, just like how we met, then moved in together. I didn't ask him where the rest of the money came from, as I didn't feel we had reached that point in our relationship where we could discuss the thorny issue of money. He seemed not to have any hesitation about it though.

"Remember, honey, just because you're not putting a penny into the house doesn't mean it isn't yours. And you see, both our names are on the contract as owners. I put down the money because you don't have much. If you did, I know you would have paid your share."

His comment reassured me. I hadn't touched my savings, but then, I couldn't access my bank account. When I left New York, Cedric set up everything for me: new cell phone, new email account, new savings, checking, credit cards, everything. He assured me I didn't need to use up my savings because he'd give me as much money as I needed. I never took advantage of him. I wasn't the kind of woman who spends every day shopping or going out to lunch with friends. I liked my tranquility, and I knew I would be content in our cozy new house with the shady garden. I didn't need anything else. Except maybe a dog to keep me company. I mentioned it to him at one point. He said sure, why not?

We moved in a few months later, in October, which was lovely that year. The leaves hadn't yet fallen, and they glowed bright red, orange, and yellow. I emptied my dozen or so boxes on the first evening, everything in its place: my books arranged on the shelves, the bed made, my clothes folded or hung up where they belonged. Even Cedric couldn't find anything to criticize. I'd had to get better at organization, because that was the only way to avoid his harsh remarks.

I had also learned how to win an argument: by never having any. I knew how he worked now. He was meticulous and controlling, and he liked to find his home exactly as he left it in the morning. One day, he even directed me to "correct" the cleaning lady I'd hired, because two statues on the table in the entrance hall had been shifted a few inches.

"Tell your Yugoslavian cleaning lady not to move things around. Shit, it isn't complicated! On top of working my ass off so you can live in the lap of luxury, now I need to deal with the help? You can't even manage a house! What are you good for? Ah yes, you're good in bed!"

I put the two statues back in place without a word.

Cedric never took the time to just be, to just enjoy our home. It was the last property on a cul-de-sac, a built-in protection against burglars and guarantee of supreme quiet, and our village was well situated, not too far from Geneva. It overlooked the lake and had a view of the Alps. I thought we were very lucky. And Cedric had achieved his childhood dream to own a beautiful home, but instead of enjoying it, he spent his weekends scrutinizing every detail and finding fault.

"Do you see how that spot on the wall is crumbling.? We'll have to redo the entire façade. Did you call the gardener? The plants look shabby and overgrown. When is he coming? I'd better be here when he comes. I'm going to give him a piece of my mind."

One late autumn day his daughters arrived for the weekend, and from how sullen they looked, I figured they weren't looking forward to spending two days out here in the country after taking a train and a bus to get here. They probably preferred seeing their friends and going out. I understood, and that evening at dinner, I tried to suggest a solution.

"You could go to your friend's house in the morning, then take the last train back at night, and we'll come and get you at the station," I said. "And I'm sure your dad will sometimes let you stay overnight at a friend's house. I grew up in the countryside, and I promise you it never kept me from going out."

Cedric grunted and said, "Easy for you to say. You snuck out to sleep around and take drugs! I really pity your parents."

The way he so casually insulted me in front of his girls made it clear what he thought of my adolescence. I wondered how he saw me as an adult. Probably just the same, a pitiful delinquent, the fragile Chloe he needed to rescue because that fit into his fantasies. I realized the only things he ever brought up about my past were the bad ones, especially the drugs, a mistake of my youth. He twisted everything and transformed even what was simply healthy curiosity into unhealthy desires or vices. He seemed to want to prove to his teen girls, to my parents, to the entire world, that he was the only reason I was still alive, that without him, I would have died on some nasty sidewalk in New York. He probably even told people I used to prostitute myself for another hit. He forgot that I had a good, clean life before I met him, with my own friends and interests and a career I loved.

By this point, we'd been together for two years, and I thought he still loved me, because most of the time, he held me up on a pedestal. I was sure the hardest part was behind us. Don't all couples grow stronger through the difficult times before hitting their stride? Maybe I was wrong. I didn't know what I was doing, so I tried not to think about it. It was easier to tell myself to just keep on keeping on. Tend to your relationship, Chloe. Don't forget your number one goal. You must never feel rejected by a man, and to do that, keep your head down and push on. Like your mother did, and in the end, she seemed to find peace with that man you so admire, your father. He was absent and never gave you any real love, but he and your mother presented you an ideal of love, an example to hold in mind and to attain with Cedric, if possible.

When we bought the new house, Cedric had said I could have a dog. I'd grown up with dogs and if I was going to faithfully replicate my mother's life, that meant it was time to have one of my own.

THIS IS BULLSHIT, NOT A LOVE STORY

So, I mentioned again how much I'd like to have a dog to keep me company during the long days alone, and he gave me permission. I wanted a young dog, but not a puppy, and eventually I found a six-month-old black Labrador, a beautiful male I named Elvis, a name that fit him perfectly. We went to pick him up a few days before my birthday, and Elvis jumped straight into my arms. I was happy, truly happy. Finally, somebody who would love me unconditionally!

I'd gotten everything ready at home to welcome our little black furball. Cedric had never had a dog, but he wanted to make me happy, his unspoken but implied condition being that I would make him happy in return. He must have figured that by letting me have a dog, I would be even more malleable.

Once inside his new house, Elvis seemed immediately at home, trotting around and sniffing everything. The weather was mild for the end of November, so I decided to serve lunch in the garden.

"Sit, Elvis."

He already knew the word. I praised him but remained firm when he started to get up. I grinned at Cedric, but he didn't even smile back. He hadn't yet touched the dog or gone near him – he was completely blank, not a hint of affection, and when lunch was over, he went into the living room to sort out our bookshelves. He liked the books organized by type, size, and author. I stayed outside petting Elvis, a bit sad that Cedric had no space in his heart for a pet. My euphoria had already disappeared.

On Elvis's first night with us, I settled him into his new bed in the kitchen. He was such a well-behaved dog. He slept through the night, and didn't make a sound, not even a whimper.

Cedric was relieved. "Actually, it's not so hard having a dog. He's like a stuffed animal. I thought he was going to bark all night."

The next night, Elvis woke us up at 3 a.m., whimpering. I got up to check on him, but I knew it was better to let him cry it out, so he'd get used to being alone at night. I went back to bed, and lay there, tense, until 6:30, when I heard him moving around, and guessed he needed to go out. I didn't mind being the one to manage this. It would pay off in the end, and Elvis would make us happy, or at least make me happy.

I decided to sign up for dog training classes. Hanging out with other dogs for a few hours every day would prevent him from being lonely, and it turned out to be good for me too. For those two hours each day, being outside with all those people and their dogs, I forgot about everything else. I didn't have to be careful what I said or did, and my increasingly worrying home life didn't matter. I could focus all my attention on Elvis and not on Cedric's mood swings. I had been finding lately that my stress level rocketed when he returned from work. Elvis welcomed him by throwing his little body against him, but Cedric would push him away with a shove. Barely saying hello to me, he would shut himself up in his office while I sat alone in the kitchen, Elvis' muzzle on my knees, his eyes looking into mine as if he understood my hurt.

I had a foreboding my dog was not going to be with me long, and I tried not to get more attached. And when Elvis peed in the living room two weeks later, Cedric exploded. It wasn't the urine on the hardwood floor that made him so crazy. It was obvious he didn't want me giving my attention to someone or something other than him, and it bothered him that an animal could come before his comfort at home.

"I want my own needs to be met, not those of some stupid dog. You love him more than you love me! But what really annoys me, even more than his stink or all those black hairs on the white tile, is that I can't host any classy parties. How can anyone do any fucking with a dog barking behind the door?"

I had to find a solution, so I asked my parents to take the dog for the weekend while I figured out what to do. We dropped Elvis off on Friday evening, and at that moment, as I set him down on their doorstep, I knew I would never see my dog again. I hugged him fiercely, then let go and turned away.

We went straight to a costume party, where I couldn't stop the tears. I locked myself up in a spare bedroom. Stretched out on the bed, I cried for a long time, my wig splayed out on the floor, mascara running down my cheeks. I didn't look like the high-class call girl Cedric had dressed me up as, more like a transvestite escapee from some seedy bar.

Cedric banged on the door finally, and demanded I let him in. When he saw me, he told me to stay there until it was time to leave. He didn't care how lousy I was feeling, he just wanted to be sure I wouldn't make a scene in front of everyone. He made it clear he needed things to go back to normal on Monday, which to him meant a pet-free house.

He got his way. We got rid of my dog. I asked him to pick Elvis up from my parents' house on Sunday and take it back to the breeder. I couldn't bear to see him. It would've been too painful for me to say goodbye. Cedric didn't even try to console me, and when he got back to the house, he was holding the dog's leash up high like a trophy.

"Won't this be perfect for us some evening, darling?" he crowed.

The breeder called me that evening to say, "Look, I know this is because of your husband. What a selfish man! I've got two words for you – good luck."

Right then, a first measure of fear filled me. I was looking at Cedric as the man spoke, and I knew I could never forgive him for the terrible thing he'd done, putting me through the sorrow of loving a dog for a few weeks, then taking it away. But I was suddenly afraid to show him how sad I was, afraid of his reaction, his contempt and derision. I walked away from him into the bedroom, and for once, he left me alone.

After losing Elvis and his cheerful presence, it was hard to get comfortable again in our house. It was too big, empty and echoing. It felt like it belonged to Cedric, not to me. He'd made it his territory from the day we moved in, leaving me only a small workshop behind the garage to call my own. This space became my writing and sculpting studio, a haven when I could no longer handle everything. A place where I could breathe.

From there, I could observe him as he went from one room to another. Very often naked. I watched him cook, and I could tell if he was in a good mood or not by his gestures. If he was happy, I knew the exact moment he would open the door and yell, "Sweetheart, dinner is ready!" Then he'd pull me into his arms and tickle me, saying something nice like, "Come and eat. I made your favorite soup." If he was on a downswing, he might not open the door at all; he'd just stand at the counter and eat out of the pot, not bothering to call me. Maybe that was better than going in, instead of being assaulted with unkind words, exasperated sighs, and glares of contempt, disappointment or anger. He never apologized. There were so many times when he should have, and so many times I held back a response, let alone a retort, but I knew better now. Avoid escalation at all costs.

I got creative in thinking up excuses for him. I racked my brains to figure out what blunder I'd committed for him to treat me this way. It took so little to upset him, and he grew more capricious by the day. I never knew when an argument would explode. He would be watching me tenderly and then his gaze would leap to something else, he would frown, and the fireworks would begin. The least little thing could light him up, like my lack of culinary skill.

"Just look at those radishes!" he said one day. "How could you cut them that way? There's nothing left!"

Then he slammed out of the kitchen into our bedroom. I found him kneeling in the corner, his face hidden in his hands, sobbing because I had made him so upset and angry with me for cutting the radishes too thin. Our guests were supposed to arrive in a few minutes, so I had to reassure him, take him in my arms, tell him that I loved him, that he was the man of my dreams, and that never again would I destroy his radishes that way.

But that wasn't enough for him. He had to draw it out, so he pushed me away. I lost my balance and fell back awkwardly onto my butt as he rushed out and ran up the stairs, then, like a crazy man, he threw himself against a wall, then another one, screaming in frustration that I would have to take care of our guests, that he was too upset to go back downstairs.

I couldn't say a word. My entire body shook. I lurched into the kitchen and stood beside the stove, frozen, staring down at those horrible drama-causing radishes. But when our friends rang the doorbell a few minutes later, Cedric came right downstairs and opened the door. He greeted them cheerfully as if nothing had happened.

"Hello there! Come on in. Let me show you around. Sweetheart, will you get the cocktails ready?" And then with a teasing tone and a wink, he added, "And don't forget to cut those radishes the right way next time."

Much later that same night, my mother called to tell me all about a concert she went to with my father. I wanted to change the subject, and tell her something about my life, that I was unhappy, that no, I wasn't being difficult, but Cedric did not treat me well. I wanted her to hear his awful insults, to know the things he made me do that were so perverted I wanted to vomit.

I wanted her to teach me how to say no and how to fight back without endangering myself or our relationship. I guess I wanted to have my cake and eat it too, but is that too much to ask?

As she went on and on about the exquisite music and the elegant dresses she'd seen, all I could think about was how to describe my daily life with Cedric to her. Mentally gathering the facts crystallized the truth: he was making me ill. I no longer knew who I was, let alone the man I was living with. He had become my sickness. The arguments he instigated now were so scary, I was afraid he would kill me. My train of thought ran away from me, and I started to panic as the culminating fact stared me in the face: escape was my only remedy.

At that instant, my mom laughed and told me how handsome my dad had looked in his rented tuxedo, and I pushed away the idea of escape. I wasn't ready. I couldn't imagine leaving, because I wanted my marriage to be a success, like my mother's was. Why did I want to resemble her so much? Why did I have to follow her example, even when her situation didn't fit mine? I wanted to tell her that it wasn't fair, that her example wasn't good for me because her life and epoch were so different from mine, and her husband was not at all like mine! So why did I insist on believing this conventional life was going to make me happy? Why did I continue to believe that my future with this man was set in stone? I couldn't unravel those answers myself. I needed her to help me, but I didn't even bother to ask. I knew she wanted only to believe I was a happy, soon-to-be-married woman. I laughed with her and after some small talk, I signed off.

"Goodnight, Mom."

"Goodnight, Chloe."

Tercio de Varas:
Dance of the Lances

The El Paseo is long over. A beginner's dance. The matador's combat against the bull will begin soon, but not yet; they are only entering Act One.

The spectators hold their breath, waiting for it to begin. They're out for more blood. The mounted picadors trot out proudly, to general applause. Everyone in the stands sits back to observe and enjoy the lance work, as the picadors test the bull's courage and stamina by stabbing him in the mound of muscle on his neck. This forces the bull to hold his head and horns lower. He is more dangerous that way, and more riled up, but he will weaken with the loss of blood. His real suffering begins now, a slow and malicious pain.

The matador observes, cranking his neck to one side and then the other, chin up, taking one step, then another, keeping his rhythm, his cape in his hand, his spine straight and as stiff as a steel bar as he makes his elegant feints. He doesn't believe in failure.

"Isn't it incredible?"

"I'm not sure I'd use the word 'incredible' to describe a bullfight. Maybe, 'intellectually interesting?'"

"Is that all you can give me? Sarcasm? Thanks a lot. Look at what I'm giving you here. A perfect lovers' weekend in Madrid, and a once-in-a-lifetime bullfight! Don't hide your enthusiasm!"

Cedric was angry, and I didn't understand why. What I found truly frightening about this tradition was how easy it became to watch the slaughter play out. Through half-closed eyes, I'd witnessed the first bull put to death. Now I was watching the second, as Cedric insisted I keep my eyes open from beginning to end.

The bull was adroit, but the horsemen maneuvered expertly, inexorably. The thud of hoofs and panting of both horses and bull were the only sounds in the arena. The lances hit home, and the bull's blood spurted. He was still strong and beautiful and belligerent, but surprised at his masters' versatility, and forced to hang his head, as a certain muscle in his neck had been severed. He looked all around – for an exit? He bellowed in defiance, yet it was dawning on him that his task might be harder than expected.

Beside me, Cedric was thrilled. "Look, the bull is weakening. They're getting him ready to submit, so the matador can do what he needs to do. What a beautiful dance! This is art!"

The bull ran straight for the wall. Wham! Head first! He almost hit the matador on his way, but swerved around him at the last second, allowing the man to keep his feet and his mastery. The audience gasped, but then clapped and exchanged comments of approval of the Varas. They seemed proud. Yet hidden behind their majestic national tradition was a death machine, an assassination.

Later, when my life became a living hell, I would understand. Like the bull bashing his head against the wall, I would do anything to be left in peace. And for a while, I did find a kind of peace. I kept my troubles hidden in a vow of silence, and in public, I spread my forced happiness. "You look so happy with him," people said. My parents should have noticed that over time I lost my shine. My body slumped, my face went empty. Why didn't they ever ask me the one thing that would have given me permission to tell them the truth?

"Tell me, Chloe, how are you? Are you really happy with this man? Does he treat you well?" No one ever asked me this, and my pride or embarrassment or fear kept me from speaking out.

I buried my old self behind this new identity. I kept my anger in check, although it crashed and scraped against the walls of my subconscious. Finally, I started thinking a visit to New York would do me a world of good, so I suggested various dates, but each time, Cedric found an excuse to push it back.

"No, not then. I was thinking of taking you to Marrakesh right about then."

"No, no, we can't. That's when we're going to Tunisia for Daniel's wedding. Like I told you."

"No, that's when the girls are on vacation, and we're going to see my mother. I already told her."

I never stopped travelling, but always with him, and never to New York, a forbidden destination for some reason. The winter months passed, then one early spring day in the third year of our relationship came a new upheaval.

Cedric was on his way home after a business trip to Tel-Aviv. His flight had a stopover in Zurich, so he suggested I drive there and meet him at the Hyatt downtown. He'd reserved a suite for us, saying he thought it could be fun.

"That way, we can drive home together and stop for lunch somewhere in the Bernese countryside. You can organize our night in Zurich with the hotel concierge – somewhere for drinks, a trendy restaurant, then a nightclub. I want to take you dancing! It's been a long time since we did that. Won't it be great?"

Luckily, he didn't ask me to look for a swingers' club. I was already stressed that I would have to drive his car, find the hotel, and plan our evening to his approval. It struck me that I'd clearly lost my self-confidence. I travelled the world, I started my life over numerous times in different countries, but I was in a panic about a one-night trip right here in Switzerland!

The weather was awful during the drive. Rain alternating with snowy slush, and the clouds were so low I could barely see a thing. My left eye started to twitch. I rubbed it, thinking it was the stress or some kind of hormonal imbalance, and started using my right eye more to watch the road. Then, just as I pulled up in front of the hotel, my right eye started twitching. My vision was now completely blurred. I blinked and rubbed, but nothing helped. I gave the keys to the valet, made my way in somehow and got to the hotel counter to check in. After telling the concierge about our plans for the evening, I had to ask the receptionist to guide me to my room. I washed my eyes and lay down, but my vision did not improve. Cedric was arriving in an hour, and I had to be ready. To relax, I took a book out and tried to read, but I couldn't focus on a single word. I decided to rest, feeling surprisingly calm – I was somehow sure this would pass. I closed my eyes and dozed off.

Cedric shook me awake. "Chloe, honey! Were you sleeping? Did you have a nice drive?"

"Call me Stevie Wonder," I said. "I don't know what's happening, but everything is blurry. Where are you? I can't see your eyes."

"I bet you're just tired. Did you make our plans for tonight?"

I got up and took a fuzzy shower, dressed and put on my makeup by rote, and we left. At the restaurant, Cedric had to read me the entire menu. That was a first! We laughed about it, though, and after eating, he took me dancing. In the darkened club, I forgot about my eyes. The next morning at breakfast, I couldn't even see clearly enough to light my cigarette. This was bad. Cedric called the doctor and as he listened, his face turned pale.

"I have to take you to the ophthalmology hospital in Lausanne, immediately. Let's get our stuff packed. We have to leave now."

He wouldn't tell me what the doctor had said to him. I'd never seen Cedric worried before, truly worried. I followed him silently to the car, and we drove for two hours. He kept quiet, holding and pressing my hand.

The doctor on duty, an internist, dilated my pupils with drops and leaned toward my face. When he examined the back of my eye, he suddenly took a deep breath and took a step backwards. "I'll be right back. I need to call the head doctor."

A nurse bustled in, then led me into an adjoining room, where she inserted an IV into my arm, saying, "Dr. Bideau asked me to give you some cortisone. He'll be here in a moment. This will take about an hour, so please, relax. Everything will be okay."

I watched the solution seep into my veins. Drip, drip. Cedric hadn't left my side, and he held my hand and looked at me solicitously with a serious smile.

The head doctor arrived and examined me. "Luckily, our internist alerted me. There's no doubt – you've suffered bilateral retinal ischemia, also called a retinal stroke. In other words, the blood flow was interrupted to both eyes. Probably for about a half an hour. It's what happens during cardiac arrest, except for you it happened in the macula of your eyes. I've given you a strong dose of cortisone, which is the best way of halting the inflammation."

He didn't say anything else. He examined the back of my eyes again, several times, as did the internist. I heard them muttering in the hallway, "...macula is ruined...exploded into a thousand pieces...never seen that before."

The head doctor came back in and asked the nurse to take blood, then have some tests run, which he jotted down. It seemed like a long list.

Then he turned to me and said, "Retinal ischemia is a risk for women on the pill who smoke. But that may not actually be the problem, because usually only one eye is affected. In your case, both eyes were affected, one after the other.

"There are several pathologies that can lead to this, such as autoimmune disorders like multiple sclerosis. We will test for all of them, but the most important thing today is to control this inflammation. You're out of immediate danger now. However, your vision has been severely affected, and I'm sorry to say it's impossible to determine if you'll regain your sight completely. You can go home, and we'll set up appointments for next week for the other tests we need to run. Are you alright?"

"Yes, yes, thank you," I lied. I was not alright and felt completely lost. I gathered myself together and got up, though. On the way out the door, Cedric said, "I asked the girls to join us at Dario's. I think a good pizza will make you feel better. Let's hurry, I don't want to make them wait."

What was he going on about? A pizza? His daughters? Was he joking, or an idiot? Everything was a blur. I felt like I'd been hit by a lightning bolt, and my vision, my favorite of the five senses was at risk. The doctor's uncertainty about regaining my vision echoed through my mind. How was I going to live if I were unable to see the world in three dimensions.? How would I drive? Or work? Or even walk around?

We got to the pizza place back in Geneva, and Cedric showed his crass unconcern for my feelings again.

"Chloe is feeling sorry for herself, girls! Guess what? She's blind! What do you want to eat, my lovies? Let's order right now, as you've got school tomorrow. Sweetheart, what would you like? Pasta? It's a bit lighter..."

Cedric kissed my cheek. Even through the mist, I could see the girls making faces at me, trying to see if what their dad had said was true. They chattered, laughed and wolfed down pizza, but I couldn't eat a bite. I just wanted to be in bed.

The next weeks consisted of endless sessions with doctors and nurses, being poked and peered at. Turns out mine was a rare case, something to be studied in light of "academic publication." This gave me one advantage: I never had to wait long for appointments. The nurses were sympathetic, which cheered me up. But they still couldn't pinpoint the cause of my ischemia.

Cedric decided he knew all about it, though. After a bit of research online, he pointed the finger at my past: drugs, alcohol, promiscuity.

Damn it, Cedric, that wasn't the entire story! I liked my life back then, and even if I didn't always know what was good or bad, I wouldn't mind reliving some of those moments again. That was who I was. Younger, crazier, carefree and romantic. I would have slept with the entire world when I was on ecstasy, and yes, I smoked far too many cigarettes, I dealt some hash, I rolled joints with one hand. So what? I was young in years, but enough of an old soul to enjoy a few human vices. I was a dusty-footed hippie, roaming the world, and I don't regret it – that's who I was, Cedric, and you should accept it.

I didn't express any of these thoughts, of course.

"What do you expect with the life you've led?" Cedric continued. "This is what you get for pushing your body to such extremes. In some ways, you deserve it. But you know that already. Anyway, I'll take care of you, sweetheart. Thank God you found me."

Cedric was setting himself up as a savior, the ultimate Prince Charming. Everyone would see him as the perfect man; no one would ever reproach him for anything. What a guy! And how lucky I was!

Without asking me, he called our friends and families to share what had happened to me. Then he spread the news out further, even to his clients and my friends in New York, who all received an email describing my "condition" in detail, peppered with medical jargon and salted with enough drama to upset them. Then I learned he was sending them a weekly health update! He was so convincing I started getting several calls a day to see how I was doing, and he demanded I answer, especially when it was one of his clients.

Allegedly, he wanted to explore all possibilities to fix the problem.

"It's Rafik, a client. Talk to him, he knows a very good ophthalmologist in Beirut, a specialist in rare cases. Don't forget to thank him. Try to appreciate what everyone is doing for you!"

Cedric didn't understand how exhausted I was. I wanted to sleep, and sleep some more, and more than anything, I didn't want to talk to anyone.

Rose called me from New York one night, sounding devastated. "Are you dying, sweetie? Is it true?"

What was she talking about? Dying? Then she read me Cedric's latest group email, one he had sent the night before:

"Chloe's situation is very unstable. She will probably be handicapped for life. She can hardly see anything. Her blindness is serious. She can no longer drive or read or watch TV. She is weak, very weak. Her doctors think it may be a very serious autoimmune disease. Eventually she's going to die."

What the hell? I was the only person with the right to broadcast how I was feeling, and I didn't want to do that. He knew nothing about it. Like how stressed I was, how terrifying it was to wake up in darkness, or how confusing it was to hear birds singing but have no idea what the weather was like. He didn't know I cried when I sat down to do my nails and couldn't even see them, or how often I opened a book in the hopes of seeing the words printed clearly. Having to push my nose against the screen to use my phone. I spent most of my time on the sofa, half-blind but hearing everything around me. Worried I would knock over another glass of wine at each meal. I moved slowly, calculating every gesture. Going down the stairs was a sporting event. I lost all sense of distance. Going into crowds scared me, and if I had to go to a restaurant, I made sure to arrive early enough to be seated first, and not have to search for whomever I was meeting. I didn't bother to look in the mirror, because the face I saw was only a blur.

Cedric didn't deserve to hear how I was doing, anyway, because he often made fun of me, treating me like a sad clown. He said it was to cheer me up. I would smile and play along, but deep down I understood my suffering belonged to me alone. My condition and how I felt became very private, a part of me I would never give to Cedric. Plus, I'd made my own connection between my retinal stroke and Cedric. It wasn't my past I needed to worry about; it was living with him. It was so stressful that my body rebelled. Maybe it was sending me a signal.

The next six months, it seemed I spent all my time at hospitals being examined, or going from one specialist to another, waiting for science to figure out exactly what was wrong with me. Nothing about it was normal, I heard again and again. The doctors did a lot of staring and speculating. "Such a young woman, losing her sight in her thirties. An ischemia no less, and in both eyes."

I started feeling like an object and wanted to tell everyone to leave me alone. But I also wanted help, a cure. During this period, Cedric changed again. He notified his office he would be working more from home, as he wanted to be near me. From then on, he rarely left me alone, and even when he did go to the bank, he would call me at least 15 times a day. If I didn't answer, he would leave me messages telling me to call him right back.

He started to focus on me, only me, but it somehow felt like a show to prove what a good husband he was. He would come check on me every half hour. "Are you okay, my darling? Do you need anything? Did you take your medicine?"

Yes, I took the horrible medicines. The prescription list from the doctor was two pages long, including cortisone, which did a real number on me. I worried about the side effects, the water retention, the puffy body. The worst was the daily shot of blood thinners I had to give myself. I would sit in the kitchen and pull out a pouch of skin from my stomach, and thwack, plant the needle and push the syringe down. Cedric liked to watch, even though he told me he hates getting shots. "Well done, honey. You did it. You see, it's not so bad." After a few months, my stomach was like a piece of tenderized meat: blue, red, swollen, bruised. Apparently, it was all for my own good.

Cedric continued researching, spending hours in front of his computer. He spoke to me with the authority of a doctor convinced he could identify the rare illness that had caused the incident.

"I've got it! Behçet's Syndrome. It must be that. I'll call the doctor right away."

It was a possibility. But I no longer cared, as I was living from one day to the next, trying to get used to being handicapped. Call it false pride, but it was more the stigma of having a handicap that handicapped me, as if someone had slapped a sticker on my forehead that read Handicapped Person. My sight was not getting better, but my brain was working hard to replace the defective parts. I lived inside my own bubble, listening to my body, and gradually my four other senses began to compensate and make daily life easier for me.

It didn't take long for Cedric's constant presence to annoy me. He had always been either loving or harsh, one or the other, so this sickly-sweet behavior confused me. I wouldn't have minded if he had always been this loving, but he had really hurt me on his harsh days, and now, his kindness threw me off. It was too much. And I was tired of him treating me like a lost cause, tired of him suffocating me with his questions and admonitions and changing diagnoses, tired of having his daughters over every weekend and forcing myself to join their conversation over meals. I was tired of his mother, tired of everyone! It was all a nightmare, and I just wanted to be left alone.

Cedric didn't realize that my outlook on life had completely changed since that day in the Lausanne hospital. It was a blurry life now. I had the feeling I was continuously underwater in a swimming pool, day and night, the same impression. And I wished it would be calmer. I didn't want to cope with his family being around so much, but I couldn't just jump in my car and get away. I felt trapped and drowning.

Cedric had a strong constitution, and he was almost never sick, although sometimes he faked it so people would pay attention to him. Like a little boy, he liked wearing a band-aid over a miniscule scratch or putting a cast over a minor strain. One time, he made me drive him to the emergency room because his thumb was swollen. During the exam, the doctor had stifled a laugh, then asked Cedric if he'd lifted something heavy. Cedric told him he'd been working with his new sports coach the day before, and lifting weights was part of the workout.

"There you go! That's your answer! It's nothing to worry about. Your thumb will heal. Have a good day!"

I was annoyed at wasting an ER doctor's time. There had been children crying in pain in the waiting room, and an old woman clutching her stomach, and then Cedric, who had pushed his way in for a swollen thumb. It was pathetic. And yet I did my duty to nurse and console and take care of him. He liked the attention.

Now it was my illness that drew a lot of attention to him; he was a victim, and he made me feel I should console him for it and tell him to buck up. That's when I came to realize Cedric was exploiting my illness, or more specifically the pity people had for me, using it as a magic spell to open new accounts at work. He would set up a business dinner, and I'd have to wear my sunglasses throughout the entire meal, as if I were blind. I definitely needed to wear glasses outside because sunlight hurt my eyes, but he insisted I wear them inside, too. He was ecstatic the first time it worked.

"Thanks to you, I just signed Tarek," he crowed. "He and his wife adored you! I don't know how many times they told me they hope you'll get better soon. Tarek opened an account today and deposited the first million euros. He's going to send a couple more next week! It's crazy how easily people let themselves be manipulated when they have sympathy for you. I love my job!"

Strangely, the stroke that took my sight helped me see the world more clearly. He was right. Sympathy did make people more compassionate. We constantly received invitations from people and accepted every single one. But this kind of exaggerated attention doesn't last forever; people's concern fizzled out, and the calls and invitations did too. I think we made them uncomfortable, not because of my illness, but because Cedric tried too hard to look like he belonged. People discovered he was simply another social climber, obsessed with power and money.

I didn't want to accept this. I wanted to believe in the Cedric I had first met, with his great sense of humor, his outsized desire to make me happy, the many ways he showed his generosity. I'd never encountered a man like him before, and despite all, I still believed he loved me, and that despite my handicap, he would always be there for me.

My handicap, however, grew more debilitating. The extended corticosteroid treatment saved me from complete blindness, but its side effects wreaked havoc on my body. As they became more pronounced, my immune system grew weaker. Every shot injected a kind of lie detector into me, relentlessly bringing up the dirt from my past. Like the parasites I had contracted years before on a trip to Africa. They took hold again, and I had to take a full course of antibiotics. All I had to do was step outside and I got the flu or a cold or a sinus infection. Aside from staying indoors, I didn't know how to protect myself.

My doctor reassured me, "It's not going to last forever. Cortisone is the only medicine that will heal your ocular inflammation, so we have to take the bad with the good. Be patient and get some rest. You look like you need it."

That goddamn cortisone! It detected lies of omission too. It exposed a little secret of Cedric's, something extremely important he'd neglected to mention. Until that point in our relationship, I figured he'd told me everything – all his dirt. But I woke up late, bizarrely late, one morning, so exhausted I had trouble getting out of bed. I felt terrible pressure in my groin, like I desperately needed to masturbate, if that makes any sense, and my right leg was tingling painfully. I'd never felt anything like this before. It was so sensitive to the touch that I couldn't put my jeans on.

I'd had enough surprises, enough suffering, and now, alone and confused, this new development overwhelmed me. Thinking it might be a UTI, I decided to inspect my vagina. With my legs spread in front of the bedroom mirror, I could see it was fiery red and covered with white dots. I immediately drove to my gynecologist's office.

"This is a full-blown eruption of herpes simplex virus type 2, otherwise known as genital herpes," he said. "I'll prescribe a medication you can take now and whenever symptoms reappear. There's no cure per se – once you've got it, it's for life. Did you know you had it? No? Better ask your partner if he's being treated. He must have given you this without telling you. Nice guy!"

Fantastic, thank you Cedric. There was no doubt he gave it to me, as I never had anything like this before, plus I always used protection and tested regularly for STDs. How would I talk to him about this without sounding like I was accusing him? I was sure this would be a touchy subject, and it would be easy to mess up our relationship even more if I went about it the wrong way.

"You look awful," was the first thing Cedric said when he came home that evening. "What's wrong with your skin? It's all irritated."

Red face, numb or tingling limbs, fever, genitals out of commission: all the symptoms of herpes. I didn't yet know much about the virus, or how I'd get used to it. This first attack was very intense, and the ones yet to come weren't a party either.

"Emergency trip to the gynecologist today," I said, trying to be firm and clear. "My vagina was irritated, and I had other strange symptoms. He told me I have genital herpes. I assure you I didn't have this before being with you, so... Why didn't you tell me? We could have used protection."

"What would be the use of telling you? You'd have gotten it from me at some point or other. It's not so serious. You just take a Valtrex and it goes away. Don't make such a fuss about something that's never killed anyone."

I could not believe it. I could only stare at him in shock. No regret, no apology, as if he didn't feel he'd done anything wrong, as if he didn't care about me at all. I was feeling too sick to deal with him right then, so I just got up, gingerly, and limped off toward the bedroom.

"Take a bath, that'll relax you," he called out after me. "Hey, I need to go pick up my mom at the airport, by the way. I asked her to come for the next couple weeks since it's gotten so hard for you to do anything on your own. She can cook some meals for you, do your nails, take you out for walks and read to you."

Two entire weeks with his mother – Geraldine, nickname Didine. I would be stuck with her and her old spinster habits all day long while Cedric was at work. Her husband had left her 20 years earlier, and she had never found a new one, maybe because she talked non-stop, even while eating, about herself or about nothing at all, in a high-pitched breathy voice that irritated me to no end.

I could hear her moving about the kitchen when I woke up in the morning. Before, I usually tried to avoid her until later in the day, but I got up and went into the living room.

"Did you sleep well?" she asked too brightly. "What are you going to do today?"

Nothing at all, my dear Didine, and I'd like to avoid you all day if possible. I couldn't stand her company, the sound of her voice, the thump-thump of her heavy steps coming up the stairs, her loud laugh and the fact that she was blind regarding her son. She wasn't a bad woman, but she was often short with me, and her deference, fear even of her son, irritated me. Being with her all day long was just too much. But I felt sorry for her, too, and I hid my feelings.

"I don't know," I said, forcing a smile. "I don't feel well at all today. I need to rest, and for once I don't have any doctor's appointments, so go ahead and plan your own day. There's some shopping to do for dinner tonight. I don't know what Cedric planned, or whether the girls are coming. Why not call him?"

Suddenly a thought came to me. I had the perfect excuse to be left in peace for two weeks: my illness. "I need rest," I'd say, or something like, "I won't be any fun, so go ahead and enjoy your time with your son and granddaughters." And it worked! The two weeks passed quickly. I stayed in bed, and they ignored me completely. I heard them in other parts of the house, laughing stupidly, arguing loudly, watching TV shows or old movies. Cedric was content to be with his family, the daughters he was so proud of, the mother he was ashamed of in public, but perfectly happy with in private. They were his family. A bit sadly, I recognized I wasn't a part of it and never would be. A unit unto themselves, why would they bother to bring me into it?

The visit came to an end finally, and Cedric's ex picked up the girls. Didine's flight left the same morning. Cedric said goodbye to me, mentioning he had something important to tell me later, and then he waited for her out in the car. She came into the bedroom and gave me a peck on the cheek, then hesitated. I could tell she felt awkward, and for once her stream of words dried up. No motherly advice about my health, no "Let's talk soon," or "Hope you feel better."

She simply turned away, saying, "See you later, kiddo."

For some reason, she called Cedric and me "kiddo," and always in an exaggerated accent. The front door clicked shut, the car vroomed off, and then silence fell, precious silence, so very rare. I got up and went into the kitchen, absolutely thrilled to be alone. My mind was a perfect, sweet blank.

And then the phone rang. "I just dropped my mom off at the airport, and I'm rushing to the office now. Have a good day, sweetheart. And get ready for tonight. I want you to be my whore. It's been a long time. I invited some friends over at 8. I love you, see you later."

So, this was what he'd meant by "something important to tell me." It meant I would not have a good day. I had expected it though. Once his mother was gone, his sexual desires would naturally come roaring back. Despite the quiet and the rest I still craved, I spent the rest of the day getting ready mentally and physically. Everything had to be perfect, of course. The mental part was the hardest because of my mood swings, which I had hoped my two-week rest would cure. It didn't.

I quit smoking after my stroke, and that wasn't easy, and then I stopped taking the pill, at which point I lost control of my hormones, and now the horrendous herpes! I needed to learn how to manage the virus, so I browsed some online forums. I found women like me, out of their depth, angry. Some of them said it had ruined their lives. Would mine be ruined too? I called Cedric a bastard in my mind, but I guess I wasn't ready to accuse him of ruining my life – I didn't even hate him for it. My misplaced guilty conscience. He'd convinced me anything bad that happened to me was my fault, because of my past. I turned off the computer and tried to focus on the immediate issue: the evening's sex party. Yet another. And there would be many others, into the foreseeable future. I jumped up. I didn't want him to be disappointed.

Cedric got home at seven. He'd done the shopping, and as usual, he made dinner while I set the table. I'd become quite good at table decoration, as that was something he let me do.

"You're so sexy tonight, darling," he said, coming over and wrapping his arms around me. "I know his wife will like you. I found them on that online swingers' site. They look really good."

Sexy? How in the world did I look sexy? But to him, any woman dressed like a whore was sexy.

Our guests arrived on time. Everything was synchronized, as they had left their kids with a babysitter and had to be home by midnight. I knew the scenario by heart. Eat a fine meal, usually a light one, so as not to ruin the after-dinner delights, because no one wants to fuck after stuffing themselves silly. He prepared fish sautéed in white wine. I sat next to the wife. I could tell she wanted to get things going during the meal, as she kept accidentally touching my hand, then my shoulder and thigh. Then she leaned over and kissed me with her mouth wide open so the two men could see our tongues at work.

Cedric always planned his sex scenes, the full agenda. He didn't ask my opinion; he simply explained the plan before the guests arrived. He didn't care about my tired eyes or my herpes lesions or my mood swings; he treated me like an object. No emotions, no getting the vibes going. No heart, no soul. An object of devotion. I went into the kitchen when he excused himself to get dessert, and I told him I had my period.

"What stops you from fucking on your period, or with herpes? You do it with me. Anyway, I can't cancel. You take care of the man this time."

I didn't answer. I would take care of the man and the woman, and no one would touch me that evening, which was rare, nearly something to appreciate. There was no way I'd join his orgy with a herpes outbreak. I was contagious. I wasn't like him, spreading it left and right. It was HIS herpes, not mine! But he still made it feel like it was my fault I had caught it.

After the swinger "friends" left late that night, he picked a fight with me because I mentioned how sick I was feeling.

"Herpes, always your herpes! When will you stop whining about your health problems? I've got the worst luck with you. You're always sick! You're so boring, ever since your eye problems. My god, just look at you! You look like hell without make-up! Luckily, I arrange these fun evenings every once in a while – at least then you make some effort. Go lie down, you look terrible."

All he cared about was whether our sex life went on. But I didn't want it anymore, not like this. What I'd been mildly curious about at first was becoming perverted enslavement, and by his obsession with it, he was also enslaved. If he had nothing planned, he spent all his free time on swingers' websites. Strangers turned him on, their bodies, penises, breasts, asses. Some blurred their faces, some left them clear, but most were average or just plain ugly. Their photos gave hints about the interiors of their homes: flowered curtains, beat-up sofas, televisions on, the woman in the foreground with red lace underwear, fake eyelashes and acrylic nails. Middle-aged women posing sexily in front of the camera, just far enough away to soften their wrinkles. Everyone seemed so pathetic.

He communicated with couples from all over Europe. Each profile was arranged according to type of desire and sexuality: bi, gay, and so on. Thousands of phantom identities hidden behind fake names. Their ads had a lot in common, variations of minor or major perversions.

"Couple seeking couple for sex games. Man likes being taken by other men. Woman is eager and likes submitting to other women."

Cedric liked to read them to me as if they were literature. If he noticed any spelling mistakes, he immediately passed them over, his rule being "no idiots." No, he only chose classy, noble, educated perverts.

He would call out to me, "Honey, can you come down a second? I want to show you something."

And me, wearily: "What is it?"

He usually wanted to know if I liked the woman's breasts or if the man had a decent cock. This pastime was important to him, so I had to show interest in it, but this bestial exchange of bodies bored me, nothing but bodies and more bodies. Hours and hours of bodies. Not that I can forget any one of those hours, the images, the sounds, the smells! A sickening smell, both rotten and strangely fruity, that wafts through the swingers' clubs and orgies at strangers' homes. The dank smell of a body that's been licked and penetrated by too many cocks, the stink of sweat and sperm. The grunts and moans of so much coming. You don't think of love, of conception; you think of death.

But thanks to my exhibitionist side, it was easier for me to get through these hours. Cedric was a voyeur at heart. Not hard to guess why, there being no reason to show off his second-rate body and prowess. Everyone knows that beauty deserves the spotlight; Cedric understood this. His voyeurism was enough for him. His eyes would narrow and focus on a scene as the action became more intense. I could see his gaze become glossy, like a dog in heat, his breathing become more of a pant and the hairs rise on his arms.

Soon, he was organizing all our trips around sex, whether in Europe, the United States, the Middle East or Asia. He took care of everything: airplane tickets, hotel reservations, and addresses to local spots that promised action. He took great care to gather details about places where he could feed his fantasies: public parks, nudist beaches, night clubs, massage parlors and even private homes. I had to pack my bag for every scenario. Daytime clothes, dining out clothes, evening attire, sexy outfits. I left my own personality behind and put on camouflage with heavy make-up, vulgar clothes and bad language. I played my part to make Cedric happy. I was an object, numb to emotion. I faked my pleasure to get it over with more quickly, but even then, he always wanted to stay until the last scene, afraid of missing out on something.

He started to get upset if I asked to leave, so I stopped trying to get away after my first orgasm. Too dangerous. I shut my mind back down and waited for another unknown tongue. If the lights were nice and low, I could pretend the blurred faces and bodies were beautiful, and that helped. I'd have less to regret the next day, as I didn't want a clear picture in my mind when I woke up. Keeping those faces barely visible in the shadows meant I wouldn't recognize anyone on the street the next day, or worse, that someone might recognize me. I desired only one thing: that Cedric wouldn't subject me to it all again later that night or the next day, or the next week.

THIS IS BULLSHIT, NOT A LOVE STORY

I wanted a break from the anxiety, but I could say nothing. I wanted to scream sometimes, from the horror and self-loathing, but it was so great it stuck in my throat. And the fact our relationship was held together by sex dismayed and depressed me. To keep him satisfied, I had to play several roles: fiancé, mistress, slut and sex slave. He bought me costumes for each role and called me an hour before getting home to tell me who I was to be. If he wanted a slut that night, I'd run a bath, shave myself to perfection, and once out of the steam, disguise myself in a thong and a tight polyester skirt. It never took long to get dressed for that role. I spent more time on my make-up: dark eyeliner around my eyes, a thick layer of mascara, bright red lipstick. There would be red streaks of it on his cheeks afterward. His fantasy toolkit went on the bed: whip, dildo, plug, black silk scarf, and he would choose what roleplay he wanted and I would obey. Sometimes I waited for him on the bed, dominatrix style. Fucking hell, he loved that. He loved whatever was lowdown and dirty, like being fucked up the ass with a dildo. I took the man's role and shoved it into him until he cried out in pain. He always asked for more. It made him super excited, and I knew his orgasm would be extra intense. I'd leave him stretched out on the ground, nearly dead. My job done for the night, I'd take a shower, dress in yoga pants and a sweatshirt, go upstairs and watch TV until he stuck his head in the door to compliment me.

"Fuck, that was amazing. Thank you, honey. What would I do without you? I have a few things to do in my office, but I'll call you when dinner's ready."

He would kiss me. He loved me.

I was no saint before meeting Cedric, I have to admit. I had a lot of one-night stands. Mornings with rumpled sheets, ready to toss in the wash. Or maybe I'd go on several dates with a man, and then came the mistakes, the awkward moments, calling him only to hear endless ringing or an answering machine. There were also flashes of tenderness, long gazes that may have been promising. So many kisses, so lovely and tender. Hope always sprang anew. Naïve and romantic, I thought a kiss could be a sign of true love, and I wanted it to last forever. I hurt myself waiting for love, something I knew little about. Deep down I suspected I was searching for the love my father never showed me.

I thought I had found real love with Cedric. Love with a capital "L," like everyone else seemed to find. We would cherish and pamper each other, say, "I love you" right out of the blue, just because we wanted to say it, and hold hands without thinking twice. When we gazed at each other, we would see our souls. We would respect each other. My True Love would kiss me without slipping a finger between my thighs every chance he got.

I began to question whether anything about my relationship with Cedric had to do with love.

"Tell me what you want. The really dirty stuff."

We were right back where we'd started. I admitted everything to him, even my most intimate sexual desires. He would often guess before I could even whisper a word. I couldn't hide anything from him. If I happened to glance at another man, or a beautiful woman on the street, it would get him going. It was like he'd bugged my brain or put a camera in my head. Nothing belonged to me, not even my thoughts.

One afternoon we were seated on a restaurant terrace with three Italian men at a table beside us. They were gorgeous. There was no other word for it.

"You'd like that, wouldn't you?" Cedric said with a leer. "To have all three at once?"

I groaned inside, knowing what was going to happen. And it wouldn't involve any handsome Italians. Sure enough, late that night he told me his plan.

"Thursday night, 6 pm. I've got it all set up."

I couldn't believe it. He'd actually organized a gang bang. There would be two men that night, who would fuck me, one after the other. I didn't want to think about it. I just wanted it to be Friday already, and over with.

This was new to me, and I didn't know what to expect, so, to relax, I had several drinks before they showed up. Cedric, the big director, prepared me. First, he told me to get on my hands and knees on the bed, then he blindfolded me. Two French firefighters came in, still wearing their uniforms, according to Cedric, who had crossed the border for only one reason: to quench what he imagined as my deepest desire. I heard them drop their heavy jackets to the floor, unbuckle their belts – thick steel buckles by the sound of it – then throw their heavy boots against the bedroom wall and shake their way out of their pants. I measured time by the sound of their discarded clothing.

"Your wife is so beautiful."

Cedric called me "sexy," but never "beautiful." They weren't violent in the way they screwed me. I could almost say they made love to me. There was even something protective about the atmosphere, except that I knew Cedric was filming the whole thing. I played my role *comme il faut*, the perfect and well-behaved wife. My restrained attitude made it possible. I should have been an actress, or maybe I was now. A porn star. But I could branch into foreign films, blockbusters, indies. Yes, I should have been an actress, I kept thinking as the two firemen slap-slapped into me.

A few weeks later, there were three men, and the following month, four men. That evening Cedric made pasta for me, to give me endurance for the night, he said. I felt like an athlete preparing for the Olympic games. I waited for them in the same way, blindfolded and posed on the bed. I promised myself I would never see their faces. It made me sick to feel their cocks inside me after their long work day, and touching their bodies, most of them flabby, did not excite me.

Cedric always set up the camera in the same corner of the room, and when I heard him click it on, I thought, "Action! Ok, fellas, we're on!" Maybe Cedric would organize a movie night one Sunday.

Each man asked me where he should ejaculate.

"Wherever you like, it's all about your pleasure."

Each one of them came with a grunt, grunt, ahh.

I tried to prevent them from getting cum on my hair, though. I hated that sticky feeling around my head, so I'd have to wash it when I showered later, then go to bed with wet hair. And be reminded of the gang of four when I saw it all rumpled in the morning. I thought of all these things while they were using me to get off. When the last of them stood up straight with a big sigh, I was happy my hair was left dry. It's the small things in life that count.

They trooped out, and I took off the blindfold and headed to the bathroom to wash off their sweat and everything else.

And that's a wrap! Yes! I'd done a good job, and Cedric would be happy, and I'd get a romantic dinner for two at the nearby Argentinian restaurant, where I always reserved our table before a gang bang session. After several months, we became regulars.

Cedric usually offered a beer to our guests down in the kitchen, clapping them on the back and saying, "After such hard work, a nice cold beer rehydrates the body."

I didn't want to see them, and had even promised myself that I wouldn't, and yet one evening I chose to go down to the kitchen while they were still there. Showered and dressed in decidedly unsexy clothes, I sat with them for a few minutes, looking into their faces. I should have kept my promise. I never would have submitted to their abuse if I'd seen them first. They disgusted me! Not only their flabby bodies but the smell of their greasy skin and their glances, sidelong, avoiding my eyes.

We went to our restaurant later, and Cedric raved over every scene. I'd worked hard for our date. And he had plenty to say. "You were so good when you took it on all fours! And that blow job – or should I say blow jobs? I didn't know you could take two in your mouth!"

Exactly the kind of declaration of love any woman would want to hear.

He talked dirty to me all the time, even when he was on a business trip, when he would call me to describe the women he encountered: their bare brown feet in the summer, the possibility they had nothing on under a fur coat in the winter, a close-fitting dress that revealed every curve. All the luscious details. As if he spent every free moment studying strangers and imagining their naked bodies. Sometimes he came home late because he'd stopped at the rest area on the way home to ogle the action, jack off in a group, or lure likely looking people for a later adventure, and I had to hear all about it. He described meetings in cafés with men or various couples to choose the next actors in our films, or without warning, he brought them directly home, where he would watch us undress and have sex.

He forced these strangers on me. If I said no, I would pay the price in another way, in private, with nobody to witness his cruelty, which had no limit. "Yes" was the only safe response. I was more frightened to deny him than to accept any sexual outrage. It felt like the beginning of a slow, hopeless death.

My poor eyesight helped him construct his game and prolong our relationship. I think he hoped I'd never see clearly again, so I couldn't react and rebel as I should have. My conscience, distressed by so much immorality, couldn't find a way to communicate with my conscious agency. I had no willpower. Moments of lucidity came over me every once in a while, and I would wonder, "What the hell are you doing? Get out of here before it's too late." But I couldn't seem to take that step. I was under the influence of this man who came home to me every night, dragging his dirtiness with him. He put a spell on me that spread through the house – every room and corner had its revolting memory. There was no way out. Cedric was always a step ahead of me, preventing my escape.

"Your car is rusting away out in the garage," he said one day. "Ana got her license, so I'm going to give it to her. She'll be so happy!"

No! That was my only lifeline to freedom I had left, in the hopes I could drive again one day. I controlled my anger, though. Tread carefully, Chloe. "But I was thinking I'd sell it. I bought it less than two years ago. I might still get some money out of it."

"Don't be stupid! Ana needs a car, and then I won't have to buy her one. Look at you, living in the lap of luxury – don't tell me you need money!"

Having my car taken away from me boxed me in even tighter, and almost made me surface from his hold on me. I wanted to move on with my life again, some kind of life, a future life, one I didn't yet know. But I had to give in, like I did to everything else. Eventually, my vision problem became the key to his strategy. It was like a child's game to him. He was so sure I'd never leave him that he convinced me too, and I stopped imagining myself elsewhere, or considering any other possible life. I would stay with him and accept everything: the money, the vacations, the attention he gave me in return for his satisfaction, not just sexual but also for making him feel I was dependent on him. And I was dependent on him, completely, as my health wasn't improving. I was weak, and my vision was still blurry. The doctors were still looking for what caused my ischemia. Cedric thought up a way to use my condition to further his goals.

"Pack a small bag, just for a couple days. I'm taking you to Las Vegas!"

"Las Vegas? But I hate that place! I've been there way too often for work. What are we going to do there?"

He didn't answer me, but showed me the first-class tickets, opening a bottle of champagne. He clinked his glass to mine. "I love you so much, Chloe. If only you knew how much I love you." I watched him, confused. What was he planning now?

He took a huge suite at the Bellagio. Las Vegas was not to my taste but still, I had never seen it as a tourist, and maybe it would be fun. Las Vegas...an amusement park for those who can't travel the world. A fake Eiffel Tower, Venice in a shopping mall, an immersion into the strangeness of history and the future, the richness of an antique city in the heart of Italy, deserted beaches in Brazil, pyramids in Cairo, or giant Buddhas in Asia, Hindu temples in South of India. I'd seen some of these places with my own eyes while travelling – the most wonderful feeling ever – but Las Vegas gathered all these places and more into one walkable town, chaotic and surreal. It was over a hundred degrees outside, so we stayed in the dazzling subterranean casino, where Cedric played blackjack and I mindlessly threw away money on the slot machines. Suddenly, I felt a hand on my shoulder, and I came to. Cedric, dressed to the nines. I hadn't noticed him leave, but he had showered and shaved and smelled like Hermès cologne.

"Go get ready. I bought you a gorgeous dress. It's in the room. I'll wait for you here."

He hadn't lied. The Dolce Gabbana dress was stunning, an absolute gem, and it fit me perfectly. I looked at myself in the full-length mirror and felt a tiny bit beautiful, a bit like my old self, with a hint of that certain elegance I'd inherited from my grandmother and my mother.

I went downstairs, found Cedric and we went out into the evening, still hot but not an absolute oven. A chauffeur opened the door of a white limo. Where was Cedric taking me? Were we celebrating the anniversary of our first date? No, it wasn't in July. So, what was it? After a few miles the car pulled into a parking lot, and there, to my great surprise, was a chapel, with a sign as big as a billboard in front:

Get married in five minutes for only $99.99!

Surely this was all a big funny joke.

"We have to get married at some point, right?" Cedric said, getting out of the limo.

Holding the hem of my dress, I climbed out slowly, and Cedric took my hand. I had only one wish: to get back in and tell the driver to step on the gas and get me as far away as possible. Isn't there a huge desert around here? Get me into the dry heart of it, I'm begging you, man, just get me out of here. He can't find me in the desert!

Cedric led me into the chapel, which had a reception desk complete with cash register in lieu of a vestibule. Plastic flowers decorated the walls, the desk and the fake stained-glass window that was too high to see out of. Its colors made psychedelic patterns float around, touching the furniture and probably my face, which already felt green.

Cedric chuckled, seeming pleased with all this kitsch. "Stay here, someone will come and get you."

Frozen in disbelief, I couldn't answer him; the words wouldn't come out. I was slightly blind, but I wasn't deaf and mute, too. Why couldn't I tell him no, no, no?

THIS IS BULLSHIT, NOT A LOVE STORY

A man dressed in white walked over to me, rubbing his hands. "Hello, young lady. You must be the lovely Chloe. Please take my arm and follow me."

Was this a horror film, or maybe a comedy? Wake up, Chloe, wake yourself up, girl. I clutched the arm of the smiling man dressed up like a TV preacher, and the action flowed ever on, like in a film. Bravo, Cedric, the perfect set design for our wedding. I tip my hat to you. You're a genius. You should have been a screenwriter.

The inner part of the chapel was more churchlike, with a dozen pews, empty of course, set in perfect rows. White plastic flowers everywhere you looked. I saw Cedric standing very still in what seemed like miles in the distance, a mirage hazing the vision, but as I approached, I saw another man beside him. I guessed it was the pastor. He pressed a button on a remote control, and music started playing. Elvis Presley's "Always on My Mind." The words seemed strange for a wedding:

Maybe I didn't treat you,
 Quite as good as I should have
 Maybe I didn't love you
 As often as I should have...

I walked slowly down the aisle leaning heavily on the arm of a stranger, thinking it should have been my father, then I became conscious of my dress – it was black. I was wearing black for my own wedding. I made it to the altar. Cedric was beaming at me, but my face must have looked completely blank.

"What a fantastic surprise, right?" he whispered. "But this is how much I love you. Even with your handicap, I want you to be my wife, my 'forever after.' Not every man would do that, but I will, sweetie. You're going to love your ring."

He turned and nodded to the pastor, who started droning the invocation.

"Dearly beloved, we are gathered here today...the bond of marriage..." Bond or bondage? "For better or worse..." Maybe the better part was still to come? "I do," came out of my mouth, and I extended my left hand and Cedric slipped the ring on my finger. It fit perfectly. Simple white gold. Goddammit, but he knew my taste. I had trouble slipping the ring on his finger, as my hands were shaking so badly. Cedric mistook my clumsiness for overwhelming happiness.

"No one will ever love you better than me," he whispered in my ear before giving me a gentle kiss.

He didn't organize an orgy for that night, which was a nice surprise. He made love to me. I twittered his nipples, of course; without that, he couldn't get it up. A half-hour later, he was asleep. I stood at the window a long time looking out at Vegas, awash in a million lights, wishing I were a reformed smoker, so I could smoke a cigarette in defiance.

Back at home I called my mom with the news. She started screaming before I could explain Cedric's maneuver, "How could you get married without telling me?" Then I could picture her turning to my father as she said, "She's crazy! Our daughter is crazy." Then she hung up on me.

With this impulsive wedding, he took me away from my family, so now my family was...him? My name was Chloe Moreau, Berkovitch no more.

Cedric's mother was delighted.

"My god! My son and this lovely girl! Married! Hopefully, there'll be a grandchild soon!"

David, the friend who'd introduced me to Cedric, took the news more soberly.

"No, you didn't, Chloe! Marriage isn't just a lark – it's an important step. And have you talked about having kids? Does he want more? In five years, you'll be forty, then it'll be too late. Do you hear what I'm saying? What's going on with you, anyway?"

I would have loved to tell him what was "going on," but I sat tongue-tied next to him, in the sunshine by the lake. I wanted so much to tell him what my daily life was really like. But I couldn't. It was like some supernatural power kept me silent, so I just looked away, shaking my head.

"You've changed, Chloe. Where's the smiling, joyful girl I used to know? Are you taking drugs again? Tell me. You know you can tell me anything. I'm your friend."

How could I have told him? Like about the previous evening, how the door had slammed when Cedric came home, how his tight smile meant a bad scene looming, how during supper he found some non-existent fault with me and wore me down until I cried. And then how, as always, he granted me absolution for said flaw, and how after dinner, he stood up and moved behind me, lifted me from my chair, pushed my face down over the table until it almost touched my uneaten, cold spaghetti, then pushed up my dress, pulled my panties out of the way and with one hard thrust, penetrated me.

That meant he'd forgiven me. "See, sweetheart? Calm down. Let it go. Everything's fine."

How could I tell that to anyone?

Sometimes I spent hours simply marveling at Cedric's brain and trying to figure out how he functioned. What are you looking for in your horrible life? What are you trying to do to me? He was neither normal nor healthy, and yet he'd never been diagnosed with a mental illness. His business fit his compulsions. He was never brave enough to reveal who he really was. I couldn't face I'd married a pathetic con man, a guy with a sick sexual pathology!

Now I understood what out "romantic" weekend in Madrid meant, and how badly he wanted to show me the bullfight. He was like the matador with his Suit of Light, his tailor-made pants and jacket. Tradition made it de rigueur, the crowd required it, but the skills had to go with the look. Cedric could only dress up in the suit like the matador; he would never belong because he didn't have what it takes. I had begun to lose respect for him, and how could I love someone I didn't respect?

We didn't go on our honeymoon right away, but when we did, Cedric managed to use it strategically. Since his mother was so delighted for us, she came on our honeymoon with us. No joke.

"I promised my mother I'd take her on an amazing trip. Where should we go? Bali? Thailand? I want to let her experience a first-class luxury hotel, a fantastic and unforgettable trip for once in her life. And combine it with our honeymoon. Two in one! Why do it like everyone else, plus we've been together a long time already, you know?"

Cedric had owed his mother a gift for some time, but this trip was simply to impress her. I wanted to tell him to take his mother on his own time, and while he was at it, set up an orgy for her, the lonely old thing.

He asked her where she wanted to go but she wasn't used to flying, and was hesitant about going to the far ends of the earth. She seemed embarrassed, and I saw she didn't want to disappoint her son. For the first time, I realized she was also a little afraid of him.

"Bali or Thailand would be great, darling. I'm just wondering if the flight will be too long. There's Egypt... I've always dreamed of going to see the pyramids and learning about its history. What do you think?"

He told her it was a great idea, but to me he griped, "How stupid! I'm offering her a first-class trip and she picks a place three-and-a-half hours away. She just doesn't get it. And besides, I know Egypt by heart. I visited it from top to bottom with that bitch of an ex-wife and my girls. I wanted to explore! And fuck! I work with Arabs all year long, and now I've got to deal with them during my honeymoon. I'm only doing this to make you two happy. If it was up to me, I'd let you go on your own."

He was hopeless. Not a good bone in his body. He thought only of himself. I finally began to understand the breadth of his selfishness, not that it mattered. We were going to celebrate our marriage in Egypt. On a camel. With souvenir photos to prove it.

In the days leading up to the trip, I wondered if this would be my last trip with him. My last October with him. I stopped myself from thinking these brave thoughts and focused on trying to experience the moment. I always loved traveling and discovering new places; at least we still had something in common.

At the airport. His mother was extremely excited. In the first-class lounge, she threw herself at the buffet. Cedric had pulled out all the stops. He even arranged for a limo to drop us off at the foot of the plane, at which she was so happy, she couldn't stop thanking her son. She was sweating, breathless with excitement. We took our seats in an empty first-class cabin, where my mother-in-law discovered how her son usually travelled. First revelation: a caviar tasting at 9 am. Second revelation: watching a film from her fully reclinable seat. She kept touching all the buttons. If she hadn't taken advantage of every first-class perk, Cedric would have made her. He kept saying, "Lie down! Eat what the stewardesses bring you! Go brush your teeth! Use that face cream at the bottom of the toiletry kit! Put on the pajamas! And don't forget to take everything with you – it's free."

She squeaked, "Pajamas! I can't sleep! I just don't know what to say, you darling kiddos. You have no idea what I'm feeling right now."

Just thank us, Didine! And stop calling me your kiddo. I'm not your child. Fucking hell. I watched her and flashed a tight smile. That's right, idiot. You're no better than your son. Catching my thoughts, I realized I was becoming mean, like Cedric. I had to stop immediately. She deserved respect and my sympathy, too. I would keep my emotions in check, I vowed. I would not show him any weakness, and I'd play the perfect spouse, obedient to every swing of his cape. If the bull could do it, so could I.

It was hot in Cairo. An intense heatwave had practically immobilized the overcrowded city. It was smothered in an endless smog, turning the dome of sky a brownish gray. It was hard to breathe. As soon as we dropped off our luggage, we had to join a tour group in the lobby to begin our six-day marathon of sightseeing.

As always, Cedric had organized every detail in advance, so his mother would enjoy our honeymoon trip to the fullest: two days in Cairo and four in Luxor, including a trip on the Nile in a small boat, meals with locals and nights in cozy hotels. We spent the first evening with Cedric's colleague Hamed, who was on a family visit there. He invited us for dinner at his parents' home. Cedric made sure I knew Hamed came from a line of high-ranking diplomats.

Before we met him for dinner, we decided to go for a drink in the panoramic bar on the 53rd floor of our hotel.

"It's incredible!" Cedric's mother cried as we walked toward the big windows.

"I hope you like it, Mom. I'm so happy to give you this trip. You deserve it."

I didn't see anything extraordinary about the view that evening, but heights are always impressive. Cedric and his mother stood before the window like a couple, his arm around her shoulders, hers wrapped around his waist. It was touching to see them like that, and I felt a spark of happiness. At least Cedric wasn't denying his origins, not here in Egypt, anyway. Back home his lies had already gone too far, and he knew it was too late. No going back now. He couldn't suddenly tell people his mother was not really Jewish, and he wasn't brave enough to tell people he'd had himself circumcised at 19 when he converted. His pride was misplaced. Cedric would never be humble enough to show even me, his wife, who he really was.

We ordered exotic vodka cocktails with fresh fruit. Didine held up her glass.

"Alright, kiddos. What's the scoop? Am I ever going to be a grandmother again? What's the news from the doctors?"

It was none of her business, but she was often intrusive like that. But what did she mean – news from the doctors? I started to open my mouth, but Cedric chimed in before I could say a word.

"You know Chloe's health isn't getting any better, Mom. The doctors haven't been able to diagnose her illness. For now, they're advising us not to hope too much, and preparing us psychologically for the possibility she may never be able to have children. It's hard for her, but that's life."

Quite the ambiance crusher. His mother gazed at me with pity. I put my head down and stared at my feet. I liked my purple nail polish. I let the conversation drift to other things as if nothing had been said. It wasn't a subject for discussion, not while on vacation, and not with his mother over drinks.

His mother brought it up again, though. "It's very sad when a woman can't have children, sad for both of you. The chance to bring a child into this world from the perfect love you share... There's nothing more beautiful. And especially with such a perfect husband like my son!"

I could not stop a rebellious thought from forming. I know what it is – a miracle! I'd never have to carry his son. I probably would have aborted any child of his anyway, without telling him. I hated that thought, though, it was so horrible, and I resented him for making me think it. I looked at my purple nails again and pasted the smile back on my face.

Hamed's family lived in the ambassadors' neighborhood in a distinguished 19th century home. A maid opened the door and ushered us in. The dark furniture, worn tapestries and richly colored rugs looked as old as the house and probably hadn't been moved since Hamed's ancestors' time. His mother welcomed us. An elegant woman, very reserved, who spoke perfect French and English, like everyone else in the family, we discovered. I noticed she was dressed all in black – she was in mourning. Apparently, Hamed's father must have died recently. At that moment, Hamed came in with his sister, her husband and their daughter.

We sat on low couches in a cavernous, ornate living room. Two servants came in with drinks and trays loaded with appetizers: baba ghanoush and hummus dips, olives and falafels, and other dishes I didn't recognize. Didine immediately stuck a pita chip into the hummus and conveyed it to her mouth, spilling a blob on her shirt and eliciting a groan from Cedric. I tried to cover the awkward moment by asking the little girl what grade she was in. This got Hamed talking. The state of Cairo's schools, the country's politics, the bank where Hamed and Cedric worked. There were long pauses in the conversation. I didn't feel comfortable, and yet I was dressed soberly and knew how to act in a bourgeois Muslim household. It was Cedric and his mother who were out of place. They knew nothing of the diplomatic world or the international culture the rest of us were so familiar with.

Cedric was wearing his blue Brioni jacket with the gold buttons. Refined Italian clothes looked good on him, but they didn't make the man, and it was obvious he didn't fit this world. His loud laughter and crude insinuations and putdowns of Arab culture mortified me. And his mother was worse. On top of her cackling and staring at everything in awe, she was wearing a nightdress. That morning she'd come to me at breakfast, panicked. "Darling, I have nothing to wear tonight – everything's dirty and wrinkled, and we don't have time to get them laundered. All I've got is my nightdress, you know, the one I wear as a sundress sometimes. It's really pretty. White cotton with little blue flowers. Do you think I could wear it to dinner at Hamed's? No one will notice it's a nightdress, will they?"

"No, of course not. Wear your pajamas! No one will notice a thing." I was simply teasing her because I thought she was joking. She wasn't.

At dinner, I was seated next to her with Hamed on my right. Cedric sat in between his mother and Hamed's mother. She rang a little bell, and servers entered with a tuna mousse. It didn't look appetizing at all. Didine gave us a tragicomic show in etiquette. As the server offered her the platter first, she tried to get my attention, hoping I could discreetly show her what to do. How should she cut the mousse? And move it onto her plate? Everyone was waiting.

"Come on, Mom, today or tomorrow?"

Seeing beads of sweat appear on her forehead, I nudged her and smiled, then made a cutting motion . After massacring the tuna, she managed to plop a piece onto her plate with her fork. Cedric tried to draw everyone's attention away with a joke, but I saw his twitching brows and knew he was furious. The servers brought in plate after plate, and as Didine made mistake after mistake, I saw Cedric's shame and mortification building. Although I pitied her, I felt relieved that for once I wasn't the reason for his fury.

Throughout the evening, Hamed's mother asked me questions: where I came from, how many languages I spoke, what my career was, who my parents were, what my father did for a living. It warmed me to feel she wanted to get to know me, to be close to me, and with a stab in the heart, I realized I hadn't felt that way in years. She wasn't at all interested in Cedric, and I could tell she felt sorry for me. Sometimes, women understand each other that way.

We returned to the hotel, and I let it slip to Cedric that Hamed's mother's interest in me and how we had hit it off had made me feel I needed to find more friends at home.

"You always have something to complain about," he said sourly. "You're never happy!"

That was certainly true. Part of the problem was that living in his world, I felt like an old, bored and boring spouse. I wanted my youth back. I was only 34 going on 35, but I yearned to be 30 again, such a great age for a woman! I was missing out on my best years, and our "idyllic" life was leading me mindlessly toward my grave, and Cedric smelled like death. This kind of clear thinking was toxic to me, a spiral into a dilemma or insanity. I closed my mind to it. I had to put on the good fight, hang on to my dream of being Cedric's perfect spouse. I still preferred my dream world. It was the only way to survive, so I would cling to hope. Even if there wasn't any.

After two days of exploring Cairo, we took a plane to Luxor, where Cedric had discovered a special hotel built on the western side of the Nile. Our rooms looked out on a flower garden, and the pool stretched out behind a line of trees. It was peaceful. The refined food helped, too, and I started to feel better, like I was on my very own "honeymoon." Where were Cedric and Didine? I didn't care. I put on my bikini and lay in a deck chair, then swam laps in the pool until I was out of breath, savoring my moments of freedom as if they were my last. To be completely alone was a rare luxury, for Cedric was a constant presence. When he was with me, he oppressed me, and when he was away, he weighed heavily on my mind.

A voice broke into my thoughts. "Have a nice swim? You're such a pro. I came to get you. We meet my mother for drinks in an hour, so that gives us some time alone. Come take a shower with me. I'd love a blow job."

And just like that, the weight came crashing down on the serenity those few minutes of solitude had given me.

The days began at dawn. It was worth it to see the sun rise from the Nile. One morning, we traveled over the region in a hot air balloon, which brought us above the heavy heat, a walk through the sky that was unforgettable. We each felt the magic of it in our own way, but for once, we were in unison, and it seemed the shared emotion rubbed off on my husband, enough for me to think that maybe he'd been a good and generous man once, but in another life. He wrapped his arms around me, leaving his mother to marvel at the view in her corner. I could feel his heart beating, and I felt safe as he cuddled me. My dreamscape, which blotted out the dark reality. I believed in his good will at that moment. I engraved this image and this feeling in my brain so I could return to it when things became unbearable again.

The rest of the trip was a flash of pyramids, history museums, pharaonic treasures, souks, traditional foods, culture, music, religion. Egypt. We concluded our honeymoon and began the trip home, back to reality. The first-class lounge wasn't as luxurious as the one in Zurich, Cedric complained. He wanted his money's worth, he said, raising his tone with the lounge attendant. He wanted her name so he could complain about her. "The service is terrible! I've asked you twice for hot milk. Twice, and you bring me tepid milk. Are you making fun of me? You don't know who you're dealing with. I'm one of this company's most loyal travelers. I'll send a letter to the management and detail your incompetence in writing, you can believe me! You don't deserve this job! You've been warned, stupid idiot!"

"Don't worry about it, darling," Didine whispered, hoping to calm him down. "I'm fine with tepid milk."

That moment revealed what a fiasco the trip had been. I'd tried to be his perfect, loving spouse day and night, but it hadn't improved things. He cut me down in front of his mother, demanded my services in the shower, even though he knew kneeling on the hard tile to suck him off bruised my kneecaps, and on our last day, he continually belittled me in front of our guide.

"How can you not know the history of the pharaohs? Look at what they've built. Do you think you have the power to destroy an empire by criticizing their ideas about death? You're so ridiculous."

He barred me from giving my opinion unless it agreed with his. "Listen and shut up," was his message. His mother, too, was on the receiving end. Like when he guffawed as she walked across the lobby in a long Mickey Mouse T-shirt on our last evening together before heading back home. "Oh, for God's sake!! Did you steal that shirt from Sarah?" This pitiful vision of Didine and Mickey remained with me for a long time.

When we finally arrived in Geneva, we brought Didine to the train station. She wasn't coming to stay with us, which was a relief to me, even if I had not minded her company on our honeymoon.

"Thanks for the unforgettable trip, kiddos. You're the best! Chloe, my darling girl, take care of yourself. You'll see, you can live without children, I'm sure of it. Keep up your pottery – that will keep you busy. My darling boy, I love you so much. It makes me so happy to see you two together. I know you take such good care of her. Such a good man. See you soon, kiddos. I love you both!"

We waved Didine off to her train. She turned around and blew us kisses, tears in her eyes. Okay, okay, Didine, let's not overdo it. Dealing with your son is more than enough to keep me busy. And by the way, I don't do pottery. I sculpt.

THIS IS BULLSHIT, NOT A LOVE STORY

"You were perfect," Cedric told me on the drive home. "Thank you for making the effort to go with my mother. I know, I know, it wasn't easy all the time. She's right, though, you should get back into sculpture."

Tercio de Banderillas:
Thrust of the Barbed Sticks

The peones *enter the arena to begin Act Two. They will assist the torero in his struggle against the bull by planting three pairs of banderillas, one pair at a time, into the flanks of the bull, unless the matador decides to do it himself.*

The two-foot-long banderillas are wooden sticks decorated with bright-colored paper and armed with sharp barbed ends. The loss of blood will further weaken the animal, but the pain will goad it to anger and encourage it to attack. The goal is to show its primal spirit to the spectators.

The event president may decide to reduce the number of banderillas, or the matador may ask the men who plant the barbs to add more. It depends on how weak or strong they judge the bull to be at that point. They don't want him to be too powerful to handle, but they don't want him to fall dead before being gloriously slaughtered by the matador.

Back in the village near Madrid, in that arena, Act One had just come to an end, the picadors trotting out. Cedric could no longer contain himself. "Marvelous!" he shouted.

"That had to be the finest part of the entire bullfight. The bull is getting tired, but he's still fighting. He doesn't give an inch. He still thinks there's hope. No clue he's going to die in the end. Are you okay, Chloe? You look a bit pale."

"No... Um... Yes, I'm fine. It's hard to watch a fight to the death. It isn't really a fair fight, because the two aren't equal. Each one wants to save himself, of course, but this is just torture. The matador makes the bull fight to entertain the crowd. It's such a morbid spectacle."

Cedric looked at me with surprise. "You're so ridiculously weak. I thought you were a strong woman, a woman with balls. It's just an animal. You're not going to get sick, are you?"

Then he turned back to look at the bull, and he started gloating, practically licking his lips. "And don't forget, the best is yet to come. That dinner plate with those huge balls! You absolutely cannot skip that. It's a must."

During our whole "honeymoon period," if you can call it that after living together so long before tying the knot, and even during our honeymoon/once-in-a-lifetime trip for the mom-in-law, I kept feeling like I was zapping over something. Oh, yeah – we were married. I was married! Mrs. Moreau. And yet whenever I reserved a table for us, I always said: "A table for two for Chloe Berkovitch, please." This was not good. I wore my ring, The Ring, displaying my civil status, which reminded me now and then I was a married woman. Maybe it was because the ceremony had been so fast. In and out of a small house made to look like a chapel, a hastily signed paper in the office of the "official celebrant, available 24/7." Cedric paid for everything with his credit card, the total of our sacred union amounting to 110 dollars. It was quite a deal, especially for my parents, since the bride's family usually foots the bill.

Ever since the wedding, my father spoke only to Cedric, the man of the house., who mattered to him now. They even started to eat lunch together. I wonder what they talked about. I never managed to develop a close relationship with my father, who did not express his emotions. No one had ever taught him how, and he never figured it out on his own. He remained focused on what he truly loved: his career as a classical music manager and his wife. A contented man. How could a person whose job involves taking care of artists not know how to express his own emotions? There was one exception: anger. He expressed that often enough, in the form of violence. I no longer blamed him but considered him a disabled person, communication-wise. But with Cedric, he let himself relax, and they would use the same vulgar language. Oddly enough, Cedric began to bring the four of us together, not often, just whenever he felt it was time to see my parents, such as for concerts my father organized, birthdays, Jewish holidays.

I no longer saw my mother one-on-one, however. Cedric had decided she was toxic for me, claiming she'd turned me into a rebel, and that she'd been a bad mother. He showed none of this when she was around; instead, he would charm her, speaking Portuguese, sprinkling a few compliments here and there: "Linda, darling, *tudo bom*?" That's all it took for my mother to blossom. Cedric had a natural talent for languages, and he imitated accents to perfection, which enabled him to elicit sympathy, to get people to trust him, and more than anything, to successfully apply his number one rule: keep in control to hold power over others.

So, my mother kept her distance from me, but not from Cedric. It was like she too was bewitched by his spell. I was stunned at the absurdity of my parents turning their backs on me, when I needed them most. Cedric weakened my emotional relationship with them by deepening his own, by manipulating them until they weren't thinking straight, and then widening the distance between us, keeping us apart, isolated from one another. Divide and conquer.

"Your daughter is doing better," he would say. "Don't you think? She still can't see much, but at least she's happier! Aren't you, darling? And you're seeing Dr. Thyssen again."

He constantly brought this tactic into play. For him to continue to be regarded as my Prince Charming, I had to be the sickly, weak woman who needed him to survive, the neurotic who needed a psychiatrist. As a result, my mother worried about my health and my father thought I was insane.

Cedric discouraged me from seeing my parents unless he was there, and I knew he meant business. I rarely saw anyone in fact. Most of our acquaintances were couples with young children and it was hard to become friends with women who were busy being mothers. Our home was inconvenient, too, since it was a half-hour drive from town, much longer near rush hour, so that meant we socialized only on weekends: brunches in the garden, early dinners in the kitchen.

But my main deterrent to making friends was Cedric, who always ended up dragging our guests into his sordid world, so they needed to drink a lot to feel comfortable. Champagne corks flew until everyone got tipsy enough to relax, but all our conversations eventually turned around sex. The women would laugh uncomfortably while the men let themselves go. At our place, they could say anything.

Why did Cedric share his perversions with these healthy-minded people? These were the kind of couples where the men might watch a bit of porn, but the women wouldn't dream of mentioning it. Like Frank and Isabelle, who may never forget their last evening with us. It happened after dessert and a lot of wine: Cedric disappeared a minute, then came back carrying a dildo and harness and my wig. He handed them to me and ordered me to put them on. And I did. I put my wig on without looking in the mirror, then the harness and dildo over my nylons. I looked ridiculous.

Cedric crowed, "Look what my wife looks like when I get home from work!" And he burst out laughing.

Isabelle stared at me in horror, but she eventually brought out an uncomfortable laugh, and Frank took photos. They thought it was just a joke or pretended to think that. But Cedric was staring at them intently, and I could tell he would have loved it if they stayed for a night of perverted sex. Isabelle noticed his gaze, and she frowned, then abruptly stood up and reeled to the bathroom. When she came back, she said she threw up, that red wine sometimes made her sick. But I'd often seen her drink red wine. Her unease and disgust were palpable.

"Frank, I'm really not feeling well. I'd like to go home, please."

Vomiting was a great excuse to say goodbye and get out of our presence as fast as possible. Frank didn't hesitate for a second. He placed his wife's coat tenderly over her shoulders, they thanked us for a nice evening, congratulated us on our marriage, and wished us all the best. Never saw them again, and it was the same for our other friends. One by one, they dropped out of our lives.

Cedric didn't seem to notice that no one wanted to come over anymore, or that we stopped getting invited anywhere. He didn't see the truth: people avoided us. When I brought it up he had an excuse handy.

"Oh, you know, people are busy," he said. "They've got their children. And on that note, the girls are coming this weekend. Sarah's bringing the present I gave her for her birthday. His name is Cactus, a King Charles Spaniel. He's three months old and you're going to love him! She really wanted that brand... I mean, breed. I wanted to surprise you. Now you can have a dog without having to take care of it! You'll meet Cactus when Sarah gets here. See you soon, *mi amor de mi vida*! Get yourself ready for tonight, I'm dying for a dirty, dirty time with you! Ok, I'm off!"

The asshole! The bastard! How could get her a dog? And announce the news so cheerfully without realizing how much it would hurt me? I couldn't believe it. What planet was he living on? Were there many men like him? I wanted to meet their wives and girlfriends and start a commiseration club. I couldn't be the only woman putting up with this kind of human being. I'd never met someone like him before. It had to be a rare case, or maybe it was just a craze – macho fever was back. The rise of the perverts, manipulators and narcissists! He was all those things, but I still didn't know what described him best. I'd never done any serious research, and I probably didn't want a diagnosis, which would have made me doubt everything, and shot all my justifications to hell.

My goal had to remain the same as when I left New York to be his wife: make our relationship work. No matter what happened, I would keep it together.

I wanted so badly to believe he was normal, at least somewhat normal, enough to build my hopes on. From the outside, our married life looked so comfortable, but I was inside it, and I wasn't sure anymore. I didn't know what to do, so I kept swallowing my anti-depressants and getting ready for his evenings, where I didn't just swallow his cum, I swallowed my own ego. I kept my bitterness from him, conformed to what he expected of me, and dutifully spent time with his daughters, his clients and the friends he still had.

The one thing helping me feel the least bit free was my writing. A relative freedom, because he kept watch on me there, too, rummaging around in my desk drawers and reading my manuscripts. He gave me little pep talks.

"You're really talented. You write well, and that story about Leo wanting to be a woman is good enough to publish. Were you a man in another life, or what? You describe perfectly what it's like to be one. Keep working on it. I can't wait to read the next pages."

He no longer had any limits when it came to my life. To his mind, I belonged to him, so that meant I had nothing to hide. He thought it was perfectly acceptable to snoop through my drawers, my dresser, my purse, my wallet, to access my bank account, browsing history, telephone bill. I used to be okay with it because I took it for a loving gesture – he was showing interest in my life – when really it was a way to hem me in, and this started as soon as I moved in with him.

"I'm organizing everything, so you don't have to bother about it, darling. Here's your phone, just memorize the number. I opened a bank account for you and put enough money in it so you can buy whatever you want. I'll keep an eye on the balance. That's only normal, since I'm paying all the bills. You see, *chérie*, I want to take care of you so you'll be happy. You can relax."

It took so long for these nagging doubts about his "love" to surface, that it was only now I questioned his "organizing everything" for me. I chided myself for having surrendered all control to him. My questions didn't last long, though. He came home with flowers out of the blue, and was so sweet to me that I persuaded myself I was worried about nothing. Did it really matter who had the passwords to my accounts? I was the one, after all, who'd given him the power. I was making stuff up – maybe paranoia was sneaking up on me on top of everything else. The only thing that mattered was that he loved me. I felt sure I was over my fear of rejection, so what was wrong with the situation? What was wrong was me, and only me, because I was the one always fucking things up! The fault was mine. I had nothing to reproach Cedric for. He was a good man, and he was deeply in love with me. He would have done anything to keep me, and to keep me under his thumb had to be his way of showing me his love.

Writing also helped me bury my doubts, as my imagination offered me a wild escape from reality. I wasn't responsible for the words on the page – stories simply sprang up to fill the empty pages, and by spending time with my fictional characters, I no longer felt lonely. They took me wherever they wanted, forbidding me nothing and never putting me in danger. Through writing, I found a part of myself again, the part Cedric hated, a free, artistic woman. He didn't want her around; she wasn't sexy enough. I had to "fix" other things about myself too. I had wavy hair, so I had to straighten it. I liked wearing flip flops, but he made me wear spiky high heels. My jeans weren't to his taste, so I had to wear the ones he bought me, or better, short skirts. He wanted me to be the woman he secretly wished he could be: a massive slut! And to get himself into the skin of that woman, he needed to see me fuck other people.

As he continued to arrange orgies for me, the range of his perverted desires grew ever wider. Bisexuality, swinging, dominatrix, gang bangs. Interestingly, he didn't like penetrating other women. I guess he had his ideal at his side. But he adored jacking off while I was being fucked hard by someone else. I understood, finally, that he wasn't really watching me; he would glance at me absent-mindedly, stroking his limp dick. He would fix my hair, proud of his work horse. But really, he was watching the man fucking and fantasizing he was in my place.

Was he a closet homosexual? I'll never know, but he didn't waste any time trying it out. I had no trouble sodomizing my husband – I told myself it's what he deserved. He had no idea I was taking my revenge when I rammed that outsized plastic dildo into his tight anus, feeling the devilish pleasure a gay guy must feel when he "makes" a heterosexual. Unfortunately, it made him come. He even acted grateful to me, as if by some miracle he was finally bringing his sexuality to light.

Cedric arranged these "parties" every few nights now, over and over. Gang rapes. Each man taking his turn. Strangers. I kept my blindfold on, never again wanting to see the sheepish faces of those men in search of love or some satisfaction just because they were horny. Cedric kept to the sidelines, filming or taking photos, recording each scene, then later, he could jerk off to his favorites in a hotel room somewhere across the globe, between two work meetings. He would call me when he was about to come, to tell me he was thinking of me. How sweet of you, Cedric. Really, how touching.

I was still handicapped by my poor vision, but since I had no choice but to accept it, I got used to it. My mother seemed sadder and more upset about than I was. Life is so unlucky, she said. She felt sorry for me, but that only frustrated me; instead of feeling sorry, why didn't she open her eyes and see how much I was suffering in this marriage? And it was not because of my weak eyesight. I felt a mother should have known something was wrong! She didn't though, not even after what happened at my birthday dinner, when the four of us went out to a restaurant. I was wearing leopard print ankle boots my mother bought for me. I had chosen them myself, and I really liked them. But when I pointed them out to Cedric, he humiliated me in front of my parents and everyone else there.

"You look like a whore in those shoes!"

I gasped and couldn't get my breath back, I was suffocating with misery, and I started to sob. Cedric's hypocrisy stung the most. It was so unfair, when what he loved best was dressing me like a whore. No one refuted his comment or confronted him for insulting me like that – they were probably too embarrassed or intimidated. Throughout the meal, tears kept running down my face. My throat was too tight to swallow a bite of food, not even my cake and ice cream. Cedric and my parents ignored me and kept eating, but there was no singing "Happy Birthday."

This was just one of so many terrible incidents of that year. I can't blame them on my parents. Yes, they should have gotten me help, as they had to have seen things weren't right, but the material comforts of my life blinded them. They must have figured my future was safe with the private banker, one less worry off their shoulders. They chose to believe Cedric treated me like a princess, at least most of the time.

"After all, he stuck with you through your ischemia," my mother said, as if other guys would dump a woman if she got sick. "You can count on him. He gave you so much attention – he didn't leave your side for a minute, and even worked from home to stay with you. And then he married you! What else do you want? You'll never be happy, will you?"

This was how my mother commiserated with me. It always turned into a scolding. She was afraid I might leave him, afraid I would escape my torturer. She had to have known.

I told myself I was at fault because I was too cowardly and too cowed to speak up. My attempts to assert myself with Cedric faltered too.

Not only did he give a dog to Sarah, and never hear a comment from me, he also wanted to celebrate her birthday in style with a long weekend in New York. Without me.

"Sarah will love it. The New York Plaza! Chez Jean-Georges! Mamma Mia, shopping, the works. We'll go in two weeks, from the sixth to the eleventh. Sarah has no idea yet, so don't tell her!"

"But I told you I was having my surgery then. I'll be in the hospital for one night and then it'll take weeks to be mobile again."

"I must have forgotten. But you'll figure it out, like you always do. You lived alone for a long time. You don't need anyone. Isn't that what you're always saying, ever since I met you?"

He liked twisting the knife in the wound like that. He had to choose those exact dates. I'd never see my beloved New York again, would I? I'd never see my friends again, and I missed Rose. But I wasn't invited. He picked the weekend to coincide with an operation I needed on my foot. The price I was paying now for all the years wearing pointed high heels, chasing fashion trends, trying to look sexy, or "professional," an absurdity that persists to this day. It was causing me incredible pain, and I was losing sleep. My doctor had decided it was time to operate, and this was the only appointment available for months.

The days passed and all he talked about was the surprise he'd set up for his daughter. My stomach was in knots as I listened to him spin his ridiculous stories, forcing a smile to remain on my face. My eyes would well up when I heard the words "New York," they provoked such strong, good memories of my past, and he knew it. I pretended not to notice his provocation, not to hear it or feel it. His two minutes of kindness per day would have to suffice for me to pretend to be happy. He had the prime position in the arena, where nothing escaped his notice. His behavior followed rituals, one after the other, slow and meticulous: after the moment of tenderness came the moment of selfishness. A honeymoon that paralleled the opening dance of the bullfight. Cedric knew by heart how to play this game. He knew what a powerful impact his words had on me.

Even after several years, I hadn't really settled into the house. My footsteps through the rooms seemed erased by his steps and his daughter's steps. He had said they would be with us every other weekend, but that was not true. They were there every weekend. I didn't complain, because I wanted him to have a good relationship with his children, and I wanted them to like me to make him happy. I was thinking of him, not of me. Never of me. I was so hurting for love, so devoid of love, that I would have welcomed theirs. I was eager to be their stepmom. But it didn't happen. By now, I thought I had never learned how to love another person, and Cedric didn't teach me. He pulled me further from their love, and even seemed to forget I was there after our last moment together before they arrived, usually in the shower. Sucking him off so I would feel loved.

On Friday evening before the surprise birthday trip, Cedric, Sarah, and her new dog trooped into the kitchen. The table was set and dinner was ready. I felt nervous. My hands were so clammy I rinsed them under cold water at the tap. I would cover my jumpiness with an irreproachable welcome. They were already laughing as they came in the door, and I assumed he must have told her about the trip. They didn't even look at me or say hello, but kept talking non-stop. I thought it was because they were looking forward to it so much. Like a young couple. In my cynicism, I didn't buy their money-distorted love, though. I wasn't jealous; I just didn't believe it. Cedric was making too much of it. It was on his face. I got the warped impression he was ogling his daughter's hips with the same perverted gaze I knew too well. Would he have ever done anything about it? For sure with his daughters' friends. He would have accused the young girls of asking for it or even openly seducing him. I'm sure that in some dark corner of his fantasies, there were familiar-looking shadows... I sat down awkwardly at the table, and got lost in dark thoughts like this, only half-listening to them talking. They seemed crazy excited about the trip.

"You're the best and coolest dad in the whole world for surprising me with a trip for my birthday! I can't wait to find out where we're going!"

I spoke without thinking, with no sense of what I was actually saying, "Yes, it's so cool to go to New York."

Cedric's face went rigid, then filled with blood, and he exploded. He shouted, he sermonized. I was a monster, a heartless bitch. He had no qualms about shouting at me in front of his daughter, and Sarah watched silently, calmly. Now I was the little kid, and she was the adult. She tried to interrupt, to take it lightly and laugh it off, but Cedric blew the whole thing out of proportion. Utterly powerless, I dropped my head in my hands and suffered my humiliation, sitting on the kitchen chair with my arms and legs tucked into a tight ball, hoping to protect myself. I folded myself up so small I felt I must be invisible.

For the first time, in that kitchen at that instant, I realized I was the bull. Cedric would kill me. He'd planted the banderillas deep, I felt their barbs in my neck and in my backbone.

After it was all over, Cedric stomped away, and I guess Sarah instinctively took her father's side, because she got up and followed him out. She never would have defended me. I was exhausted, and thought I'd better go spend the night in the guest room. The white walls hummed with a carefree vibe, like a child's bedroom. But it reeked of sex as if all those awful sessions I'd endured still lingered in the air, the curtains, the carpet, everywhere. I lay on the bed, my mind a whirl, my body limp, and for once, Cedric ignored me. This surprised me, as he'd always refused the idea I sleep anywhere except in his bed. After resting a while, I got up and fished out some paper and pen from a side table and wrote him a letter.

I knew it was a waste of time. My words would make no impression on him. I wrote him so many letters over the years, expressing my frustrations and hopes he would realize he could be at fault too. Not such a waste of time, though, as it did me good in a way. Did I write from my heart, or soul, or my brain? Maybe all at once. At least someone was recording our mistakes and gathering our excuses. It was absurd, but because I love him, I always made excuses for him and convinced myself I was at fault and Cedric was innocent. He never responded to these missives, never offered an apology or showed the least sense of guilt or accountability, or even willingness to consider changing his behavior.

Like always, I made the first steps to make up after my colossal mistake of letting slip the Sarah's birthday surprise. I didn't want to suffer the entire weekend. I slipped back into our room and into our bed, and found he wasn't sleeping. My punishment was to be ignored. Without a word, he gathered me into his arms, and a few minutes later, his cock was inside me. This was how he forgave me. He confirmed it later that night, when he finally whispered a few words in my ear: "Suck my cock, you big slut, I know you love it." Then I knew it would be easier in the morning, and the weekend just might pass without any more hostility, and it did.

Cedric brought me to the hospital early Monday morning, but once we got to my room, I told him he didn't need to stick around. I wanted to be alone. My foot didn't belong to him. At least something still belonged to me. I wasn't worried about my surgery; I even caught myself looking forward to it despite missing out on New York, because it meant a few days without having to deal with his moods and a few nights without having to fulfill his dirty fantasies. He didn't argue about it, and said he'd come back after the surgery. Alone in the room, I sat on the edge of the high, hard bed clutching my blue gown, which gaped open at the back. I looked around the bare hospital room, then out the window. The sky was gray, as was the hospital building. I sighed, feeling gray too, and old, hopeless, and sad.

As soon as the nurses wheeled me back into my room, Cedric arrived with sandwiches.

"You look so tired, sweetie. I hope it doesn't hurt. Here, I brought you your favorite cheese sandwich. What an exhausting morning I've had. There's so much work I have to finish before we fly to New York. Only two more days – hey, I better check on the flights!"

He got on his phone and confirmed their departure. Even if I didn't want him around, I thought it was cruel to crow about the trip when I couldn't go. My foot was going to be immobilized for nearly a month, but he didn't care. Instead of his usual fussing over me, he planned to leave me alone, high on painkillers, and walking on crutches. This time, I really would have to take care of myself, and I suddenly felt misgivings. I'd gotten accustomed to his pampering.

"Are you sure you can't put it off a few weeks? I could even go with you if you wait until next—-"

"You can't possibly think I'd cancel my trip with Sarah to take care of a fucking invalid?" he interrupted. "You're already so annoying with your stupid eyes. And now it's your foot. What do I give a shit about your foot? Or your minor little surgery! You should have rescheduled it, instead of whining about it now. You only care about yourself."

He stormed out, furious that I didn't care about his big plans. I gritted my teeth. Splurging on his daughter was more important than caring for his wife's health. His favorite expression, "my poor wife," used so often to stun the public, and the way he would tell everyone that without me, he was nothing, but at this moment, I was nothing to him, or worse, I was an annoyance.

How could he say all that, when a minute earlier, he was saying "I love you?" Did he know what love was? Or was it a calculated statement cooked up in his disturbed brain to disable me?

They had given me all kinds of drugs, including morphine, otherwise I would never have mentioned their trip, and I certainly would not have texted him, which I did, immediately and impulsively. I told him the truth, desperate to make him understand how he was hurting me. My hand shook, but I hit "send."

"It's you who only thinks about yourself, not me! You don't give a shit about my foot, about my pain! You don't give a shit about me! You think you love me because I obey you and perform to perfection whatever you expect from me. On paper, I'm the perfect wife for you but not in your heart. If only you had one! No need to answer."

My phone immediately started ringing, so loudly it startled me. Cedric. I took a quick breath, suddenly frightened to face his reaction. I picked up.

"You see how you act when you're not the center of the world? There's really something wrong with you, woman. What a terrible way to react. You're just jealous of my little girls, and you resent any smidgen of happiness I can get. It's a good thing I'm going away and leaving you – I wish it were a lot longer. If I stay with you, you're going to infect me – you hear me? You're a disease!"

Click.

He was never going to change. It was all about him, always Cedric. And I was sick of it. I had a flash of all our fancy trips, chasing after him through the airport, my suitcase knocking at my heels. I told him so many times how nice it would be to walk together, calmly, without so much stress, but he ignored me, and never once turned around to see if I was still there. I should have run the other way, taken another flight, headed somewhere else. Tears flowed down my cheeks. Why could I not leave him?

He picked me up from the hospital the next morning, sulking. He was angry with me, but I tried to ignore it. He begrudgingly carried my bag. I struggled along on my crutches, which I would have to use for the next several weeks. I couldn't wait for the next day, when he would leave me alone in the quiet house. Not a sound, not a word, not a look, released from his presence, which, even when he was silent, was such a heavy, gnawing weight. I went straight to bed when we got home.

"Sorry, but I'm going to have to sleep on your side of the bed until I'm healed," I told him as I climbed in awkwardly. "I need to keep my foot elevated and without the duvet on it."

"You know I sleep badly on your side. So now because of you I'm not going to get any sleep and I'll be exhausted at work and for the flight. You really should have had the operation another time. You could have put it off or not had it at all!"

Always the same accusing manner, even though he knew I had no choice in the matter.

In the morning, his suitcase packed, I said goodbye to him on the front steps. He didn't kiss me, and he told me not to expect him to call me during his trip.

But probably because he hated the thought of losing control of our relationship, he started emailing me from noon on. Vacuous love letters that had no effect on me. I responded with a few words, then went back to resting. I watched movies stretched out on the sofa, rested some more, savored the silence. It had been so long since Cedric, no, the enemy, I thought with a wry smile, had left me alone! It was different from his business trips, and I think it was because of my text. It had broken a thread of his web around me. Still, I had a creepy feeling he was watching my every move.

Rose called me from New York. "You'll never guess who came to see me this morning. Cedric and his daughter! They just showed up without any warning. Did you give him my address? And how come you weren't with him? You didn't tell they were coming to New York. What's going on, Chloe?"

She said it was weird to show up like that, and I agreed. Cedric had only met her once, when I was still living in New York. But he hadn't stopped by that morning to say hello – he wanted to show her what a great man he was, that he loved me even when I wasn't by his side, and so he had to go and visit my best friend "for me."

"I don't want to intrude on your relationship," she continued, "but something Cedric said really upset me, about how he'd never have kids with you, that you're not stable, and can't be a mother because of your vision problems. Plus, he said he doesn't want any more kids, but didn't tell you so as not to hurt you. He told me not to say anything but well, it's me, Rose, your friend, and you should tell me if something's wrong! He acted so weird. He's not hurting you, is he?"

Faced with that question so abruptly, my mind froze up. I hadn't admitted anything about my disastrous marriage to anyone because I'd barely begun to admit it to myself. Maybe our relationship was a bit abnormal, but I wasn't living in a horror film, was I? "No explain, no complain." My sense of reality was warped, just like for the bull. Despite the first cuts, the bull doesn't yet hate the matador. He's just angry. He doesn't know what he's in for.

"Cedric hurt me? No, he's not a mean guy," I said, laughing away her question. "I'm glad he went to see you; hope he gave you a hug for me. And isn't little Sarah sweet?"

I was such a fucking idiot. Instead of opening my heart to my best friend, I shielded Cedric once again, and steeled myself for his next charge. For this was a new part of his dark game. He was very subtly hemming me in. Instead of telling me from the outset he didn't want another child, he'd lied, insinuating that it was a distinct possibility, a natural part of the whole "traditional family" concept he'd dangled in front of me. The man who brings home the bread and protects his clan and the woman who cares for him and the home. And has his children! I think if he'd given me a definite "no kids," I would have stayed in New York. I should have asked him before moving to another continent, but I wasn't ready for kids then anyway. Now I felt relieved there would be no child with him, no link to keep us together. He couldn't even stand a dog; how would he put up with a screaming baby?

After the trip to New York, Cedric's verbal and sexual aggressions became more extreme and more frequent. Until then, he'd only shown me certain aspects of his personality, but now he ensconced himself in an identity he created: Cedric, the product of a tortured childhood, whose *modus vivendi* was revenge on a father that left him. He'd already brainwashed me into believing that demeaning me was a sign of love, and subjugating me was a sign of my respect for him, but now that he couldn't organize any orgies because of my foot, he decided to satisfy different kinds of his sick fantasies. His latest was to sell my used panties on the internet to strangers, for exorbitant prices.

"Yes! Sweetheart, come look. Your blue silk, you know, those stained ones, went for 1200 euros! We're eating out tonight! Get me something else of yours that I can sell. No, wait, I've got a better idea. We'll take some photos, some very exciting ones!"

It was late, and I was tired, but he managed to make me star in a staged torture scene. He shoved a cane up my ass, and then used the timer so we were both in the pictures. They sold very well. Thanks to me, we fattened up our end-of-month revenue. Cedric really got off on being able to indulge in his own perversions and make money from it.

When I was fully healed, Cedric went back to his former twisted habits. But instead of taking me to a 5-star restaurant on what he earned from my stinky underwear, he saved it up for long "romantic" weekends. Nothing to complain about as far as the destinations: Prague, Paris, London, Nice, Budapest, etc. Rooms in the finest hotels. Art museums, cocktails in the trendiest bars, elegant dinners, wonderful days that, unfortunately, never failed to end in a previously organized sex party with multiple strangers. This last part was not an option; it was the main feature of Cedric's "all-inclusive" package.

As the months passed, though, his sexual aggression became the least of my worries. He now began to use his words to chastise and torture me, and that was more difficult to cope with. He would whisper some horrible insult into my ear and finish with a sadistic laugh, leaving me paralyzed, crushing any bit of self-esteem I had left.

His constant, ugly comments, his "playful" pinches or flicks when he passed by me, his lewd sideways glances were a daily harassment. Those early days of having too much time on my hands were over. Now I raced against the clock to make sure his home and his wife were impeccable when he opened the front door, so I wouldn't merit his stinging criticisms, and too bad for me if anything was amiss.

One day my esthetician messed up my eyebrows. Crow black with venetian blond hair! I panicked. I knew Cedric wouldn't let it pass, plus, we had people coming over later. I scrubbed them as hard as possible to smooth out the color, plucked as many as I could, used light eyeshadow on them, foundation. Should I try bleach? No, I drew the line at that. The black would fade after a few days, and the problem would be solved.

But that was not good enough for him, never for him, and he vented his irritation that evening in front of our guests.

"What is that horrid color! You look like a vampire. How could you allow that to happen? You're sick, I mean, really crazy! You can't even handle a simple thing like giving the right directions to your stupid esthetician? And by the way, I fucked her before we met, did you know? I had to have my ass waxed, and I jumped on the occasion. And she sucks dick like a champion! Look at you! What a shame!"

I felt like curling up in a ball.

And I will never give myself a manicure again. Cedric could not stand the smell of nail polish remover. When we first started living together, I did my nails in the bathroom on Saturday mornings, but after he started complaining about the smell, I moved the operation to a weekday morning, or avoided it altogether if he was home. But with his keen sense of smell, he detected the slightest molecule, even hours after my nails were dry and looking pretty for him. He railed about "his one rule," that there could be no trace of that smell in his house. One day, I finally decided to do it outside on the back deck. Safe! He'd have no reason to reproach me.

I put everything away in the bathroom and dropped the cotton ball into the kitchen garbage can. Big mistake.

"What's that horrible smell?" he said as he came in the front door a couple hours later. "Did you do your nails in here again? I can't believe it! I told you I hate the smell of the remover."

"No, I did it outside. This nice shade of pink, see?"

He just stood there, head thrown back, sniffing. "Where did you throw away the cotton balls?"

"In the kitchen trash. I thought it would be okay," I said in a soft voice.

The bag was empty save the little white ball turned pink by the polish. He grabbed the bag and brought it out to the bin at the bottom of the garden, and marched back with a hard smile on his face. I knew that whatever awaited me would not be nice. It didn't come right away though. It's as if he had to think long and hard to come up with a fitting punishment.

About a week later, he woke me up at the usual time. He'd already dressed and made my coffee. As usual, I got up and drank it while it was hot, smoking my cigarillo, reading the headlines. My morning ritual. Before leaving for work, he told me to use the bathroom "one last time." I did as he asked me, but I was starting to tremble, then he told me to take off my bathrobe and kneel down in the kitchen next to the radiator. Again, I did as he asked, and there I was, naked on the icy kitchen tiles. I didn't understand where he was going with this until I saw him come back with the dog leash we bought for Elvis.

I'd often wondered when he would bring it out. Cedric got rid of my dog, but he kept the leash, saying it'd be "good for something or other." He never forgot those kinds of things. I should have known from the beginning that his words promised actions. And here we were...the hour of punishment for my minor mistake had come. I'd figured he was keeping it in wait for some sexual use, so this must be-—What was this? A surprise. Not a good one, not a good one at all.

No, he wouldn't dare do that. I thought for a second he was going to whip me with the long leather strap and its metal buttons. But it was worse. He tied my hands behind my back with a rough rope and then calmly put the leash around my neck, tightened it carefully, as if he didn't want to hurt me, and locked it to the warm radiator.

"Do you know why? I don't like to be provoked. Next time go to some salon and get your nails done! I give you more than enough money to pay for a manicure."

He stood in front of me now and shouted, "Never again. Do you hear me? Never again do I want to come home and smell that disgusting nail polish remover!"

Now he kneeled next to me and caressed my hair, my shoulders, my cheeks wet with tears. "My sweet, sweet Chloe, this is the only way you'll ever understand. The heater will keep you warm. I won't be home late, I promise. I love you, sweetheart."

I spent the entire day attached to the radiator. If someone had predicted this would happen to me one day, I wouldn't have believed it. An entire day sitting, kneeling, leaning, crouching, never finding a comfortable position, on cold kitchen tile, a prisoner. Punished for a fluffy bit of cotton.

During those long hours I kept wondering just how far he could go. Scenarios of him torturing and killing me kept making my heart race, but I always pushed them away, both to calm down and to avoid acknowledging it was possible. I spent the hours going over the last several years of my life like the plot of a film. The first time our eyes met, the first time our hands and then our lips touched, the first time he penetrated me. That next morning, and my eagerness to get back to New York City. That stupid romantic letter of his. Probably an example straight off the internet. I digressed into ever more sour thoughts and even some vicious chuckles. My stomach growled and I was thirty. I went back to the movie plot, trying to figure out my character's motive for giving up everything for him? Love. Of course, it was love, like in all the other movies, the most powerful motive on earth. But I knew I didn't love him now. He killed it that day. Who had I loved, I pondered. Ah, I'd loved my dog Yasco, the black lab I got for my 17th birthday. Yasco proved to me kindness was simple, a word or gesture freely given. Cedric had never shown me true kindness because he always required something in exchange. This was not love.

I ruminated on all the horrors of my life with him, and how they had so gradually escalated that I kept taking them in stride, making excuses for him, resigned to be a good spouse – at least his version of what that meant. Thinking about the bullfight kept me occupied for a few hours, as I analyzed its movements as the three acts in a play, and how Cedric and I represented the main characters. Eventually, I entered a netherworld of darkness and fell asleep.

I awoke with Cedric poking me in the arm. He was sitting cross-legged in front of me, staring at me with one eyebrow raised in appraisal, and for a moment, there was only the sound of our breathing. Conversation was not necessary. He untied me.

"I'll run you a warm bath with plenty of bubbles," he said cheerily. "I did the shopping for tonight. I'll cook you something delicious. It's over now, you were good. You see, it's not so difficult, is it?"

Like an obedient little girl, I hobbled into the bathroom, stretching my sore limbs and aching back. He ran a bath and I slipped into the bubbles. I listened to him moving around in the kitchen, the utensils clinking against each other, and I prayed he wouldn't come and bother me, that for once I could relax in peace. What was I going to do? I understood now I was living with a sick person. My heart started racing again and wouldn't slow down. I couldn't control it this time. My mind, no, my whole body was screaming at me to see the truth: think hard, Chloe, you know you haven't discovered everything, he's planning other things, you've only touched the surface of his depravity.

What does he really do all day? Nothing stops him from looking through your desk, so he must be watching you as well. I wouldn't put it past him to have a camera hidden right here with its eyeball open to the tub.

I shook my head and took some deep, slow breaths, then dunked my head under and thought. How had I gotten to this point? I suddenly remembered the film *Sleeping with the Enemy*. No one writes a story like that, about a wife forced to escape from an abusive husband, without there being a grain of truth in it. But how could I be in any of this? I wasn't Laura Burney. Not me! But like her, I'd have to make my escape.

I let out my breath, raised myself and shook my head like a wet dog. This was it! I forced a smile on my face, head high, shoulders back, and stepped out. I would prove my real worth to the world, and somehow survive to live a peaceful life. I deserved that much, and no one, not even Cedric, would change that. In the bathtub, after a day spent attached to the radiator, I realized how far he really would go, and my realization was like opening a prison cell window and letting in light. Now, I'd have to figure out how to open the cell door. It wasn't going to be as easy as packing my bags and walking out; I would have to prepare a strategy. I'd never been confronted with a psychopath like him. As I dressed, I defiantly repeated over and over in my head that he was the one who should have been locked up.

THIS IS BULLSHIT, NOT A LOVE STORY

I've had my dose of bad experiences, but this topped them all. I've also had a few vices of my own, but I dropped them and became a better person for it. Cedric's vices only multiplied. I wasn't about to show him I understood him now, though, because risking a confrontation might mean risking death. I wondered if he was capable of murder. He was too shrewd to leave marks of physical violence like a black eye or cuts and bruises in places visible to others, but how many more crushing humiliations would it take to lead me to suicide? Like the matador, he had manipulated me to the point I was completely under his power. This was a shock because it was so gradual, and because I thought it had been beyond my control, that I played into his hands because I loved him so much I was powerless to do otherwise, no matter how much it chafed me. Over time though, his behavior repeatedly brought up questions, and I knew better now. I was finally convinced that all was not normal. Now, the game could begin. I got dressed, put a cowed look on my face, and went back to the kitchen.

I lay in bed awake for a long time that night, planning my moves. More than anything I needed to understand his Machiavellian universe and how his twisted brain functioned. But where would I start? Or rather, when? The downward spiral began when his perversion made itself known, and my dreams of being a "good wife" turned into a nightmare. He acted as if I had unlimited tolerance for pain, that I could withstand the worst. I did, too. "The bull has to have balls!" Cedric liked to say. I accepted his emotional, physical and sexual abuse just to be with him, to feel loved instead of abandoned.

I realized patterns from my childhood had influenced my choices. Cedric even looked a little like my father, but he was nothing like him. My father was overprotective of my mother out of kindness, his gifts to her were spontaneous, and his love ran deep. Cedric protected me like a scrooge protecting a pot of gold and as a way to control me, , his gifts had a price, and his "love" was a mockery. Because of my unresolved traumas, I had thrown away my dream of independence and blindly put myself in danger.

So many humiliations had accumulated across the days and months and years, barbs planted in my neck, one after another! I didn't fight back, first out of reluctance to give up my hopes for us, then out of his manipulation of me. And I won't do anything yet, I thought, out of fear of him.

Cedric had tried to stamp out the very idea of doing something for myself by making me believe I belonged to him. But my old self wasn't completely crushed, only hidden beneath layers of numbed compliance. I would have to search for it. I realized I'd also been hiding behind a façade of blaming others, too, angry with the entire world, but not with Cedric. I was unable to blame him as I had no idea what a normal relationship looked like.

Over the weeks, I observed him closely. I guessed there weren't many men like him, so frustrated and uncomfortable in their own skin, men with a lot of money, but no inner wealth. They think they're perfect but they're deaf to their unhappiness. They pretend to be happy and to be able to make the entire world happy as well, but they're empty inside, with an intense need to destroy someone else so they can feel alive. That gives them pleasure. My husband was one of these men.

I braced myself to battle him by picturing him as that handsome, cold, perfectly prepared matador, whose barbs have struck their mark. Despite all the wounds, the bull's eyes fill with rage, and he manages to stand up. Victorious. The bull will not give up.

Cedric called me from the office one afternoon. "Guess who I'm having coffee with right now?"

Wary, I said, "I don't know."

"Whalid. I've invited him for drinks on Sunday night. See you soon, honey."

THIS IS BULLSHIT, NOT A LOVE STORY

His memory was incredible, a steel trap. More than four years had passed, and yet Cedric hadn't forgotten. Whalid was a bartender at a place we used to go to, and whenever he served us drinks, Whalid and I always flirted a bit. It was innocent; nothing ever happened, not even a clandestine brush of hands. I believe in fidelity. Whalid was just having some fun chatting up a slightly older woman, and for me, it was a break, a breath of fresh air. I was usually surrounded by Cedric and his clients, who were so much older than me I was bored to tears. So what if I secretly imagined how it would be to sleep with a hot young bartender? My thoughts belonged to me. But Cedric noticed right away. To his twisted way of thinking, if he could accidentally run into Whalid, then I could, too, meaning I could cheat on him, and since Whalid was handsome, I wouldn't be able to resist. And he wasn't about to let that happen.

I knew what kind of impossible situation he was setting up for me, and I did not want it. On Sunday nights, we relaxed in front of a good movie eating a pizza, and I looked forward to it all week. A direct "no" would never work, so I put on the charm when Cedric got home, trying to make it sound enticing. Nothing would convince him to cancel or change the date, though.

"Stop complaining," he said. "I'm giving you carte blanche for Sunday night, instead of a boring old movie. Do whatever you want, it's my gift to you. You want it, don't you?"

My fate was sealed. I was to fuck the young stallion, and that was it. Whalid would get to satisfy his fantasy about me, thanks to my own husband. Caught in a trap again, but that word "no" wouldn't come out of my mouth. Such a useful word, and yet I still couldn't drum up the courage to say it. What was I afraid of, though? Cedric would act proud of me, and then he'd leave me alone for a few days. I understood what was behind it: if he set it up and staged it for his own pleasure, I couldn't cheat on him with Whalid.

That night I pulled out all the stops, drinking glass after glass, trying to disappear into the wine bottle and never come out again. When the time came, I undressed and started to dance. Whalid's eyes widened, his mouth gaped as if he couldn't believe it. He was in his early 20s, and he'd never seen anything so surreal. It was certainly strange enough – Cedric had set up the living room to resemble a strip club, complete with pole. The music was too loud, bottles lolled about the low table, we were smoking cigarettes, and the smell permeated our clothes. After a strip-tease worthy of a pro, I undressed Whalid and kneeled down to take his cock in my mouth. Cedric was filming, and I shot him the sluttiest glance I could, so that he wouldn't know he was torturing me. At one point, he had some problem with the camera, and I took the chance to escape into the guest room with Whalid. By the time Cedric came in, the young man had slipped inside me and for a moment, I had the feeling, finally, that someone was actually making love to me. He even whispered into my ear that he'd love to see me again, alone.

The next day, Cedric had to go on a business trip, but before leaving, he made me look at the photos he'd taken of Whalid and me, naked.

"I sent them to him, just as a souvenir," Cedric said, laughing.

This was too much. For the very first time, I told him "No, it's not okay. Look, it's my body. I decide who you can send photos to, naked or not. I can't accept everything!"

"You're not going to bitch about it after you acted the perfect whore! If that's what you want, I'll erase everything. We'll never go out again, we'll never see anyone. We'll stay at home. You make things into such a big deal. It's just some photos!"

Then slammed out of the house as if he were the victim, leaving me shaking with rage.

Like a spoiled child, he couldn't stand to be told no. He always turned his mistakes around on me: if something went wrong, it was not his fault, he hadn't done anything wrong, it was my fault. And he never said sorry, ever. He disgusted me.

"You won't touch me ever again!" I screamed into the empty house. I didn't want him near me. I didn't want to give him anything, but I felt I'd never escape his grasp. I wanted to die. Yes, I wanted to die, right then, as my life at that moment wasn't worth living. I wanted to put a bullet in my head. Boom! Right to the temple, no chance of survival.

There was no gun in the house, though, and to me, that was the only possible way to end it all. I wasn't interested in passing out drunk or drugged in a bathtub, or cutting my wrists. Nope. Nope to hanging. We had some good rope, but I had no confidence I'd tie the knot right, and I didn't want to dangle ridiculously in the living room, which was the only room with crossbeams on the ceiling. And if it did work, I pictured myself dead, cold, my face turning blue...

I shook my head to rid myself of these thoughts. I wouldn't give him the pleasure of knowing he'd had the power to make me kill myself. I felt my strength returning, my guilt fading. I owed him nothing. Suddenly, I belonged to myself again. I had a flashback to New York, to the time before we met, and I saw myself at 30, full of the confidence that had attracted Cedric to me, the very confidence he'd tried to drain from me. I saw that strong woman with her defiant shoulders, her direct glance. I wasn't tall, but when I walked down the street in Manhattan, I felt six feet tall, and I grasped at that feeling, knowing it could get me out of the mess I was in. Finally. It took me five years, but I was coming to my senses.

He needed to understand that our marriage was collapsing. But I didn't know any safe way of telling him or making him see. I couldn't come right out and say, "Fucking hell, Cedric, you don't make me happy! Look at my empty face. The old me is gone. Look at my haggard eyes. Look at the despair there. Can't you see how much damage you do? You need help." He'd refuse, get angry, get violent, then pretend everything was fine and dandy.

But by the next afternoon, I felt under his thumb once more, and the image of a gun hovered before my eyes. Cedric had weakened me, decimated my pride, and I'd gotten discouraged to the point of lethargy, until I no longer wanted to do anything. He had burrowed into my inner life, taken away my privacy and stolen everything from me. Controlled everything about me. I resented that he had stolen my dream of a better life. But then I thought of a way to get back at him, and my blue funk dissipated. I would sleep with another man without his permission or knowledge. Instead of killing myself, I would wield sex as a weapon and fight my way to freedom. I tried to gear myself up for it by pacing around the living room thinking, "I can do this." I wanted to explode, but I couldn't do that without breaking something. I felt like the bull at his wit's end in the arena. How would he have reacted? He would drive his horns into his adversary, without a second thought! At lightning speed and in a blind rage, he would gore the matador, shoot him into the air, watch him fall mercilessly to the ground, chest and stomach ripped to shreds and the crowd screaming its horror. Then he would walk out of the arena with his head held high.

Just thinking about Cedric was poisonous. It was now or never. My computer was on the kitchen table, and Cedric would be gone until the next day. I stared at it, my hands trembling, but ready for what I was going to do. Light the fire. Whalid wouldn't say no. I sent him a message on Facebook: "How are you?" He answered within seconds, as if he were waiting for this.

"Great, and you? Your husband just called me. Isn't that weird? Crazy coincidence. He asked me if I was in Paris right now, saying he's there for work. Until when?"

"That is really weird. He's gone until tomorrow night."

THIS IS BULLSHIT, NOT A LOVE STORY

"So, you're alone?"

We made plans for him to come over at 9 pm. Not for a drink, not as a friend, and no stage props or cameras. He wasn't coming to watch me pole dance or sit across from him at a table.

I emptied my mind of all these whirling thoughts and took a bath. I had no idea what the consequences of this single night would be, but I had to do it, that was all, fidelity be damned. Needing some moral support, I called Rose and told her, finally, about my disastrous marriage, about our deviant sex life and how it included other people all the time. I didn't give her too many details though because I was too ashamed. But even if she could not envision what our sex life really involved, the horrors it involved, I felt lighter and less lonely after opening my heart to her. Then I shared what I was about to do with Whalid. She approved and said I should take back what belonged to me. She was reassured even. Her voice on the other end of the line calmed me down, and when I hung up, I smiled.

This was a big step. My sexuality would belong to me. Cedric wouldn't decide anything for me. I chose my clothes for the evening, comfy jeans, a simple T-shirt, and my favorite square-toed shoes. The kind of thing Cedric would only let me wear at home. I could hear his snide comments: "What the hell is that outfit? No ass, no tits, you're ugly, go change!" I looked in the mirror and liked what I saw: a woman who didn't overdo it or doll herself up to look sexy, an elegant woman with natural sensuality and confidence that solicited respect. Come back to me, Chloe...

Whalid arrived and I poured us some whisky. We talked about his future in the hotel business, and he asked me some questions about my work – not one mention of my marriage or that sordid night with my husband. Cedric had vanished from view. I tried to remain aware of the experience, the here and now of my act. Adultery, my sole, precious instance of it, the act that would break the chains around my life into pieces.

He kissed me, awkwardly at first. A bit disappointed, I decided to take over, and everything happened very quickly after that. Sweater removed, then shoes, socks, pants, everything. We were naked and honest about what we were doing. I led him by the hand to the guest room, just as I'd done before. I had enough respect to keep him out of the marriage bed. Cedric would have detected his cologne anyway.

Whalid was not a particularly skilled lover, but I didn't care. I wanted him inside me. I closed my eyes, and pictured my husband far away in the distance, just a spot on the horizon. I had no regrets, but felt a touch of sadness, and even desperation. I didn't show him my feelings while we had sex, and when we were tired out, he dressed, and we said goodnight. Not another word. I didn't want to lay there in his arms or for him to sleep beside me; I wanted him to leave, and quickly, to close the door and not look back.

It was done. I had committed the worst. Two human beings had spent a moment enlaced, kissing and loving each other, and it would be our secret. I sat down in the kitchen in my bathrobe. The sight of my lipstick on the edge of the whisky glass sent me a few hours back. I quickly scanned the room but there was no sign of Whalid's presence. Cedric would never find out unless Whalid told him, and he had no reason to do that. I went to bed, feeling good.

I didn't know Cedric had installed cameras around the house and paid a hacker to tap my phone. I was aware he monitored my Facebook account and read my emails, but I thought I was safe otherwise. He was always with me unless he was traveling, and even then, I felt his presence so strongly it was like a second skin, like his brain was wedged inside my own brain. Long ago this had felt comforting. I never thought he would spy on me, so I wasn't on my guard, even if every now and then I had a creepy feeling that someone was watching me. I'd always put it to my having a guilty conscience. But now I was guilty of a marital transgression, I didn't feel guilty at all.

Cedric didn't call that night. He'd told me that he wasn't going to, which was unusual in itself, but I didn't believe him. Cedric always called, every night and sometimes more than once. But that night, nothing.

He came home the next day in a very good mood.

"Hello, my darling, how are you? You smell good. You're so lovely."

"I'm fine. How was your trip?"

The next morning, he was strangely tender with me, solicitous of everything, constantly asking me how I was feeling, or what I wanted to eat. Did he know how fake he sounded? Was he worried about our marriage? This new act sure worried me – it had to mean something ominous.

We left for Zurich after lunch to spend the weekend there. An hour into the drive, he reached for my hand, and asked me for the first time, "Honey, have you ever cheated on me?"

He said it in such a syrupy voice. I wasn't thinking about Whalid, and I didn't feel bad about what I'd done. I'm sure Cedric fucked plenty of prostitutes in Asia and probably a few Lady Boys, too. I never tried to find out or imagine it – that was not worthy of a nice housewife, plus I think it's awful knowing everything about another person. He, on the other hand, had invaded me, swallowed me whole in the effort to know me through and through. We should have remained two completely separate human beings.

I simply stared at him, unable to come out with a lie or the truth. I've heard Mossad agents have an effective technique to get their enemies to talk. First they manipulate, then they hit. It took him only a few hours to worm the truth out of me. He didn't have to hit, or yell at me or blind me with fluorescent lamps, he didn't need to stick my head under water or shock me. He just kept at me during the long ride, over and over and over again: "You're sure you have nothing to tell me, you're sure you didn't cheat on me while I was away?"

Finally, I talked. "Yes! I did it! I didn't want to cheat on you, but it was the only way I could think of to show you I can't do this anymore. I've told you again and again I can't stand the way you speak to me and how you use me. You don't listen to me! I'm so unhappy in this marriage."

He threw my hand away. He didn't say another word, but I knew his looks, and this one was smug, not angry or sad or jealous, just smug. I couldn't tell what that meant, and not knowing unnerved me. We finally reached our hotel in Zurich. The weather was grim, the air cold and damp, and the whole city dripped with sadness.

In our room, he blurted out, "I've thought about it, and I forgive you. I have to do it now or I might never be able to do it."

We were stretched out on the bed, and he wrapped his arms around me. Had he considered what I'd said about his treating me badly? It was too soon to forgive me. A normal person would not have reacted that way, so this made me even more nervous. But he played the jovial, loving husband all weekend and I went along with it.

When we got back home, he told me to make an appointment with our family doctor, explaining that what I'd done "was abnormal" because someone with a life like mine doesn't do such things. He brought up the emotional problems of my past, insisting I was tottering on the edge of a nervous breakdown, and even offered me some Xanax "to calm down."

I made the appointment, knowing Cedric would make it himself if I didn't. Since my ischemia, he attended all my doctor's appointments, and this one was no different.

"So, what brings you in? You called about her medication. What's going on?"

"She's having a Borderline Disorder episode, Doctor. Go on, Chloe, explain what happened."

Doubled up in my chair with my head down, I looked like the class clown in trouble for some mischief. It wasn't my husband beside me; it was my father, and I was 12 years old again, my world crumbling around me. The doctor waited for my explanation, but I said nothing, so Cedric stepped in.

"It's simple. Chloe cheated on me with a young man, the son of one of my clients even! And just to send me some message, she says. Is she insane? She needs medication and maybe psychiatry, and she might even benefit from a stay in a hospital. What do you think? Do you think she'll ever be healed?"

"Listen, Mrs. Moreau, your husband's right to be worried about you. What if he came home one night, and you'd slit your wrists? I'd like to put you on anti-depressants and have you see a psychiatrist. I'll give you an address for a colleague of mine. He's very good. And remember, there's full-time care if you feel you need it."

I turned and looked out of the window. I didn't want to look at either of them, the man in his white coat or my husband playing his violin, out for pity. I wanted to be anywhere else. But of course, I would have to explain myself to some stranger about how I'd slept with another man as a call for help. "Admit" to an act that had nothing to do with mental illness. I wanted to send that message to my husband, not to anyone else; it was personal. But it didn't matter, the finger remained pointed at me. My error gave Cedric the chance to up his game. He wanted to send me to a psych ward!

As we left the consultation, he gloated.

"You see, you haven't healed at all. You're 'borderline' and probably bi-polar as well! You'd better go see the shrink he recommended. He's going to send him your file, anyway, so I don't think you have a choice."

I couldn't prove to him that everyone is a little "borderline." I knew how far I had come, what I had sorted out in my life: anorexia, anxiety and all the rest. Before meeting him, I was on the right path, I knew that. He had no right to send me back down that road and I wouldn't let him do it. I was strong enough now to overcome his influence. I would go and see this psychiatrist, but not for his reasons.

A deep tension set in between Cedric and me, as real as between the wood and the concrete of the house, two materials that were no longer compatible. Cedric kept looking at me like I was ill. He understood physical pain, but he always said mental suffering was weakness, and he would use this against me until I died.

I decided I would no longer show him my emotions. From one day to the next my face shut down, covered by a mask I put on at will to guard myself. Behind it, and in my daydreams, or late at night, I imagined myself without him. I didn't know when I would leave him, but I pushed myself toward it step by step. When I woke up or snapped to, the image disappeared, as if I was not quite ready for the great escape, and besides, I no longer remembered what freedom was like.

I could have used my mother's help, but she didn't want to "interfere" in my marriage. We didn't have the same vision of life. I was a woman who wanted to be a loving wife, but also wanted freedom, no matter what, and she was a post-war woman, uncomfortable with women's rights. It would have been improper of me to reproach her, because two generations separated us, and two different histories. Plus, she had never stopped loving her husband, and I had never loved mine – it had been a gut-wrenching hold he had on me, but not love.

She did let me have a piece of her mind, of course. "You're not a child anymore. You don't need me. Just take care of your looks and be happy with this man! He gives you all a woman needs."

What she didn't know, or refused to see, was what a tyrant he was. I couldn't count on her help even now, when I had reached the breaking point. And yet, when I introduced Cedric to her and my father in the beginning of our relationship, she had frowned on him. I guess the prospect of me settling down into a life of conventional comfort must have reassured her – both my parents wanted me to be happy and stable. Cedric had said nasty things about her back then, but she didn't know that, and he acted so winningly to her, she wouldn't have believed it.

In the end, our marriage woes were no one's business but mine and my husband's.

When my mother announced that she had breast cancer, Cedric went ballistic. "Great, so now you're going to spend day and night at her bedside, you're going to pout and complain all the time and you'll never fuck me again! You're such a piece of shit. I'll have to get a hooker if this continues!" How does a person even respond to that? I was terrified my mother would die, and I would have to suffer through it without his support.

Ignoring his frequent comments, I started helping my father, visiting my mother in the hospital, trying to comfort her and distract her from the pain and possible outcomes. I stopped thinking about my own problems. If only I didn't have to go home! I wanted to move in with my parents, and I dreamed, absurdly, of being a kid again. I needed to be strong though, as my mother would start worrying if she saw my weakness, my father would be annoyed, and Cedric would be very happy. I tried to give her the little strength I had left. I could still make her smile. She couldn't bear wearing a wig, so I helped her find brightly colored turbans, outsized earrings, and "happy dresses." She spent the summer looking frail but beautiful, hiding the effects of her chemo. I said "She won't die" so many times I became sure of it.

Since Cedric was still making all our decisions, he organized our life behind my back, never asking me what I thought or what I wanted. It didn't matter to him that my mother needed me. He arranged my life, and I had to be there for evenings with friends or his clients, outings with his daughters or the unexpected visit from his mother. He was in charge. Either I was "in," or I was "out."

"One of my most important potential clients is coming to Geneva this weekend, so I arranged to have tea with your parents on Sunday. His wife and your mother will get along really well."

I tried to dissuade him. My mother was still undergoing chemo, which tired her out. She couldn't do anything halfway, though, and her notion of having guests over required everything to be perfect. She would deep-clean the house, bake a cake, get out her gold-rimmed porcelain dishes and fancy teapot. She would never admit she was overextended. I called her to offer to help and to apologize for Cedric organizing this without asking me, but she brushed it all away. I gritted my teeth thinking about why he did it: his eternal social climbing. My parents had a beautiful home, so his clients would be impressed, and my mother would charm them with her well-chosen jewelry, her beautiful, flowing clothing, her cosmopolitan polish. My father would want the event over with as quickly as possible, as he had other things to do on a Sunday afternoon than play the worldly man with strangers. He hid it well from them, but I noticed it as soon as we arrived.

The tea and cake came out at just the right time, and the conversation began. I stayed discreetly in my corner and observed. Cedric explained my father's background in a few words, focusing on how he had managed some of the greatest musicians of our time. He mentioned a few big names, of course, but his clients didn't recognize them. Their taste was limited to Arab music. The husband talked about his career in the merchant trade and when he mentioned a Brazilian port he'd been based in briefly, I saw my mother's eyes fill with tears. She recounted how her father had established his wood processing business there. They began swapping stories, sharing good memories. Cedric looked ecstatic. Clearly, dollar signs were flashing across his mind, for through his adroit maneuvering, he'd won the client's trust, and he would open a fat account or two before returning to Kuwait.

This success led him to use my family for his own means several more times. He believed in his natural charm, and now he seemed to feel he belonged to their social class. He thought my parents were naïve, because most people would have seen what he was up to, and balked. I wondered about that, too, and also why they never asked me about Cedric or whether my marriage was happy and why they acted as if material comfort alone makes a person happy.

As the weeks passed, I kept casting around for ways to safely end our relationship. Pack up and escape? That would require putting a lot of distance between us, but how much would be enough? I wished I could be indifferent; it would make it easier, but I still looked at his face, and I hadn't moved into the guest room, even if we slept with our backs to each other. I put it off breaking the bond.

Instead of making my great escape, I ended up convincing myself I really was at risk of mental illness. The blown fuse, the destructive woman, unable to be happy. Cedric had guided me so far away from my true personality that he'd weakened me, using the same tactics the matador used with the bull. I knew I had to save myself.

I had just enough sense left to merely pretend to return to my borderline behaviors, as a last-ditch strategy to defy him. I exaggerated my "episodes" and my melancholy, giddiness, everything that indicated a spiral down. It was risky, because at times I almost lost control.

I was so afraid. I had thought I could tame the devil, but now he truly frightened me. I was fragile, and I tried, in vain, to understand what he was thinking before it was too late. He was always a few steps ahead of me and had been from day one. He'd found the perfect victim to satisfy his compulsions, he'd seen it all. He used my weakness, and my instability made it possible for him to conceal his own mental disorder. He didn't care at all about my psychological state, but maybe, just maybe, he'd get winded always running so far ahead.

I provoked him one night a bit too much.

He screamed, "You're hysterical, I'm going to take you to the doctor. There's something wrong with you, little girl, you're definitely crazy!"

I lost control, my mask fell, and I shook my head back and forth, screaming that I couldn't take it anymore. I tried to run away and lock myself up in the guest room to calm down. Impossible. I kept running but he followed me all over the house, grabbing me and pinching my arm. I begged him to leave me alone for a few minutes, but he wouldn't let me go. He was smiling euphorically, nearly demented, then he forced me to kiss him and I gave in. There was no way out; I couldn't refuse him, because he was stronger in every way. Fucking me would end our argument. He came hard inside me, his way of forgiving me, but he was raping me, each time it was rape. We fell asleep wrapped up together as if there was nothing violent about our sex.

And next morning, he whispered in my ear, "I'll call the shrink. You'll see, everything will be fine."

THIS IS BULLSHIT, NOT A LOVE STORY

I should have called Dr. Thyssen, the therapist I'd seen on and off since I was a teenager. Out of pride, I didn't want her to be right when she said my relationship would never last, that she'd seen it all. It didn't really matter because Cedric wouldn't have let me – she was my ally, and he knew it, which made her his adversary. Cedric wanted me to see Dr. Trévoz, the psychiatrist our family doctor had recommended.

The next day, he dropped me off at his office, on the ground floor of a house in a village on the outskirts of Geneva. There was a sign on the door that said to ring, come in, and take a seat in the waiting room. I carefully opened the door with the feeling of trespassing on a private residence. A few minutes later, Dr. Trévoz came in and ushered me into the consultation room.

My hands were clammy. What the hell was I doing here? What did I have to talk about – an imaginary illness? At least five or six years had passed since I'd had real need of a therapist, but now, at the order of my husband, I had to spill my guts to a psychiatrist who knew nothing of my life. Cedric was a genius. He would maintain his role as the victim, and I would be the neurotic.

Right from the outset, Dr. Trévoz turned me off. Ugly, unkempt clothes, ratty furniture, zero charisma, cold and clearly awkward. Had he become a shrink to deal with his own problems, like others I'd come across? His piercing glance seemed to take me in all at once, and he didn't smile as he greeted me, but his voice was calm, pleasant even, and I became a bit more reassured as he took me through the usual formalities. I gave him an overview of my past and the problems linked to my behavior, then talked about my retinal ischemia. He told me I was lucky not to be completely blind; otherwise, he was distant, taking notes without talking or looking at me much. I started to squirm in the straight-backed chair. Noticing, he indicated the couch. The old leather creaked as I lay down, and the stuffing sighed as the air escaped.

"And your marriage?" he said, broaching the main subject.

"What about my marriage?"

"Are you and your husband happy?"

I shifted uneasily, and the couch sighed again. What should I tell him? Yeah, it's great, as perfect as the first day? But this man was giving me a chance to admit what was happening, and I pushed myself to let it all out, to tell him how Cedric treats me, to tell him everything. I felt it was a "now or never" moment.

There was a long moment of silence while I gathered my courage. Dr. Trévoz prodded me, saying, "I'm not here to judge you. I'm simply here to listen to you and maybe help."

I needed to trust him that not a word of this would leave the room. As a doctor, he must hold to professional confidentiality, and nothing could change that. This was my chance to get it all off my chest.

"I'm not really sure where to start," I said, and then my throat tightened, and I started to cry. I let myself go, not even trying to maintain any semblance of composure. I cried for several minutes, sobbing with my hands cupping my face. After so many years of never saying anything to anyone, how could I describe my day-to-day life, let alone our completely fucked-up sex life? And then what, ask him if all that was normal? My head cleared as anger rushed in. The tears dried up and I began to talk, letting it out without a pause, practically vomiting my narrative of how Cedric treated me, his insults, humiliations, putdowns, and then I reached the part where I had to describe our intimate life. Intimate! The word had nothing to do with our relationship. Our sex life was more public than private, no restraint or respect, and it wallowed in the dregs of immorality. I was off the couch and pacing the room by this time.

"I don't want anything more to do with it," I shouted, then abruptly lay down again.

It felt liberating to finally get it all out, down to the disgusting details, and Dr. Trévoz didn't interrupt me. Tears were still running down my face, and I had to blow my nose half a dozen times. I was suffering, my entire body in pain, the pins-and-needles kind.

I wrapped up by telling the doctor about the day Cedric leashed me to the radiator, the day Cedric had gone too far, and I knew I could break with him, and that my infidelity was a direct result. I took a deep breath and stopped unloading the harsh truth of my life to this complete stranger. I sat up and looked straight at the psychiatrist.

"So that's my marriage, Dr. Trévoz. What would you say about it?"

"Would you agree to have another session next week?"

I left feeling overwhelmed, light-headed from emptying out so much bitterness and pent-up emotion, and relieved to have heard my own thoughts articulated, to hear what my soul was screaming to say for so long. My story terrified me.

Cedric was waiting for me in the car, on time as always. I didn't want to talk about the session to him, so all I said was that I'd see the doctor again the following week.

"But what did you talk about? Your behavioral problems? I hope you talked to him about that."

"Yes, yes, I told him about my past. And he asked about our marriage."

I bit my tongue. Why did I say that last bit?

"I see. You mentioned our sex life? You're right, my love. And maybe we need a little break from all that. It's maybe a bit out of control."

Why the leap from our marriage to our sex life? How did he know my conversation with Dr. Trévoz would focus on sex? Cedric creeped me out. I went quiet until we reached the house. His daughters were waiting for us.

I was hoping for a sign of some kind, a pointer on how to keep fighting in a void, a guide on how to escape without any help. Fucking fate! Sometimes I hated fate for putting me into such a horrible situation, and "love," I was so disgusted by this emotional stranglehold called love. What happened to me was so wrong, but I had to admit I had made wrong choices, too. Did God know what was happening, and not doing a thing to help? That would make him one fucking pervert, too.

With Cedric, I became a robot, I kept my mouth shut, I dutifully took the medicine the doctor prescribed. I went to see Trévoz every week and while he barely said a word, I never stopped talking. I felt lighter and stronger – I think I was unconsciously preparing myself to fight my torturer.

Cedric was often traveling for work during this period, but he no longer took me with him, and sometimes he didn't even tell me he was leaving until the night before departure. To him, I was a "thing," his thing, so what did it matter if I knew his comings and goings? Same with our sex nights, which had dwindled to about once a month: he would spring it on me at the last minute.

"Go get ready, our guests will be here in an hour. I'll make dinner while you go do your make-up – you look like an old cleaning lady. And shave your pussy this time. I don't want to see a single hair. I want to imagine I'm licking a teenager." The horrible thought came into my mind that what he really meant was he wanted to imagine doing it with one of his daughters. I hated him for putting a thought like that in my head, another to add to the horrors and insults buried deep, where even he couldn't read my mind.

My brain was no mystery to him, though, and his perversions didn't simply go away when I started seeing Dr. Trévoz. But now he used more cunning to get what he wanted. He created a new set of rules. Ever since I cheated on him with Whalid, the Swingers' clubs were out. He didn't want to risk me enjoying an encounter with a stranger, exchanging phone numbers or making plans to meet in a hotel. He needed to be in control. But he did want to enjoy showing off his trophy, so one night he put his plan in motion.

"Come on, we're going to go out. Put on the garter belt and stockings I gave you for Christmas, and the black Louboutin boots. But nothing else. Wait, put on your dark red lipstick! You're so pale. Let your hair down and put on your coat."

"But it's freezing outside, and I'm already exhausted... I thought we were staying at home nice and quiet tonight."

That made no difference to him. He bundled me out the door, me in boots, underwear and a coat. Oh, and red lipstick.

"Where are you taking me?"

"Don't be worried, darling. Don't you trust me?"

I nodded, thinking, "No, Cedric, I haven't trusted you for a long time. I'm afraid of you."

He stopped the car at a highway rest area, one I knew only too well. Even in subzero temperatures, there'd always be some weirdo hiding in the bushes, waiting for the appearance of the divine. It's me, gentlemen. Some of you have seen me before, for others I'm truly of gift from God. Or Lucifer.

Cedric changed the setup this time. He got Elvis's dog leash out of the glove box. I had been wondering when he'd use it again. It wasn't to a radiator this time, but out in the cold. I would have preferred somewhere warmer. He put the leash around my neck and led me to a big tree, attached me to a branch, then took off my coat. He said in a soft voice, "I'll be back."

He disappeared, leaving me shivering and sad. A few minutes were all it took for a small troupe of hungry men to appear.

"She's all yours," I heard Cedric say. "She's just waiting for it."

He was going to leave me to them, to a bunch of lecherous men, with their filthy dicks. I couldn't believe the insanity of what was happening. How could he? He'd promised me all of this was going to stop, and I really believed that my sessions with Dr. Trévoz had made him understand he'd gone too far. I closed my eyes and waited anxiously. I could hear the familiar sounds of Cedric setting up his tripod and video camera somewhere close by. I was going to star in a horror film now!

I told myself I could do this one last time, get over the pain of it, hope there would be no STD consequences, swallow my pride. After tonight, it's over. Never concede to him again! Please, God, make it so these guys haven't ejaculated for a long time, so they'll come in five seconds or less.

The leash kept me from fighting or trying to run away. One after the other...finally it was over, and Cedric unleashed me, threw me my coat and led me, limping from the pain between my legs, to the car. Back home, I showered gingerly, then went to find Cedric.

"I thought this was all finished, Cedric! Why did you make me do that tonight?"

"Don't lie! I didn't make you do anything. You wanted it as much as I did, so stop accusing me. It's not a good idea to tell your doctor everything, you know. Just tell him the truth, tell him you're really sick, tell him you're the one who's the pervert. Before you came into my life, I would never – do you hear me – never have done anything perverted. It's you, dear wifey, who's the slut here. You're the one who brought me into your sick world. Just ask my ex-wife, she'll tell you our sex life was completely normal. It's you who's abnormal! No matter what you do, you will always be the one everyone considers the sicko. You got that?"

So, Cedric was threatening me, and what was that mention of my psychiatrist? I now added paranoia to my constant feeling of defeat. For weeks, I'd felt Cedric was spying on me, night and day, with his microphones and hidden cameras. I couldn't find them, but I knew they were there, and adjusted all my behavior to that knowledge. So, maybe he was paying the psychiatrist to spill what I talked about. No, that was impossible. A doctor has to honor patient confidentiality. So, maybe he'd hired a private detective to bug the doctor's office, to follow me, spy on me! I never imagined he would go so far, but in words and deeds, he'd already gone way farther, so why not that?

In the end, I decided I was just being paranoid.

I always kept hoping he would consider our relationship objectively and prove to me he could change. One night months earlier, he had given me a glimmer of hope. He had been drinking for hours and became weepy, maudlin even, and he admitted he treated me with disrespect and even cruelty and made no honest effort to help his daughters and me connect emotionally. He then made a solemn vow to confront his own weaknesses, and to go see a therapist to work through his painful past, instead of always blaming his father to excuse his own behavior. He admitted he wasn't acting out of love, but out of revenge, to punish me and make me suffer.

After hearing his confession in his own words, I believed in him, and thought he had the courage to change, to throw down his sword and cape. But now he'd proved the opposite, with that dog leash, poor Elvis's damned leash, and his video camera. And now his hint about knowing everything my therapist had heard. That got me extremely worried, not about the future of our marriage – that was doomed – but about my very life. I started to pay more careful attention to him as he spewed his vitriol, and I had to face it: he or someone else was spying on me. He was repeating my own sentences back to me verbatim, throwing them into my face with a gloating look on his face, as if he were proud of his cleverness. He described specific moments he'd stolen from my day.

Had he hidden a microphone in my purse? Was he in the next room or even hidden in the same room during my sessions with Dr. Trévoz? Everything became frighteningly obvious. It was no coincidence when Whalid told me Cedric called him to see if he was in Paris, or that our family doctor had taken his side. He must have called him before my appointment to give him a completely exaggerated picture of my behavior.

Were they all in on it, everyone, even my parents? My father had suggested I get some help, and my mother was treating me like I was possessed. Cedric had managed to make my family turn their backs on me.

Please, everyone, it's not me. It's him, Cedric has done this, has manipulated all of us, so don't believe what he says. I'm begging you to help me.

From that point on, Cedric treated me like I was mentally ill. He kept telling me that everything I did, and everything I felt, had something to do with my "disorder." And he wasn't shy about talking about this in public.

"There's nothing I can do," he would say. "It's how she is. But she's getting help. It isn't easy to live with someone who's so imbalanced. I'm phobic about illness and I'm terrified of hospitals. And look what I ended up with! She's quite the gift. But I can't imagine living without her. Love doesn't make sense, does it? She's the only one who fulfills me sexually. Look at her, doesn't she just reek of sex?"

His blunt, vulgar language no longer shocked anyone in Geneva's high society, which seemed to have accepted him. If we went to charity dinners, he never bought raffle tickets; he explained he was doing his charity work at home, taking care of his "sick" wife, maybe hoping some sympathetic patron would pity him enough to give him a huge wad of cash. He continued to present me as being nearly blind, and made me wear my sunglasses when we went out, day or night. I ended up with an entire collection.

"Here, wear your Prada's tonight, you look better in them," he would say as we got ready. Of course I looked better. They hid the dark circles of sleep deprivation and the unhappiness that was slowly destroying my face.

"You see? You need to get with it and listen to me. Remember, it's my way..."

Cedric's favorite saying was, "It's either my way or the fucking highway!" I should have kept track of how many times he threw this in my face. It was how he ended our arguments, always getting the last word. He was so sure I wouldn't move out, that I'd never leave him, that my world would crumble without him, and I'd be nothing, because before him I hadn't counted for much at all. Everyone seemed to believe that now, as his savior approach had done the job. From the outside, everything about him looked perfect. I had a perfect husband apart from his brutally honest way of talking, maybe. "But that was just Cedric," they'd say with a snicker. If only they knew what I knew. Watch out, Cedric, I'm about to get on your "fucking highway." I can't wait to get away from you.

The ambiance at home was heavy, tense and awkward, and we hardly spoke to each other. It couldn't last much longer. Constant pressure gnawed at me to hurry up and find a safe, permanent way to escape. Finally, I decided to suggest getting some distance between us.

"Maybe I should go stay with my parents for a bit, a few weeks, maybe a month? That might help us make the right decision about where we're going as a couple."

He agreed with me, for once.

"It's true. We're headed straight for a wall, and I can't take it anymore. I need to focus on my work, but you're making it impossible."

I understood. He didn't give a shit about me or our marriage, only his job, his priority.

But my parents didn't want me around. I could feel their reluctance when I asked, even though I'd told my mother in private I desperately needed some maternal comfort. I didn't have any friends who lived nearby who could take me in, so I needed to look farther afield, out of Switzerland. I didn't have too much time to think about it, though, as Cedric was stressing me out, in a rush suddenly to get me out of the house.

"I said you could leave, so hurry up and figure out where you're going, and remember, you pay your own way. You can move into your office in the backyard – that won't cost you anything, or insist your parents take you in. If no one wants you, that's your problem, but I don't want to see you anymore. When you get back, we'll figure out if we have a future. Or not."

I had to get out of there. I hadn't spent all my savings from working in New York, as Cedric hadn't touched it. At least, I hoped not. I should have enough to buy a ticket for somewhere far away. But where? I invited myself to Sunday brunch at my parents' house, hoping they would relent, or that my mother would give me an idea. I couldn't stand another meal with Cedric's daughters and my mother-in-law. Without warning, he'd brought Didine to stay with us and the way they kept looking at me was making me crazy. What had Cedric told them? I felt so awkward with everyone. I was under so much stress that I kept breaking into cold sweats, something I'd never experienced.

I waited until Sunday morning to tell Cedric I was going to brunch. We'd just woken up. I had to spread my legs to get him to say "yes." His panting, his heavy, sweaty body over me disgusted me, but I slowly counted to ten, and it was over. He came and I could get up, take a shower, then call my mother to ask her to pick me up. I needed to be with my own family. Even if my father couldn't stand me, maybe my mother would understand why I was so upset.

She waited for me at the end of the block. I'd asked her not to park in front of the house, as she would have felt obligated to come in and say hello to everyone, and I didn't want to waste any time. When I opened the car door, I felt a rush of tenderness. My mom. Her face was closed, but I knew her heart was open to me. I asked her to turn off the engine. The problem was how to explain my unhappiness. My parents wouldn't understand unless I went into detail, and that I would not do. Bruises would be the kind of proof they needed, not words. Words didn't mean abuse, and I would never admit to his sexual depravity or the humiliation of the leash. So I told her we wanted to try a temporary separation because I needed "some fresh air," and assured her we would get our marriage back on the right path afterwards. She didn't seem surprised.

"I am worried about you," she said. "I think you should stop writing. You're torturing your mind. Was that story you gave me based on your life with Cedric? It's too much – sometimes you need to take a step back, make sure you're not exaggerating. You complain far too much. But it's your choice, of course."

She was shifting the subject. It wouldn't be easy to confide in her about my fears. I could tell she didn't want to hear it, and she definitely wouldn't want to help.

"Writing it all down helps me deal with the pain of it. And I'm scared—-"

I couldn't finish. She was not ready for the whole truth. I believed my parents loved me, even my father. He wasn't a bad man, even if he sometimes flew off the handle. For him, speaking harshly didn't mean "I hate you;" it meant there was confusion between his emotions and his body. He was a poor communicator, but he would protect his wife until the day he died, and since I was her daughter, he'd protect me too, even if a bit begrudgingly.

Our talk in the car led us nowhere, because I couldn't tell my mother the truth. She ended up lecturing me about how a woman's happiness depends on her ability to conform to her husband's expectations.

"It's how our society has worked for so long, so why try to fight it?"

The gulf between us was so wide I couldn't even make the attempt to shift her in my direction. I felt pulled between two worlds. I had tried, willingly, to consent to what society wanted me to be, just like my mother advised, but I had to get away from a dangerous situation. Cedric was making this all too clear.

"I can't do this anymore, I really can't," I said. "But don't worry about me, Mom, you know me, I always find a way. It's not working now, but I'll see my way back to a good place."

What she wanted for me was to conform and be happy about it, but that wasn't what I wanted. For my sake, she needed to learn I was unhappy in my marriage, and why, but when we arrived at their house, I realized she did know, because she took a deep breath, grabbed my hand and whispered, "I hope God is with you. I mean it."

She knew something deep inside me had changed, that the machinery was turning, and nothing could stop me. I watched in wonder as her eyes filled with tears.

"I feel so helpless, but I came up with a possible solution. Our Brazil trip is coming up. We're planning to be there for a month, so come with us. Get your ticket and come."

This seemed like the ideal plan. It had been ten years since I'd been back to Rio, and I could spend time with family, cousins, aunts, my brother and my nephew, the perfect solace instead of being alone to face my ordeal. Once inside, though, I felt my father's coldness. It enveloped me, unspoken but strongly expressed in his narrowed lips and the pointed look at my mother. Right then my father hated me.

A horrible feeling that tied my stomach in knots, and even made me afraid of him, just like I was afraid of Cedric. I could tell my mother didn't know what to do. But that day her maternal instinct kicked in, and she tried to take my part when I asked him about their trip to Brazil, coaxing him into a better mood. I nudged her so she would ask my father. She finally broached the question.

"Why not have Chloe come along? Wouldn't it be fun to get the whole family together in Rio?"

"I'll come if you ask, Dad." I believed in the plan. A miracle, too good to be true.

"Of course, sweetie," my mother said. "He'd be delighted if you could come, isn't that so, my love?"

But he just grunted and kept eating, his mood darkening again. After brunch, they went into the kitchen, where I could hear my father grumbling about plans changing, the inconvenience and expense. In his stubbornness, he wouldn't give her an answer, yes or no, but I knew already I wouldn't be going with them.

My mother came out to the terrace and sat down next to me, looking flustered. She coughed awkwardly and mumbled that we'd "have to see" about me joining them on their trip to Brazil. I would have loved so much to hear her say something more comforting, like, "I know you're suffering, my darling, and you don't deserve it. But don't worry, I'm here for you. You know how your father is, the old grouch, but someday you'll find out he loves you."

Even better, she could have said she'd persuade him to ask me to come along, but she wasn't brave enough to attempt it. I didn't resent her, but I missed her like a little girl misses her absent mother. It's strange to feel so rejected by your own family. I swallowed hard and did what I always do: I made her feel better by giving excuses for her failures, and lying that Brazil wasn't such a good idea anyway, for this and that bogus reason. But this meant I had to move fast, as I had only a few days to find a solution. I knew Cedric wouldn't give me any extra time. I immediately picked up my phone, called Rose and asked if she would like a visitor the following week.

"Why are you even hesitating?" she said. "Get your ticket and get over here! Give me your dates as soon as you can and tell that asshole you're going to New York. He'll be so annoyed. I cannot wait to take care of you, my girl!"

I hung up, relieved. Forget Brazil. I could see my mother's relief when I told her about Rose and New York. My relief was enormous; it felt so good to take back a small measure of control. I borrowed her computer and started checking flights for New York, and the prices were reasonable. I didn't wait another second, I got out my credit card and bought a ticket.

Once I was home, I told Cedric. "I'm going away for a month."

"So, you'll be staying at your parents' house while they're in Brazil?"

"No, I'm going to New York to visit Rose."

This meant open revolt. He'd kept me away from the city for so long. For the first time, his ego took a serious hit. It wouldn't be the last. He squinted his eyes, and his lips tightened in a flash of rage, which he quickly hid behind a mask of indifference.

The days flew by. When anyone in our entourage asked about my plans, I explained that I missed New York. "And my friend Rose has been asking me to visit for ages. Cedric is delighted, and a little time apart will do us both some good." I didn't tell anyone our marriage was imploding, but I think people suspected what was going on. They knew Cedric's personality, and they'd begun to watch me carefully, especially after all his insinuations about my mental stability. "New York would do me good" was the general consensus.

Both Cedric and I were looking forward to my departure, but not for the same reasons.

"I can't wait for you to go," he said one evening. "You'll see, you can't live without me. I'm the only man for you." Such confidence paired with such modesty was a rare gift indeed.

He took me to the airport, but stayed in the car, engine running. He gave me only a perfunctory kiss, then looked straight ahead. I got my suitcase out of the trunk by myself and didn't look back. The only thing I wanted to see was my departure gate. My head high and a smile on my face, I walked into the airport. I had done it, one step forward. I couldn't wait to be in the air at 30,000 feet.

My dream went up in smoke, literally. People were hurrying in all directions, talking and gesturing. What on earth was going on? I looked at the Departures Board. All flights cancelled. All over Europe, planes were grounded because a volcano in Iceland had erupted. Eyjafjallajökull hadn't erupted for almost 200 years, and it had to pick the day I was to leave? I couldn't believe it. Fucking fate. Europe was paralyzed by an ash cloud stretching across the sky from north to south. Airplanes grounded, and no hint of future flights. The check-in agent was soothing. "Stay home and we'll keep you informed." She didn't understand my emergency. Stay home? What home? With Cedric? No, I had to leave!

My departure date had been confirmed, and Cedric hated whenever anyone went back on their word. I called him anyway.

"I know. The volcano, all flights cancelled. You told me the 15th, and this is the 15th. You know what you have to do. Don't come here. Send me a message when you finally get to New York. If you ever get there!"

He laughed viciously and hung up.

The only solution was to go to my parents. They were supposed to leave for Brazil the same day.

"I can't leave today, Mom. You saw the news. Your plane was cancelled too? I don't know where to go to wait. Can I come to your house?"

"Go home, my dear. It's your home. I don't understand, Chloe – you're married, aren't you? You shouldn't come here when you have a husband at home."

"Please," I said. "I'm begging you, don't shut the door on me like this and don't ask me any questions."

She hesitated. "Ok. I'll warn your father."

I took the bus. My husband had rejected me, and my parents pretty much had as well. I felt so alone, abandoned. I pushed those thoughts away, though, using my therapist's pep talk on myself: Gather your courage, Chloe. You've got a ticket to freedom. Or at least to New York City, to your friend Rose. She won't judge you.

But I had only escaped one crushing tension for another: instead of Cedric as matador, it was my father. I couldn't figure out what he had against me, so I couldn't address the problem. Zero communication. He wouldn't even look at me. I knew how he functioned, though, and this meant he was eventually going to explode, I just didn't know when. The volcano's ash cloud might take days, even weeks, to clear up, so I would be there a while. I was as discreet as possible, but my very presence disturbed him, so I kept to the guest room, I made as little noise as possible, and showed my face only at meals. And then at breakfast one morning, I caught my father's eyes and saw the matador.

"Why the hell are you cutting so much bread?" he said.

His excuse for an explosion. He grabbed the knife from my hands, nearly cutting my finger. I said nothing, just left the room, like I always did. No one spoke in this family. But I slammed the door to the guest room, which was stupid. I was no longer a child, I fumed, I'm a woman now, not a little girl. You can scream at me as much as you want, but I won't stand there and take it. Not from you, and from now on, not from any other man!

THIS IS BULLSHIT, NOT A LOVE STORY

I didn't deserve to be treated this way. I felt like a tiger locked in a cage, and had to get out, so, since it was a sunny day, I took a bus downtown and walked around until I found a café with a terrace. I sat in the sunshine, enjoying the fresh air and space. No one would yell at me out here. I had lunch, then took the bus back to their house several hours later. Without saying a word to either of them, I went into the guest room and locked the door. After my father's explosion I figured it was better to stay out of his way. I wasn't interested in making up with him, and I didn't even want to hear his voice. I didn't want to hear Cedric's voice, either. I wanted to hear my own voice, the one that would tell me the truth, but I think I already knew – I would leave him when I got back to Switzerland. It was difficult to admit, for some crazy reason. I needed Rose to talk some sense into me, and I needed time to cut myself off from Cedric. No contact with Cedric for four weeks – that ought to wean me from him. And I wasn't going to risk letting him know I intended to divorce him. That would put me in real danger. I suddenly longed to be in New York. This was all too serious, and I was tired of the drama. A few minutes after climbing in bed, I got a message announcing my flight would leave the next morning. I sighed in relief and a smile came to my lips as I closed my eyes. For once, I slept well.

Still, after the long flight, I was exhausted when I arrived at JFK. Rose was there as promised, waiting for me outside the baggage claim area. I had to go right up to her and shake her arm, though, as she didn't recognize me. That hit me hard. Had I changed that much? She hadn't changed a bit.

"How was the flight, Chloe? It must have been so tiring."

The ever-tactful Rose, she knew not to ask me too many questions right away. I wasn't ready to talk about the last few months anyway. I wanted only to breathe in New York. May is one of the loveliest months of the year there, when the city has turned the corner on winter, spring is in full swing, and the hot, sultry summer hasn't yet settled in.

We found a taxi and climbed in. Rose had insisted on meeting me, although I would have preferred the time to myself, to rediscover the city from inside a cab smelling of the spicy food the driver had probably had for lunch. But I was happy with Rose's hugs and sincere smile in exchange. She chatted about her daily life. Rose had a good set-up, with her own events company and a bustling social life. She was a contented 40-something who, like so many women in the Big Apple, focused on her career and never wanted to depend on a man. She'd been in love many times, and always with good men, but evidently, they were never good enough for her, because each time the question of settling down came up, she broke up with them.

Rose was obsessed with her own idea of marriage. She'd met a guy named John, who was as fiercely independent as she was, she said with a laugh. They didn't live together but they often spent the night at each other's place. No promises, just living for the moment, but she thought they might have a future. I wasn't envious. My day would come. I needed to understand how I'd gotten into the mess I was in, and to accept who I really was and what I really wanted before I could even begin to think about finding my match.

Like me, Rose was a huge fan of the West Side. We made fun of the stuffy Upper East Side. I loved her apartment on the top floor of an old building, especially its roof terrace looking out over the city. I left my suitcase in the hall and rushed up to the roof. I've never yelled so loud in my life. "Yes! Yes! Yes!" Rose hugged me. She could tell I was living through something very difficult.

That month-long "temporary separation" was a turning point for me. I took things day by day, woke up when I wanted, stayed in bed and let myself think of nothing. Rose made coffee for me and left early. It took me several days just to get a little energy back. I called my friends, made appointments for lunch or Happy Hour, and Rose came with me. I had forgotten the lovely spontaneity of urban life; I had missed the sirens and the nonstop noise of the city that never sleeps. I missed all of New York, which suited me like a part of my personality. And it was here that I gathered the energy to put my life back in order.

I didn't bring up what had been going on in my life, and Rose didn't push it. It was like Cedric no longer existed, until the morning Rose called me out of bed. "Chloe, come and see. There's a bouquet with your name on it."

Cedric wouldn't give up so easily, it seemed.

It was a huge bouquet of flowers that took up the entire table in the front hall. Dark yellow chrysanthemums. Didn't he know those were tombstone flowers? Of course he knew – this had to be a message. My husband had sent me a funeral bouquet. Rose noted my rising panic.

"Are you okay? There's a note, too."

"I'll read it in my room."

So, Cedric wasn't going to leave me alone. Damn. What happened to the "no contact" order? But he wouldn't soften me up with a bunch of macabre flowers and a letter filled with lies.

"My dearest, A bouquet of chrysanthemums for you. Strange, I know. This variety is called 'Golden Flower.' But you're worth more than gold to me, so I chose them. I can't stop thinking about you. About us. About our unexpected meeting in that nightclub when you stepped out of the shadows. Five years. We got married like two crazy teenagers, like our love would never separate us. I've made mistakes. I have. I admit it. Please forgive me for how I've messed up – unable to bring you into my world, unable to let you create your own. But I do let you keep writing and take time for your writing and sculpture. I loved you so much, I didn't see your weaknesses. You confided in me, but I didn't realize how much your painful past still haunts you. I wanted you to be happy and I would have done anything to see you find it. I feel like I've failed. You're the only woman I ever introduced to my daughters. I never imagined it would be so hard to create a new family. I should have tried harder. And maybe you could have made a few compromises. No one is perfect. That's no secret. I gave you everything. And yet you always seemed sad with me. I'm sure New York is good for you. It's your town. I'll let you visit whenever you want, but come home, Chloe, come back to me. To your life...with me. I still believe in it. I love you. I'm waiting for you. You're worth more than gold to me. Love, Cedric."

I didn't want to reread the letter, but I threw it on the nightstand instead of ripping it up or burning it. I didn't believe a single one of his sentences. I'd learned to read between the lines. He was asking me to forgive him and accusing me of being at fault at the same time. He wasn't soul-searching. He'd lost his prey, and he was hunting her down, that's all. That letter sent me straight back into hell, but I told myself it was over, he had no power to send me into a black mood, and I wouldn't let him con me ever again.

"But think of what you're losing."

"I'm sure he loves you."

"Look at your life, at the travel. You have everything you need. And life is easier when you have money."

I heard the same thing over and over from friends who weren't married, or friends who couldn't understand, or who weren't in my situation. My decision was made.

The days passed quickly, unlike the lagging days in Geneva. I walked in Central Park every morning and after a few weeks, I began to look healthier. My energy returned, my mind cleared, and I felt

160

my old tenacity coming back. My priority? Prepare myself mentally and physically for my return, to be ready to reclaim my life and launch myself into a Cedric-free future. When I found I had only a few days left, I made a list of new rules for fighting my matador.

I must hide my transformation into a war machine. I had to remain powerful by remembering I took care of myself just fine before meeting him. I must overcome my fear, not let him intimidate me, let his insults and vile actions slide over me, and above all, I must not give up.

After tucking my list into my purse, I forced myself to stop thinking of what awaited me and focus on being here in New York City. I would let its strength fill me. I'd breathe in its vibrancy to the fullest, knowing that when I got back, Cedric wouldn't give me time to breathe. He'd put me to the test right away, and not let up until I was dead, vanquished, or free. I hoped for "free."

I never did confide in Rose beyond a sketch of my situation and my plan. When the time came, I would tell her my whole story, but it was still too soon, plus, it was far from over. She tactfully kept from inquiring, and simply showed me she was there for me by sharing her time and her good humor, long nights of laughter and a feeling of joie de vivre I hadn't felt for ages.

One evening, Cedric called me on Rose's phone. I could hear his voice on the other end of the line, but I hardly listened to it, and hardly replied. I was paying more attention to my body's reaction: clammy hands, racing heart, drooping head. I hated feeling that way, and resented that he caused it, so I told him the connection was bad and we could talk when I got back to Geneva, then I hung up.

My last day came, and Rose decided to take off work and spend it with me. We walked for miles, snacked on street food, dined in a fine restaurant, and laughed and talked for hours. In the evening, she stretched out on my bed and watched me pack my suitcase. The mood was sad, and I could see she was concerned about me, but I kept a smile on my face and reassured her about my future.

"Don't worry, Rose, everything is going to be fine. And thank you so much for taking me in! Without you, I wouldn't be feeling as strong as I am today. I'm ready for this, and besides, no one can leave him for me – I got myself into this mess, and now I need to go home and take care of it as soon as possible. Believe me, I'll be okay."

"I know, Chloe, you're such a strong woman. But I'm here for you. Just call me, anytime. And keep me posted!"

I insisted on taking a taxi. I hate goodbyes, and this one would be hard. Again. I was leaving my favorite place in the world for the second time, this city that had anchored me when I needed it. New York would give me the courage to succeed. And the thought I would be back would buoy me through the hard times ahead. I hugged Rose, wordlessly, keeping my tears in check. She understood. Then I left Manhattan behind, staring out the taxi window and wiping the tears from my eyes. That month of May had allowed me to step outside my hellish former life, like stepping out of time to regather. Now I could step back in and deal with my situation.

New York had given me a kick in the ass, and told me, "If you can make it here, you can make it anywhere, so get to it!" I had made it in New York years ago, and I would follow its motto to the letter. Go to hell, Cedric.

There were no exploding volcanoes this time to cause delays, but the minute I took my seat in the plane my anxiety level skyrocketed. Four weeks of tranquility had been only a temporary reprieve. Now it was back to cold sweats then intense hot flashes, then a dizzy spell, shortness of breath, the whole works.

When I lived in New York, I loved going to JFK and boarding a plane, anticipating adventures in some foreign country, the sudden pull of gravity at take-off throwing me back on the seat. It was all so exciting to me. And then I had the joy of taking the plane back home, to New York, so unlike going home to Switzerland with Cedric at the end of our many trips – those homecomings were gloomy to me. And now here I was again, not looking forward to going home. I waved goodbye to the skyscrapers one last time, reliving the moment five years earlier when I'd headed off into the unknown: life with Cedric. Like that time, he would be waiting for me at the arrivals gate, but everything I felt and thought about him had changed, darkened, and I was no longer in love with him.

I went through passport control then through the exit doors. So many eyes on me, and on each side, sudden rushes of people toward each other with open arms, smiles, laughter, tears, shouts of joy. But Cedric wasn't there to welcome me with hugs and kisses. I scanned the faces all around, close by then farther and farther, until I saw him, leaning against the Hertz counter like a statue, just staring at me. I stopped, too, even as the world continued to dance around me. It wasn't like a scene in some blockbuster romance, although Cedric was approaching me in what seemed like slo-mo. Was he afraid of me, was he admiring me? He grabbed me by the waist and kissed me passionately.

Then, looking very serious, he peered at my face before pulling me into his arms again, suffocating me.

"You're so beautiful, Chloe. It's so good to see you."

In the car, I folded my hands to avoid placing one on his thigh by habit, which I usually did in the car. He glanced at me and then focused on the road, with a slight smile on his lips. He placed his hand over mine. I didn't take it.

"You're cold. Did you miss me?"

Oh yes, terribly! I thought about you night and day. That's what he wanted to hear, but I couldn't lie to him.

"New York did me a world of good."

Cedric smiled as if that were the right answer, and put on some music. We hardly spoke for the rest of the trip home, which seemed to take forever, and even though it was a sunny June afternoon, everything around us looked sad to me. As we drove through our village, the knot in my stomach grew larger. We reached our cul-de-sac and a heavy weight settled on me, and then, buried at the end, our happy home, unsmiling. He parked the car near the gate, the motor stopped, and there was no turning back. He carried my suitcase in. Nothing had changed. That should be a good sign when returning from a trip, but I knew it included Cedric, too, and that was not ideal.

It was a Thursday, so our housekeeper was there working in the kitchen. I said hello to her and went to unpack my bag. Cedric greeted her as well and then came into the bedroom, zeroing in on the clothes I'd laid on the bed.

"What are those pants? I won't be able to see your gorgeous ass in them! Throw them out! Did you buy them in New York?"

He launched this at me in a friendly tone, as if he was teasing. It wasn't a reproach, as he was in a jubilant mood. But commenting about my pants was his way to put me on my guard.

The background hum of the vacuum didn't bother Cedric – it gave him cover for any noise he wanted to make. He led me into the bathroom, no questions asked, turned me around to face the mirror, placed my hands on the counter and pushed my head down, then unzipped. Ass up, hurry hurry, like an animal in rut, not a single kiss or other sign of love. Our reunion. He pounded my body and came fast. I kept my eyes closed rather than seeing it all in the mirror. He pulled up his underwear and jeans, re-buckled his belt. He hadn't taken off his shoes. He brushed his lips against my cheek, but I kept my head down.

"Welcome home, darling. Take your time to unpack."

He went out, then I heard him speaking to the housecleaner. I stood up straight and stretched, and finally looked in the mirror. Who is that woman? My god, you look so sad. That won't do. Keep your wits about you, Chloe. You can't let your guard down for a second. This is just the beginning. You're smarter than him, and stronger, because you can keep your rage in check and he can't. Keep it all in, and pretend all the way out of this marriage. Besides, he's done much worse than a quick fuck in the bathroom.

The housekeeper was getting ready to leave. I had the sudden urge to ask her to stay and eat with us, to sleep between Cedric and me, and protect me from whatever could happen.

"Bye, Mrs. Moreau. See you next week. Have a nice weekend."

I was alone, no witnesses, just Cedric and me, exactly what he wanted.

"Now we can finally be alone, just the two of us," he said with a sigh of contentment. "Go take a bath and I'll get dinner ready early. You must be exhausted."

I wasn't going to spend hours in the bath this time. He was waiting for me; I could feel it. It was no longer necessary for him to sit next to me to feel how desperately he wanted to ask about my trip, and to talk about himself. He needed me to join him in the kitchen. Quickly.

A bottle of rosé was on the coffee table, along with two glasses and some olives. He poured me a glass.

"Come here, come and sit beside me. Tell me about your trip. How's Rose?"

"Good. She's great."

"Is that all you're going to say? What are you afraid of? Wasn't it good for you?"

"It was amazing. It was really good for me. I saw all my friends. I felt that special energy of the city. Yes, Cedric, it did me an immense amount of good."

His smile was hiding something, but he kept quiet about it. We were not tender with one another. We were both acting really awkward.

I gave him more details about the trip, but he wasn't really listening, and suddenly he interrupted me. He couldn't wait another second, as some question or other had been on his lips since I began talking. He stuttered the first few words, and seemed almost uncomfortable, embarrassed. This was the first time I'd ever seen Cedric like that. What the hell was it?

"I need to ask you something, but I was waiting for you to get home first, because I didn't want to ruin your vacation."

"What is it? You look so serious. Go on, ask me."

"While you were away, I got an anonymous phone call. From a man. He spoke with an English accent."

He got up and started walking back and forth, until I got impatient. "And...what did he say?"

"Apparently, you've been making money as an escort girl!" he said in a rush. "He said he had proof, photos of you."

This was just too much. I wanted to laugh but repressed it. I was supposed to be the writer who made up stories, not Cedric. Such a lie! I thought hard, as I knew this had to be going somewhere, since it came out of Cedric's mouth. Where on earth could he have gotten this idea? I searched my memory but came up with nothing. It was completely absurd. I had never sold my body. I looked him straight in the eye.

"You couldn't possibly believe such a thing!"

"I talked it over with your old school friend Annie. She's known you for a long time, and even she had doubts. And while you were away, she gave me a lot of support. Annie's a good woman."

He'd thrown suspicion upon me and made her doubt me, I suspected, just like he manipulated everyone else around him, so why not her too. He'd nearly succeeded at driving me crazy by his insinuations. What was true, and what was false? Anyone could betray me at this point, so I had to be careful, doubly so with people I thought were my friends. I couldn't trust anyone anymore, and Annie was now first on that list. It only half-surprised me. She'd been wanting to sleep with Cedric from the day I introduced her to him, I'd seen it in how she fawned on him and always tried to touch him or sit too close to him. Go for it, Annie. He's all yours.

But this was serious – Cedric was not only a liar, but capable of inventing false proof, meaning he could even get me arrested, or shut up in a mental institution! There were no limits to his perversion. He was mentally ill, and such a total bastard. I remained outwardly calm, though, and didn't try to defend myself beyond saying flat out that it wasn't true. I would not play his game – it was too late for that. My month away from him had removed some of my fear and I was clear-headed again, but I would need all my wits to beat him. I needed time to figure out how to respond to an accusation that came directly from his sick brain. I would have to use my healthy brain to stay a step ahead of him.

"Anyway, that's what I wanted to talk to you about. I'm sure you can see why I might be a bit suspicious. But since you tell me you haven't been selling your body, I believe you. Dinner's ready, so let's eat. You love fish."

While we ate, Cedric told me all about his month. It sounded like he'd seen more people in that time than he and I had seen the entire year. He laughed as he described the impromptu suppers with friends, the "wonderful" brunches in our garden and "magnificent" weekends with his daughters, making it clear his life had been much more exciting than the usual grind. What was his goal, to make me jealous? I didn't feel a shred of jealousy – I didn't care one way or the other. I threw in a "Cool" or "That's great" from time to time, and then I said in a neutral tone, "You see, Cedric, you can have fun without me."

Big mistake. I opened the door for him, and as soon as he started to reply, my entire body tensed, and I felt the tingling heat at the back of my neck, the trembling in my fingers. I concentrated on my breathing and tried to detach emotionally. I became marble. His bitter voice brought me upright and I stared at him.

"You're jealous! What did you think? That I'd spend all my time waiting for you in front of the TV? Do you think I can't live without you? Don't worry about me, honeybunch. The day you leave me, I'll have no problem replacing you. The girls are already lining up."

He jerked up from the table so fast his chair fell backwards.

"Go on, clear the table and go to bed. You've got nothing better to do than criticize everything I do instead of being happy for me. You're so worthless. I'm going to call that guy back and have him send me those photos of you. Fucking whore!"

Yes, I was home. Here was the proof it wasn't a dream. He just laid out irrefutable proof he was a narcissist, a horribly perverted one, and I knew for a certainty that Cedric was a murderer, a killer of souls. I probably wasn't his first victim. He must have honed his skills on women even weaker than me, more malleable, romantics who would do anything to keep their man, broken women in search of their perfect "other half." But I doubt any of them lost sight of reality as deeply as I did, and for so long. They must have escaped in time, had more respect for themselves. My puerile curiosity for extremes had pushed me too far, but I had finally reached my limit. Now it was time to face reality.

Cedric went upstairs to watch TV and I cleared the table as he'd ordered. I didn't cry. I was no longer angry or upset or depressed, which surprised me, to tell the truth. I felt like I could ignore his insults from now on, and that made me feel strong. I savored the last few moments alone, then I went to bed without another word to him. I was no longer afraid of him.

Tercio de Muerte:
Ballet of Death

Bullfight, beautiful perfect bullfight. You make death into a work of art.

This is the matador's moment of artistic glory. With a red cape in one hand, and a sword in the other, he must anticipate and counter the animal's every movement if he hopes to deal the final, fatal blow. If he does not, the ballet of death might end with his own.

As the sun was setting over Torrelaguna, Cedric and I watched the final act. The death scene, the last fifteen minutes of the corrida. The crowd was euphoric and impatient.

"Look around us, Chloe! What a feeling, what a crowd! I've never experienced anything like it."

He was astonished. He was joyful. We'd reached the moment they were all waiting for. Killing the bull. What a sordid affair.

Fifteen minutes, the "official" time allowed for the death. Five minutes before the end of that time, the president proffered his first judgment, determining that the matador didn't yet deserve to be called the winner, and three minutes later, he gave his second judgment, the same determination – giving more time for the matador to do his work, but also more time for the bull to figure things out and turn the tables on the matador.

"Aviso, aviso," the crowd screamed. They whistled and hooted. They wanted blood? A vanquished matador? Inconceivable. But it was all confusing to me.

"What's going on, Cedric? Why does everyone look so unhappy? What are they upset with the matador about?"

"You really don't know anything about bullfighting, do you? The president wants to give him more time, and he has the right, but it shames the matador. Plus, there's a theory that says the longer it takes, the more chance the bull has to realize the enemy isn't the cape, but the man. And then he can directly attack the matador. What a show! I hope he'll do it. Look at the bull, he still has some power left. He could gore that man to death."

I silently begged the president to give the bull extra time to conquer his opponent. Now that would give the crowd a real fight, worthy of its name. Would the matador deliver the final, fatal blow? Would the bull be stupid enough to forgo its chance? I wanted to jump down from the bleachers, race toward the animal and whisper in its ear, "The president is giving you extra time, use it wisely, kill your adversary. What? You can't? Your conscience won't let you? Don't miss this chance, bull, wake up!"

The crowd was screaming, "Toreador, on guard!" straight out of Act 2 of Carmen. My head was spinning with the noise. I couldn't stand it anymore. I wanted this final combat over with.

I hadn't seen my parents since returning from New York several weeks earlier. My mother had called me once to see how I was doing. I kept things vague.

"Everything's fine. I got home fine. See you soon."

She had survived cancer, so she would survive the dissolution of my marriage. I didn't have time, right then, to take care of her, and anyway, she had my father. I had other things to worry about.

Day after day passed. Cedric, me. We no longer knew how to be with one another, and whenever he was in the house, the atmosphere was suffocating. He would bait me, trying to see if I'd rise and bite. He hadn't yet understood that my eyes were open to him now.

The only thing I believed in was my ability to outsmart him. I still searched for a way to escape my unhealthy situation, out from the walls of a house that vibrated with hatred. I had to arrange it so the decision seemed to be his own, so he could feel in control, so I waited for an opportunity. I felt stifled being in a place where all my cries for help were in vain – there was no one to hear them. I had to figure it out myself, though, and not count on others. Like Annie. Cedric had told me things only Annie knew, so I knew she'd betrayed me. I wouldn't let on that I was aware of her betrayal, though, when I saw her next. She might be useful to me later on, plus her husband was a lawyer, and he could give me free advice. But what a mistake it had been to confide in her!

Nothing would surprise me anymore. Human beings in all their splendor, capable of the worst. And my friend Christelle had warned me.

"Annie isn't on your side. While you were away, Cedric had me and Doug over for lunch at your place. Cedric told us you guys were having trouble, but he said he loved you like crazy, and couldn't imagine living without you. He left the table at one point for about fifteen minutes, and when he came back, he told us he was talking to Annie. He wanted to show us an email you sent her from New York. Apparently, she forwarded your messages to him! He tried to show us his phone, but I wouldn't read them, neither would Doug. That's none of our business, but I wanted you to know you can't trust Annie."

Too bad I didn't believe her, but at least now I thought I could trust Christelle.

Cedric and I met Christelle and her husband Doug in a sex club, but we became friends afterwards. We never had sex together after that first night. And right now, they were the only friends among all the other "friends" here that I felt I could rely on. I even shared a little of what was going on in my life then, the torture of living with a man I desperately wanted to leave.

Cedric and I hadn't talked about separating; we were still at the constant fighting stage. This was the first time we were actually behaving like a normal couple. Fights, stormy silences, falling back in and out of love, short separations. So many others have experienced the same, except in my case, I only pretended to fall in and out of love, and I hadn't yet tried another separation.

The game was over, and we were about to fall apart. A failure for most people, a victory for me. Especially if I could make him believe it was what he wanted.

He quit organizing his gang bangs, stopped calling me over to check out some woman online, no longer showed me off in the middle of the night at the highway rest areas, gave up selling my dirty underwear. It was wonderful, such a relief that all that horror was behind me. With a vicious smile, I stuffed plastic bags with the wig, the ugly skin-tight polyester dresses and the thigh-high boots he used to make me wear, then threw them into a dumpster far from our neighborhood. I felt like a criminal getting rid of the evidence, and it felt good. I tossed the heavy make-up, and even let my hair go back to its natural curl, instead of straightening it as he always insisted.

Cedric no longer invited me to his professional dinners. According to him, he told his clients we were re-examining our way of life, and had decided it was better not to mix private and professional. I preferred not to imagine what he was really telling them. Probably something along the lines of my having serious psychological problems, how difficult it was to live with me, his fears that I'd be interned in a psych ward at some point.

I also stopped seeing his favorite psychiatrist Dr. Trévoz. He hadn't been a huge help, anyway, except that I'd been able to articulate what I'd never been able to say to anyone else. I needed help to get through the next few months, however, so I called Dr. Thyssen. She would listen to me without judging, and never point a finger at me and say, "I told you so."

"It's Chloe Berkovitch. I need to see you. It's urgent." She gave me an appointment without hesitation.

Cedric may have given me a pass on the sexual abuse, but he continued to attack me emotionally, testing me constantly. But it didn't work. I endured it all, and even managed to say "no" from time to time. Like when he invited me to Roland Garros. Every year, he made me go with him because his "besty" Martine had VIP passes to share, and I always told him I wasn't interested in tennis. When my vision was affected, I tried to excuse myself by saying I wouldn't even be able to see the ball, but he always bullied me into going. And this year was no different. Except he added an extra dose of cruelty:

"Do you want to come to Roland Garros? Martine has it all set up. She doesn't really want to see you, but she loves me and feels obligated to invite you as well. So just let me know, because I need to arrange things. I warn you though, if you come, you'd better be on your best behavior, and no sulking. No one needs to know our marriage is on the rocks, especially because I do a lot of business at Roland Garros. Celebrities will be there, and Martine has already set up a meeting with Jean Dujardin. He wants to open a Swiss bank account. Isn't that cool?"

I said no. He thought dropping names would make me leap to accept his insulting invitation, like I was some groupie. Cedric, don't you see how pathetic you are? I would have loved meeting a big-name actor like Dujardin, whose work I respected, but it would be excruciating to see Cedric fawning all over him. Plus, by stipulating what clothes I would wear, what sunglasses, hairstyle, makeup, jewelry, my very words, I would lose control. And I wouldn't give in anymore.

"Thanks, but I think I'll stay home, if that's okay with you. It's supposed to be sunny this weekend, so I'll simply enjoy the garden. Thank Martine for me."

Two can play at this game, dear Cedric. He shrugged his shoulders and left without another word, and two days later he was on a train to Paris. Peace! The weather was perfect, warm and not a cloud in the sky. On a whim, I called Christelle and Doug to come over that evening. They were the only couple in our crowd that I felt even a bit connected to. They liked going out, and they didn't have kids so they could be spontaneous. I wanted to feel a little of what I'd felt during my month in New York. Drink a glass of wine, maybe go dancing. When they arrived, I was still getting ready. I'd lost the habit of choosing my own clothes, according to my own moods, so I had gone through my closet and tried on a dozen different outfits, which now lay in a pile on the bed. It was easy in New York, because I'd packed only a few things. I had to keep reminding myself I could wear whatever I wanted. I could be casual, because that's who I was, and I wanted to pay attention to the truth of myself.

I finally put on my favorite jeans and a T-shirt and looked in the mirror. I liked my reflection – I hadn't seen myself looking so relaxed for a long time. I was no sex object, I was Chloe, myself.

"What are we celebrating, Chloe? This is the first time we've hung out without Cedric. Does he know?"

"Why should he know about every single thing I do? This is a free country."

It hit me – we would celebrate freedom. I hadn't understood until that second. I had succeeded at imagining myself without Cedric, but I hadn't yet envisioned the process of getting divorced from him. Free of him! That was changing, but I couldn't rush it, reminding myself the only safe way to swing a divorce and escape him was to manipulate him into believing it was his decision. That he remained in control. But not tonight, I thought with jubilation.

We went to a bistro on the lakefront and sat on the terrace drinking wine. Doug was always fairly quiet, but Christelle seemed subdued tonight as well, like she was mulling something over.

"How are things between you and Cedric?" she asked.

Things? The question was pointed, but posed in this vague way might mean they wanted to avoid an awkward discussion. I blurted out the truth anyway.

"You mean how is our marriage? I'm going to leave him."

I said it. I managed to say it, and I felt proud of myself.

Christelle took a deep breath, then said, "Listen, sweetie, I've been worried about you for months. He screams at you practically every time we go out together. But I figured he's just hot-tempered, and that he must be good to you, too, or why would you stay with him? I should have asked you if everything was okay, but I didn't like interfering in your marriage. We're so stupid. I'm sorry, Chloe, I should have talked to you about it before now."

Doug reached out and put his hand on my shoulder. It felt so good, so comforting.

"We're both sorry, Chloe."

"It's okay. Hanging out with you two tonight makes me incredibly happy. You're the first people I've confided in, and please, let's keep it between ourselves for now. Don't say anything to Cedric especially! I haven't told him. But nothing can change my mind. I have to leave him."

I felt so happy to be taking control of my life that I got tipsy that night. My husband would oppress me no longer, or at least not much longer, I added as a caveat to myself. After dinner, we went to a club, and I danced up a storm until it closed. Doug and Christelle dropped me off at the house as the sun was rising.

I woke up around one in the afternoon, when the phone rang. It was my friend Sylvie.

"Hey you, I'm near your house. How would you like to come walk the dogs with me?"

I told her yes, of course, and jumped out of bed to get dressed.

Cedric had introduced me to Sylvie, a writer. She lived in her own fantasy world, and I liked her from the moment we met. I trusted her. We didn't see each other often, but we talked on the phone and took walks together occasionally. This time it was a very long walk, the mountains in front of us towering over Lake Geneva. We walked arm in arm, and she encouraged me to talk. She could tell I was unhappy, and without realizing it, I told her everything. Not about the fights or the insults, or the psychological war Cedric had been waging against me since the very beginning. I told her what I could never manage to say to any other friend. About our abnormal sex life, the abuse, the dog leash. All of Cedric's sick fantasies. I recounted my nightmare to Sylvie, scene by scene.

"Get away from him!" she said, when the rush of words finally ended. "Don't wait. Men like that are dangerous. Get the hell out of there now. Don't be afraid – you'll see life is fantastic once you're away from him. You need to go see a lawyer. You were married under what marital agreement?"

Sylvie's question stopped me cold. What marital agreement? I signed the marriage contract in that Las Vegas "chapel" without reading it, and Cedric had done the paperwork once we returned to Switzerland. I had no idea where it was even filed. Everything was mixed up in my head. With no concrete information to give a lawyer, I would waste his or her time and my money, so I needed to do some research first, and that meant rifling through Cedric's office. That was a scary thought – what if he caught me? There must be cameras hidden in there, and he would know, like he knew everything about me.

THIS IS BULLSHIT, NOT A LOVE STORY

It was just one more proof of my absurd recklessness. I used to be good at doing things on my own, but I didn't even understand the legal aspects of my own marriage. I'd thrown myself into the role of wife in a conventional couple, without checking that the man filling the husband role was not a narcissistic pervert.

Sylvie explained her own divorce to me, I recorded all the information on my phone. The smallest details were helpful, even if her situation was nothing like mine. The word "divorce" hadn't been part of my vocabulary, but it was now, and I could accept it instead of going back to the eternal idea, the lie, that I had vowed to be the perfect wife, and make my marriage work no matter what. Sylvie ended by hugging me and urging me to leave him right away, but I knew that was a bad idea.

"He'll never let me just leave. He would see that as me winning and him losing, and he can't swallow that. He'd chase me to the ends of the earth to get back at me!"

"But there's no alternative, Chloe. Your marriage is over. Maybe you could get him to agree to a temporary separation and then just let it stretch into a permanent one, until he eventually files for divorce. If he calls tonight, suggest it to him, and begin the process. It's important. And remember, you're not alone – I'm here for you."

Those two hours with Sylvie meant the world to me. My adrenaline was high, my pain was transforming to power, and I was as excited as a little girl. I felt that magical buzz of a new adventure on the horizon, far off still, but hovering there. My life wasn't over.

Cedric called me just before his gala dinner at Roland Garros. I turned off the lights and the music I'd been listening to, and focused all my attention on his words and his tone of voice so I could gauge his mood and guide our conversation the way I wanted it to go.

"Are you having a good weekend without me – not too lonely?" he said. "It's so amazing here. I'm freaking out, meeting people I never thought I'd meet."

He went on for a while about his "amazing" VIP encounters, the matches, and how much business he was generating. He enthused about his upcoming dinner with the movie star. Since he seemed in such a good mood, I broached the subject.

"That's wonderful for you! Listen, there's something we need to discuss, and it can't wait for you to get back. I've been thinking about us, about how I've disappointed you in so many ways, and I realize I'm holding you back. That month apart did us a bit of good but not enough. Maybe we need a real break. I don't mean break up forever, but I can tell you're not happy right now. A trial separation would allow us to make a decision, not something hasty, or due to some fight or argument. What do you think?"

"I've thought about it, too, and I agree. Let's talk about it when I get home. Just know that you have nothing to worry about, financially. I'll give you enough every month to take care of yourself. Start looking for an apartment, a studio. Ok, I have to go. Goodnight, and see you tomorrow night."

I hadn't said the word "divorce." I didn't yet know much about what a divorce involved, especially from a man like him. Did we need to make our separation official? Did we need a lawyer to file papers for that? Then I started thinking about how oddly understanding Cedric had been, and his voice so gentle talking about money. I hadn't expected that, and it nagged at me. It was too good to be true. But I tucked that thought away, turned the lights back on and hit "play" on the sound system, poured myself a whiskey and thought about my future.

The good news was he'd said I could go. Sylvie had been right about suggesting a trial separation. It would be best if I left as soon as possible, so I decided to start looking for an apartment the next day. But where? Geneva? Lausanne? Where were my friends? Who were my friends? After five years, my social life had changed, and though I knew a lot of people, I could consider very few of them as friends. Why the fuck had I wasted five years with this guy?

What about New York? It was enticing, but so far away – I shouldn't leave Switzerland until I put my strategic plan into action and we were finally divorced. And I doubted I could easily recover that old happy life of mine in New York City. My only possibility, I determined, was to find a quiet apartment in the backwaters of the Geneva suburbs.

The rest of the night and the next day, I felt completely unmoored. I wandered through the big empty house, telling myself to think, to be calm and clear-headed. There's no rush. Think of the next five years, the ones you can't yet imagine, but where you will no longer be raped, abused, chained to a radiator, berated and controlled. Smile. Think of signing your torturer's death warrant. That's already a good start.

When I met up again with Dr. Thyssen, she began by saying I didn't look well and had lost too much weight.

"It's because I'm under so much stress," I said. "I'll gain the curves back later. That isn't what matters."

One session wasn't enough to tell the whole story to her, but I made a good start, and she listened patiently to what she then called "your version of events." It turned out Cedric had come to see her a few months before and poured out a different version, his version, and described me as being completely unhinged.

"He recounted incidents in which you were violent with him. I was worried about you, but you must know I can't intervene without your consent. Your mother also called me. I could tell she was extremely worried. She thought you had fallen through the cracks again, and even suspected you were taking drugs. I can't tell you what she said, but she didn't paint a pretty picture. I can show you one thing, a letter Cedric sent me a few years ago."

She leaned toward me, and for the first time, she took both my hands in hers.

"Chloe, I've known you since you were sixteen, and I have faith in you. Together, you and I will find out what's true or not, and how to deal with it."

She pulled a letter from her files and gave it to me. I recognized Cedric's stiff, precise handwriting. He began by sharing his belief he couldn't make me happy. Every line was a lie, but I had to admire his skill in manipulation, because from apologizing for his inadequacy to "help" me, he gradually switched to blaming me. Among his heap of falsehoods, he accused me of perverting him, of wrecking our furniture and paintings during fights that I started, of biting his daughter, of hitting him with a frying pan, and the worst, of threatening him with a knife. He wrapped up by writing that I was the most odious woman he'd ever known.

I dropped the letter on the floor, and lay back on the couch, unable to look at Dr. Thyssen or express my horror. No tears, no words, even my heart seemed barely beating.

"Chloe, I know those are nothing but lies, now that I see your reaction," she said. "What matters now is you get control of your situation and move out as soon as you can. But be careful. Tread lightly. Make sure he doesn't see you're afraid of him. Especially that. And don't show him you're stronger than he is. Be like you've always been with him, docile and pleasing."

Docile and pleasing. Was that how I came across? When I was seeing Dr. Thyssen in the early days of my relationship with Cedric, I thought it was because leaving New York had been such a huge rupture that I was becoming depressive again. I told myself then I didn't regret my return to Switzerland, for I was finally going to experience True Love, with Cedric Moreau. My future husband couldn't possibly have anything to do with my difficulties, and Dr. Thyssen hadn't been able to dissuade me from that. I should have listened to her, because she'd quickly seen something was wrong with Cedric. I wished I'd seen that letter long ago.

I left the appointment on very unsteady feet. To gather my thoughts, I walked through the streets of Geneva, feeling like I was wrapped in layers of wool. I didn't hear the city noise surrounding me and hardly checked before crossing the street. What should I do?

Cedric had "given me my freedom" and yet I didn't know how to get out the door. Where could I go? And where was my happy ending, the one everyone always talks about? I sat on a bench finally and devised a plan. I would create a file and gather my proof, overlooking nothing, and I would keep it a secret. The first logical step was to consult a divorce lawyer. How do people do this? I didn't have enough money to shell out 300 bucks an hour, but I needed an expert to figure everything out. There had to be a solution for people in my position.

The next day, I asked Sylvie and she gave me the number of a legal service for people needing advice at a reasonable rate. She also told me what I needed to hear most, the promise that everything would be fine.

I didn't even have time to make my first move before Cedric had everything wrapped up. At 9 a.m., my coffee in hand, I heard him come in through the front door. I hadn't even heard him leave, and yet we'd slept in the same bed. Where had he gone so early in the morning? He sat beside me and smiled.

"I'm just back from the lawyer. I'll be sending you the written paperwork for our legal separation. We're not talking about divorce, right?"

Hilarious! For once he was saying "our," and in respect to a separation. I thought the word "our" indicated union, but for Cedric a union was a dictatorship. He wrote the laws, and he built the walls, like the wall in his brain, now crumbling, between what was healthy and what was evil, like a traitor, a liar, a thief, a destroyer of hopes. He'd shown me everything while keeping it all cleverly hidden from my whitewashed brain.

Cedric read me my rights as if I was being arrested, as if the electric chair were waiting for me at the end of the hallway, as if I were a condemned woman. But he's the murderer, Your Honor, I swear on a stack of bibles it's him.

I saw I was about to enter a crazy world of lawyers and bars, judges and laws, knowing nothing of what applied to me and what I could ignore. Nothing. I knew about manipulation – my husband was an expert, and my conception of lawyers was that they were in the same trade: the liar's trade, the manipulator's trade. I tried to keep my hopes up, though. I had figured out his game, and although I was only half-listening to him, I nodded, pretending to pay attention until his monologue ended. Remember: docile and pleasing. But did he really think I'd let him just take over? I also knew how to enlist a lawyer and send him a catalog of rights.

It turned out fairly easy to do. The lawyer Sylvie recommended, Mr. Bola, put me at ease right away, as soon as he closed the door, in fact. I felt safe. I handed him the only paperwork I had, our marriage certificate. Cedric had assumed I'd see a lawyer, and he made me a copy, officially translated by a certified legal translator. As usual, Cedric in control, prepared for anything.

I handed it to Mr. Bola, who looked it over. "I see you were married under a joint property arrangement."

He continued his comments, complete with definitions and processes, but it was all in legalese. It sounded like he knew what he was talking about, but I understood only about half of it. The gist of it was that I would get half the proceeds from the house, and best of all, be able to do it without a battle. I wanted to avoid that at all costs, not only to save my dignity but possibly my skin.

"So, I don't have anything to worry about?" I asked him. "I don't need much to cover my expenses while I get back on my feet, but with my handicap and because I haven't worked for five years, would it be reasonable to ask for alimony? I have no idea if that even exists anymore, or what I'd get. I guess it's based on what he earns – which is about 30,000 Swiss francs a month, excluding his bonuses."

"Did you bring any of his salary slips with you?"

I'd planned to. I looked through the desk drawers and files in Cedric's office two days before this meeting and found his salary statements. I made a copy of the most recent one, which I put back, then I hid my copy in a notebook and then hidden that. That was the first time I'd ever snooped through his things, and I felt awful about it. I compromised my values because I couldn't think of a way to ask Cedric outright for his salary slips. Survival instinct, I guess.

But that morning, as I was getting ready for my lawyer's appointment, the salary slip was nowhere to be found. It wasn't in my notebook, or in any of my files. I looked everywhere. Cedric couldn't have known about it, because he was at work when I rifled through his office. After he said goodbye that morning, I heard his car door slam and the engine start. He was definitely not at home. It was a mystery – but the image of a hidden camera popped into my mind once more, and again, I dismissed it.

"I made a copy of the most recent slip, but I misplaced it," I told Mr. Bola. "The figures are correct, though."

"If that's the case, Mrs. Moreau, you can request a sizable amount. Not only are you eligible for disability insurance, but you have no revenue."

He took out a calculator and diligently tapped away, then said, "You can expect to be awarded at least two years of alimony at approximately 7000 Swiss francs per month."

I gasped. He smiled.

"An insignificant amount in relation to his revenue, Mrs. Moreau. You mustn't let yourself be taken advantage of. Present the figures to him, that's my advice. And know that the law is behind you."

Astonished, I listened to the lawyer continue to explain what I should and should not do, my eyes widening. He assumed I would behave like so many other women, who treat their divorces as a kind of business deal. I had no desire to go down that road, or to let my divorce become my second life. I wasn't looking to get rich or get revenge; I just wanted to get away from Cedric as quickly as possible. I didn't go into this with Mr. Bola, who wouldn't be my lawyer anyway; I just needed his help to get some idea of my situation. I left his office feeling somewhat relieved. Cedric and I simply needed to find a compromise and I was sure we were nearly there. After all, he was the one who agreed so quickly to my suggestion of a temporary separation. Maybe too quickly, I remembered with a start of apprehension.

Having decided to walk downtown to have dinner somewhere, I returned to the question of that salary slip. It was impossible I had misplaced it. Could Cedric have pretended to leave, and snuck upstairs after me? I scoffed at that; I would have known. Something else was bothering me, too, something I finally had to confront. After a recent trip to Korea, Cedric had told me he'd seen a friend from college, Adam, who was living in Seoul. They talked about their home lives, and Adam confided that his marriage was on the rocks. Suspecting his wife of infidelity, he'd put microphones and miniature cameras in their home, and watched his wife day and night, finally catching her with her lover. Cedric eyed me strangely as he told me this story, with that weird gleam in his eye I knew meant trouble.

"I could have done the same after what you did," he said. "Bugged the whole house. I would have known right away about Whalid. Anyway, it was cool to see Adam again, and his idea isn't so bad."

He acted like he was joking but I knew Cedric believed he was invincible. The link between his salary slip and his friend who took himself for a spy was too obvious, and my suspicion of him using microphones and cameras now grew too strong to ignore. I would have to keep that knowledge to myself though, and maybe even use it to my advantage. My God, I thought, I'm no longer the naïve, "docile" Chloe I used to be.

I chose a restaurant with a terrace and sat down at a table for one. I would have to get used to that. The waiter had just brought me a shot of vodka when Cedric called me, and I downed it in one gulp. His increasingly frequent and frenzied calls no longer upset me like they used to, as they showed he was losing confidence, but I figured the alcohol would help me project my old self, compliant Chloe.

"What did your lawyer have to say? I'm sure he told you the same thing I did, right?"

"Just about. He asked how much you made, and he said that by law..."

"What? By law? What law? I'm not giving you a penny over what we agreed on. Do you hear me? It's not enough to destroy me emotionally, you want to steal my money, too!"

"Not at all, Cedric. That's not what I was trying to say. The lawyer only mentioned how the law should be applied in a case like this. That's all. But we'll find a compromise, don't worry."

I kept my tone cool, which irritated him even more. He was screaming "We agreed!" so loudly into the phone that the people next to me stopped talking, like they were trying to hear what was happening at my table. I turned red with shame, something I was far too used to. After he screamed some more, then hung up on me, I ordered a second vodka. I fumed about his accusation I was going back on my word. What had I agreed to? I never signed the papers his lawyer had sent, or ever said I was alright with any deal. I was furious, but I wouldn't give in to it, and I repeated my mantras about keeping calm, about being too smart and too strong to let him manipulate me. I repeated "do-cile, do-cile."

I got home late, having just barely caught the last bus of the evening. I'd had several more vodkas, and I tripped a bit on the front steps. Cedric was waiting for me in the kitchen.

"Where have you been? You look drunk. Fuck, you're pathetic. Fine, I'm going to bed. Are you coming?"

"A bit later."

Why was I still sleeping in our bedroom? And how on earth could I stand another night beside him? But he hadn't said I could sleep in the guest room, and without his explicit approval, I didn't dare risk another explosion.

The next morning, he brought up the separation. "I think we should hire one lawyer for both of us."

"Sure, maybe you're right. Annie's husband knows Mrs. Frey. Everyone says she's really good."

"No chance. A woman? And her! Never. She'll destroy me. Don't you know her reputation? We'll hire Jacques. He did a good job in my first divorce."

"We're pretty close friends with him, though, so that might not be such a good idea. We could at least get another recommendation. A completely neutral lawyer. What do you think?"

I was on eggshells, thinking of what Dr. Thyssen had said. Don't oppose him, use gentle persuasion until he agrees. And he did agree to at least meet me halfway in this. He told me to take care of it.

Using my therapist's protocol, I didn't call Jacques, but his wife. I wasn't taking any chances with anything. Every detail mattered right then.

"Stephanie, how are you?"

"Chloe! What a lovely surprise. I'm fine, how are you?"

"Quite frankly, things are just so-so. Cedric and I are separating, at least for a while. We've both agreed we need some space. I'm calling because we're looking for a lawyer, and I was hoping you could ask Jacques for a recommendation."

"Of course, I'll ask him, and he can call you back directly. But what happened? You seemed so perfect together."

"Appearances can be deceiving. Thanks for your help. Have a good evening, and I hope I'll see you soon."

I didn't waste a moment. I'd already wasted too much time, and I launched into action. I felt a strange dread, almost a premonition, of what the coming days might bring me, and I felt I needed to get ready, and in short order. Like in a Sergio Leone film, one of those Westerns where people have to be constantly at the ready because the next moment may be their last. I couldn't die now. Hopefully, I still had some good years ahead of me to find happiness. I'd lost five years with Cedric, but I didn't want to die without experiencing real love in an honest, enduring relationship. You can't invent that, or dream it up, and if didn't endure, if my real love story did end, it would be the kind of end that burns, that destroys and breaks you. I yearned to feel the kind of love that deserves being experienced, even at its painful end. A true love story. And what I'd had with Cedric was no love story.

I didn't want him to yell at me anymore. I didn't want to be manipulated, or have him turn every situation against me, or tell people crazy things about me, I didn't want to always be at fault. I didn't want him, period!

I promised myself that from then on, I would hold my soul close to my breast, keep it warm in the cup of my own hands. I promised, rashly, never to give it to some man again. It was mine, and even though it was broken, I would put the pieces together. I began doing that by adding "Cedric Moreau" to the list of bad things I had lived through, the last one needed to topple my fear of rejection. Enough was enough. I saw I had been lost in denial, that Cedric had buried the person I'd been before. I'd become an idiot, a brainless robot. Each time I had tried to assert myself, Cedric had managed, by word or gesture, to get the upper hand.

I wished my mother could have been there to help me, but if she knew everything, she would have been so ashamed of me, she could only have rejected me, left me for good. And how could I tell her about all those perverted acts? It was too humiliating and intimate, too raw altogether. She wouldn't understand I'd done those things against my will, under the powerful influence of a dangerous man. So, I couldn't ask for help from her. I wanted her to be proud of me, and believe I had healthy values. I wished she would stop judging me so harshly, and for her to see that my father's shadow was all over this toxic marriage of mine.

Cedric handed me our separation agreement a few days later. It noted our current situation in a few lines only: the legal framework of our marriage, his personal debts, my alimony.

"Tell me, honestly, if I give you this much, you have nothing to complain about."

I read the document again. It had no legal value, even I could see that, and he'd forgotten to clarify what we would do about our photos and films. All of those dirty sex scenes just sitting amidst the documents on his computer, probably on the cloud too. Someone could find them. We needed a clause to forbid either of us from showing them to anyone, but how could I make sure to get this in there without a major tussle?

"I'm fine with it, but I'd like you to add one thing – that all photos and videos featuring our sex life be destroyed. It's important for both of us. Imagine if one of your colleagues or clients came across them. You might damage your reputation or your career."

His career and his social status were worth more than anything to him, and this way I thought he would be sure to accept.

"If you're going to be like that, I'd like to add something to annoy you, too. Once you're gone, you're never allowed to set foot again in this house. You can take your photos and shove them up your ass."

I didn't see a connection between destroying proof that could harm us both and forbidding me from coming back home, which I had no intention of doing anyway. It made no sense, unless he was expecting me to back down on this important part of our agreement, and know for the rest of my life that one day some photo of me – in full sexual glory – might show up on Facebook, in someone's email, on a porn site. No way!

I sat unmoving at my end of the table and stared him down as gently as I could. At his end, Cedric did not move an eyelash. He seemed like a wild animal waiting to pounce. The minutes stretched out until my feet and legs began tingling. It was too much for me. I got up, scooped up the papers and started to walk out, but Cedric grabbed my wrist as I moved past him.

"I have an idea – let's go erase all the photos and videos together. Stay here. I'll go get the USB key and the video camera. Let's watch them all one last time."

I didn't want to see those pornographic scenes. I wanted this to be over as quickly as possible. A flash. Thousands of photos of me in motion, now frozen but ready for the web to bring them to life again. Cedric came back with his technology, set up his computer, and slipped in the USB.

He took my wrist again and pulled me over.

"Why are you shaking, Chloe? You're not afraid of me, are you? Take off your clothes and come sit on my lap."

"That's alright, I'd rather sit on the chair next to you."

I wished I could tell him the whole truth. "You disgust me. Your entire being disgusts me. Your lewd gaze, your thick eyelashes, your green eyes, your Grecian nose. Your confident way of marching across a room makes me sick. And yes, I'm afraid of you. You've frightened me more than once. And now you want me to sit on your lap? And then what? A little slip of cock without my permission? Like you've done before? You raped me so many times these last five years, I'm nothing now. No, that's not true: I'm your sexual object, to be used however you want. That's all you want. You're crazy and I don't want to be anywhere near you. I don't want to smell you, listen to you brag, hear your heartbeat, brush against your pale skin, deal with your moods or your tailor-made moments of joy. You're dreaming if you think I'm going to give in again to your dirty wishes."

"Take your clothes off, now!"

"Oh, Cedric, we can erase these photos without a re-enactment. I'm not in the mood, but maybe later."

"What the hell? Don't you get it? You do what I tell you. I'm the one who decides, I'm the one who has all the proof of your deviant sex life."

"It's also proof of yours, but I would never use those photos to hurt you. Would you?"

"Shut up!"

He grabbed my arm, then tore my dress open, just like in a porno film. Actions that may have appeared to be consensual, when I was still compliant to his every wish, were all the more abhorrent to me now, and I fought back. This was not an act of passionate love; this was violence. He was going to rape me, truly rape me. Rape isn't a fantasy: it's an act of extreme violence. Screams, cloth ripping, underwear pushed to the side, hair pulled tight, tears streaming, lipstick smeared, mascara running. What should I have done at that precise moment? What did I have left, except play my role of the helpless woman? And I was helpless, for he was stronger than me.

He pushed me against the kitchen counter, undid his belt, unbuttoned his pants, then pushed against me. His eyes bulged with rage and desire, and his mouth was fixed in a sneer. Suddenly I thought of that horrid letter he sent to Dr. Thyssen. He claimed I threatened him with a knife. There was a knife on the counter right next to me. I could grab it. What was I thinking? How on earth can a person come to this, to pick up a monstrous kitchen knife and point it at a man trying to shove his dick inside you? And he'd done it before, many times already, shoving his dick inside me without my explicit consent. And I had never fought back or even refused him. Why was I going to threaten him now? And what was I capable of doing? Could I kill him? Yes, I could!

Rage exploded and filled my mind; my body seemed to act on its own, grabbing the knife and pushing it against his throat. It nicked the skin, and a pearl of blood slid down his neck. He froze, eyes open in wonder.

"You're insane!" he said with a gasp. "Put that down right now!"

"Promise not to touch me, or I'll kill you."

I saw his fear. Finally.

He dropped his hands, and I let him move away, but I did not put the knife down. I gripped its handle like it was the only thing that could save my life. Cedric put his clothes back in order with shaky hands. His forehead was dripping with sweat, and he glared at me before sidling out and shutting himself up in his office. I could not move for a few minutes, the time to understand what had just happened, but I slowly came back to myself, and dropped the knife in the sink like it was diseased. I slid down to the floor, put my hands together and prayed to God to come to my rescue.

Cedric called to me later from our room, "Come to bed. We don't have to talk about all this. We're both at the end of our ropes. I still love you Chloe, and I will always love you. I hope you know how much I'm going to miss you."

I went to him, reluctantly, but I needed comforting, desperately. I let him take me into his arms like he was cradling an infant. I felt so tired, so confused. His fleeting tenderness would not change my mind, though. I had to leave.

The next morning, Cedric insisted we deal with this issue of the X-rated photos and videos. He brought his computer out to the kitchen, and this time he made sure there were no knives around. I saw I wouldn't be able to avoid the parade of photos, so I sighed and sat down. I knew this was a waste of time anyway. I wasn't stupid. Cedric had copies of everything, tucked away on a USB key or hard disk in our safe, and he'd changed the code.

While going through the files, he kept making comments. "Look! Remember that? Yeah, baby, that was so nice. I must say, sex with you was really good. Come sit next to me, so you'll be sure I'm erasing everything."

I watched the photos as they flicked across the screen, for the last time watching my body used as an object. I felt nauseated, but I forced myself to stay where I was and make sure he didn't "forget" anything.

"Go get the video camera from our room and see if there isn't a film," he said after erasing the computer files. "I think I might have missed something."

I suspected there was something he wanted me to find, and sure enough, there was a saved recording. I sat down on the bed and hit PLAY. The camera jerked a bit as Cedric placed it on the nightstand, his face, close to the lens, looming large and distorted. Then he lay back on the bed, naked, and blindfolded his eyes, pushed a butt plug in his ass and hung weights from his nipples, then started masturbating like a maniac. His mouth hung open like it was receiving a cock, and his tongue going back and forth. I watched, shocked.

"It's maybe a bit much. Maybe." Cedric said over my shoulder. He had silently padded in. "You were in New York. I had to find some way to pass the time!"

I erased this last video, wishing I'd never seen it, and resenting him for tricking me into watching it. If I only I knew how to get at his copies of everything. Otherwise, I'd never be safe. That risk of being exposed would always haunt me – images of my naked body, or starring in an orgy, or being abused in the bushes of a rest area. Will they be tacked up on a wall somewhere or used as a profile pic on some sex site?

I didn't nag Cedric about it, as I wanted to avoid more conflict. I knew only too well his shadow would always follow me, and the photos would always lie in wait, so why bother to keep insisting we include a formal clause in our separation agreement? I took Cedric's word, the word of a liar, that he'd erased it all. I let him have the last word.

I had to choose my battles, and this wasn't one I could win.

"Your lawyer said 8:30!" Cedric complained, looking at his watch for the third time. "He's ten minutes late. I hate people who aren't on time. Can't you even find a lawyer who can keep an appointment? Call him!"

I was praying Mr. Girod would arrive soon. I called him, and said he needed to get there as quickly as possible. My tone was dry, distant. I didn't even recognize myself.

He arrived a few minutes later, to my relief. Cedric stretched out a hand in greeting and pasted on his urbane smile, the one that charmed the pants off everyone, the con-man smile that swindled the whole world.

"You're not very punctual for a lawyer – I hope you're not late like this for court!" He gave a fake laugh. "Just kidding. My wife has indicated our situation to you, of course. Here is the legal separation document we prepared together."

Mr. Girod took his time reading it before offering any comment.

"Mr. and Mrs. Moreau, after reading this I'm persuaded it would be more expedient to move straight to a divorce. It would be much quicker and save you money. That is, if a separation were to end up being permanent, because you would only file once, rather than doubling all the expenses. And if it's truly meant to be, you'll get back together either way."

I remembered what the other lawyer, Mr. Bola, had said: "Ask for a divorce straightaway, and get everything agreed upon upfront. If you wait, you run the risk of getting nothing, and you may also be held responsible for his debts. I don't think you want to find yourself in that situation. Believe me, the law is well conceived, but you have to do things correctly from the get-go."

Wise counsel, since Cedric had accumulated debt over the years, even before meeting me. Debts he simply shrugged off. He wanted to live the way his wealthy friends and clients lived, as if their habits rubbed off on him and made him forget he wasn't in the same class as they were. I didn't want anything to do with his money, but I didn't want to be liable one day for his hundred grand or more of debt.

Cedric surprised me by laughing. "Just like Elizabeth Taylor and Richard Burton, huh?" The lawyer's comment about getting back together if we really loved each other seemed to tickle him. I laughed along with him, letting him indulge his little fantasy, but I was horrified at the thought of starting that nightmare over again. No thank you, at least not with Cedric.

The lawyer asked us for certain documents and official paperwork he would need to draw up the divorce contract. Cedric told him to wait while we got them. I found a copy of my disability insurance and brought it back, and Cedric came back carrying two binders, a green one with his tax documents, and a yellow one with colored dividers testifying to his faultless organizational methods. His salary papers were arranged in the section labeled EMPLOYMENT.

"You're very methodical," Mr. Girod said approvingly. "That will make everything much easier."

"These are all copies, so you can keep them."

While Cedric bent over to point out various figures, I snuck a peek at the fat yellow binder, and noticed a divider labeled CHLOE. Cedric had a file on me? What would be in there? Photos? Letters? Insults? I turned my attention back to the two men, but I was too distracted to understand what they were saying. I needed to know once and for all if he was spying on me. If so, to what extent and to what end? How far would he go? Maybe he would kill me in the end, Cedric, the serial killer who prepared the act in minute detail. Maybe I'd be a headline one day in the newspaper.

I came to when Mr. Girod pushed his chair back. He gathered his papers as he stood up.

"That's it for now. I've made my notes, and I'll send you a divorce proposal next week in line with your separation contract. If you both agree with everything, we can have this finished up in two months. My office will be in touch with you."

Once Mr. Girod was gone, Cedric picked up his binders, a satisfied look on his face. "He seems competent. He's right, divorce is the best option. Have you started looking for an apartment? The sooner the better."

He went back into the office with his file box, then came out holding his coat and briefcase.

"I'm off to work. Because, unlike you, I have a career."

And then he was gone. I waited an entire hour after the car was out of the driveway before moving. I had to know what he was hiding in that fucking file.

My hands were clammy, and I was sweating as I searched for that yellow binder. I thought it would be difficult to find, but he hadn't hidden it; it was right in his desk drawer. I opened it. There was the purple divider with my name on it. Cedric hadn't noticed that I'd seen it, which meant that Cedric didn't see everything. He was not as invincible as he pretended. I never had thought he was extraordinarily intelligent or more creative than average. He was mediocre, and he was a very disturbed man.

When I opened it and started reading, my mouth gaped and I shook my head, feeling horrified. A detective could not have done a better job at creating a file on someone. He'd gone through all my files and drawers, as well as the boxes I'd stacked in the garage, and taken photos or photocopies. There was my resume, which was not even on my computer, and all the letters I'd written, happy letters or moping ones, newsy ones or lovey-dovey ones. I read some of the notes he jotted throughout them: "You're the destructive one; this is totally false; you're the one making me unhappy; I'm not crazy, you're the nut job!" In one big envelope were naked photos of me, from static poses to active sex. He'd printed out certain conversations he'd had on online swingers' sites, talking about me. His comments were filthy. He'd sold my body to these people for ridiculous sums, and he'd kept all the offers, waiting for the highest bidder. There was also a letter from his daughter Ana, in which she vented her hatred of me. She called me mean and violent, and she begged her father to kick me out. That one broke the dam, and I started crying. I couldn't continue. I closed the file and put it back where it belonged.

I crept out of the room in a daze, went into the kitchen and poured myself a glass of wine, even though it was not even lunchtime. I was so shocked by what I'd seen that I couldn't gather my thoughts. How could I ever understand behavior like that? Who was Cedric Moreau, really? I didn't know this person I'd been sharing my life with. Only the devil could lie and roll in filth as much as Cedric did. Only the devil had such a remorseless gaze, and only the devil could cry without suffering and laugh without joy. Cedric did not experience emotions like normal people did. He had to be the devil.

I closed my eyes and took deep breaths, telling myself to control my own emotions if I wanted to make my escape. Don't believe a word he says, or panic when he insults you. Don't rise to the bait or break apart when he puts you down, when he hurts you. Be like him: push your emotions to the side and get your way through connivance.

That weekend, Cedric finally gave me permission to move into the guest room. First, I had to give him one last blow job to keep him happy. As usual, he whispered, "I love you," when it was over. I felt his pulse racing, and I wished his heart would simply stop beating. He thought I was crying because we were separating, still certain he was the perfect man for me. He thought I would come crawling back to him because I was useless and unable to make it on my own. No, I was crying from shame, and I would never crawl back.

So, I moved into the guest room. I started looking for an apartment in Geneva, to get myself settled in a city I didn't even like. All that mattered was starting my life over, and I had to start somewhere. I tried to think of it like a layover for a long flight, and it didn't matter what city it was in. I soon found the perfect apartment, a large studio in a building from the 1950s. It had charm, a huge balcony with a view of the lake, and very good vibes. It was being renovated when I visited and could be ready for me by the time I had to get out of our house, as Cedric had ordered. I nodded to

"It's great," I told the real estate agent. "I'll take it. I can bring you the paperwork today. You're sure I can have it by July 7th?"

"It should be ready, yes. We'll need two months' rent paid in advance and proof of revenues, such as a salary statement. Here's the contract to fill out."

But I had no salary – I was on disability and had no other revenue until the divorce was formalized and I started getting alimony. I could not let this apartment slip through my fingers. I was already imagining how I could rebuild my life in those 500 square feet. I wasn't going to give up because of a technicality; I needed this place. I called my mother, and after some awkward chitchat, I got down to business.

"I need your help, Mom. I found an apartment, but I need to secure it. I can pay the two months' rent, I think, but can the lease go in your name? Please!"

"Your father will never agree, Chloe. He doesn't even want to speak to you right now. He thinks you're ruining your life. You'll just have to work it out with Cedric."

And that was it – she wouldn't budge. I was surprised at her hard tone but had no time to wonder about it. I turned to Christelle and Doug, who squirmed at the idea of putting their names on the lease, which was only natural. A divorcee with no job, a whacko ex-husband... I realized no one would willingly take that kind of security risk to help me, and I was on my own. The only option was to ask Cedric to give me back access to my accounts, and to secure the lease for me. I groaned, as that was the last thing I wanted to do. I had no choice but to follow my mother's advice, and that evening, I asked Cedric for his help.

"I found a little studio, but since we haven't signed the divorce papers, I can't move on it. Since you want me to leave as quickly as possible, will you sign for it? Here are the papers, and a check for the two months' rent to transfer. I do have that much in my account, right? Please, Cedric, I won't ask you for anything else."

"I knew you couldn't do anything without me," he scoffed. "You can't live without me. Fine, give me the fucking papers and let's be done with it. You're so useless."

His insult did not touch me. I wasn't afraid of starting a new life, as this wasn't the first time I'd packed my bags and headed into the unknown. I had moved a dozen times. And there was no difficulty in dividing up our stuff: Cedric made it clear he was keeping everything except what I brought from New York. I had used my disability payments to buy the living room sofa, the kitchen chairs, some throw pillows and other decorations, but he wouldn't let me take them. Same for the wedding presents, even the cutlery my parents had given us.

"You can find nice stuff at IKEA. They have complete sets in boxes. That's what I did after my first divorce."

What could I say? Fuck it, I would start over from zero and leave behind everything that might trigger a bad memory anyway.

In my mind, I was close to the finish line. The rental agency received the contract and payment and confirmed the lease was mine. I would leave Cedric July 7th. I could get to work now to find boxes and start packing my things, stacking them up in my room. I didn't want to leave anything in the hallways. I had a month, and I couldn't forget anything, because once I was gone, I'd never set foot in that rotten house again.

I began with my books and CDs. I took a long time to check the bookshelves because of my poor vision, but I didn't want to leave Cedric even one of my books, or any of my music. The housekeeper helped me stack the boxes in the guest room. I took my clothing from the bedroom and hung it up in a cardboard closet, carefully wrapped my paintings in thick blankets and swaddled my sculptures with bubble wrap.

Cedric tried to claim my statue of a beautiful, curvy woman out in the garden: "You're not leaving it? You gave it to me as a gift."

Just hearing him say that made me no longer want it. That would be my final gift to him, and he could also keep the naked photos of me he'd enlarged and hung on his office wall. I pictured him showing them off to his new friends, bragging about his ex-wife, and then adding, in a sad voice, that even though I left him, I'd always be his one and only. The old pity play.

I should have been more careful when I first met him, should have seen his faults. I would never have lied to myself the way I did for five whole years. But that was in the past. Each day my understanding of reality grew starker. I'd kept it in the shadows throughout my marriage, but now I saw him in all his ugly, mean pettiness. I imagined a nice, calm future without him. That was all I wanted, and to get it, I had to control my feelings. I couldn't break down in front of him; that could come later, after I got through this last excruciating month and made my move.

If he was at home, I almost never left my room, saving the packing for when he was gone. The boxes stacked up, and eventually, I had just enough space to walk between the door and the bed, with some open boxes full of clothes I could use during this limbo period. Because I was surrounded with only my own things, that small, crowded space gave me an odd sense of freedom.

THIS IS BULLSHIT, NOT A LOVE STORY

The rest of the house no longer belonged to me. I was a stranger within its walls and Cedric made sure to play it up by pointedly ignoring me or treating me like a stranger renting a room. Our meeting with the lawyer seemed to have put a natural end to our relationship. We hardly spoke during the first two weeks following it. He didn't touch me, or kiss me, or force me into any orgies. No more aggression, no more insults, and sometimes, in an automatic sort of way, he even smiled at me and said goodbye before leaving for work, always catching himself before adding his customary "See you tonight, darling." He left, he came home. I did the same.

It was a relief, but it also felt bizarre and very awkward to live this way. Like a kid before summer break, I started counting down the days before I could leave, 13 more at that point. I wrote the date in my calendar. Life could begin again on July 7th.

The only person I asked for help was my mother, and this time, she said yes, she could drive me to IKEA for kitchen supplies. I kept stealing a look at her fixed face on the way there, wondering who this woman was, a stranger or a helpful mom? Was she disappointed, angry, ashamed? Was she on my side or Cedric's? I didn't ask her, and she barely spoke, not even to ask me how I was doing. She followed me around the store, IKEA with its suffocating happiness, and that annoying series of arrows to finally get to the kitchen section. I kept my head down, trying to contain my bad mood, caused by my mother, who could have shown me a bit of compassion, or treated this shopping trip as an adventure, a celebration of a new beginning, but no, it was the opposite. The heavy atmosphere between us made me feel uneasy, awkward, and I rushed through my purchases, just to get it over with.

Her coldness worried me. Why on earth was she so distant? Was she rejecting me? Didn't she want to see her daughter happy? Not a single kind gesture, not even a kiss on the cheek. She and my father were breaking my heart. I wasn't going through a normal breakup;

I was getting away from someone who had hurt me and threatened me still. Yet they kept defending him. They told me to stay with him! The only conclusion I could come to is that he had lied to them about me. Probably to everyone around me. Had he completely brainwashed them?

She dropped me off at the house without helping me bring my bags in, and as I watched her drive away, I started crying. I felt so alone. I told myself not to hate her or my father, though, as they didn't understand me or my situation, and I couldn't bring myself to explain, because I would have to bring out the whole mortifying truth. I hoped I would have the courage someday, and that they would believe me.

After adding my IKEA purchases to the ceiling-high towers of boxes in my room, I went into the garage to dig out a box of old letters and photos I'd stored there. They were. Looking through the photos, which dated from the time before I met Cedric, sent a flash through my brain. What about all the photos Cedric had developed? He'd often come home with envelopes of photos, crowing about the shock on the face of whoever developed them. He was proud of shocking people that way, for some reason.

I had forgotten about all those shots, and I needed to get them, so that evening, I asked him. "Before I forget, Cedric, you're the one who has all our printed photos, right?"

He groaned. "You're certainly thorough. Yes, they're in the safe, and so what? You want to destroy those as well? You're not done annoying the fuck out of everyone, are you, Chloe? It must be tiring to be such a bitch. You think I'm going to publish them in some magazine, or send them out as Christmas cards? Come on, Chloe. Don't you trust me?"

"I'd appreciate if you could just get rid of them, please," I replied as calmly as possible.

THIS IS BULLSHIT, NOT A LOVE STORY

Instead of doing that, Cedric had the good taste to place them side by side on my bed the next day while I was out, so that I could destroy them myself. He left a note beside a disgusting photo of me he'd taken during a gang bang:

As you've requested, my dearest Chloe, I'm returning your photos. You'll know what to do with them. I've cum enough on them by now. So long.... Cedric

He hadn't lost his sense of humor evidently. I ripped up the photos one after the other, which felt great. Too bad I couldn't rip up the memories they brought back or pile them up and set them on fire. Over the years, I had tried, unsuccessfully, to convince myself it wasn't really me in those photos, doing those things, to find ways to soften the violence and blur the images. It would take decades to do that, if it was even possible.

I found our wedding photos that day, too, in an album stuck between two art books, one on Mapplethorpe and the other on Rodin. I saw no connection between our hokey marriage in Las Vegas and those two geniuses. I hadn't looked at those pictures in years. Cedric and I were posing, and our cardboard smiles only accentuated our disconnection. Our wedding seemed surreal, a complete fake, like a staged event in a reality TV show. I closed the album and put it back. I didn't want it. The title of the album made me laugh: Welcome to Paradise. Cedric had written this himself. What a narcissist! A paradise where he got to play out his sick fantasies. I wanted off this tropical island I was trapped on; maybe I had "island fever." Then I realized I would be off it, very soon, and a jolt of stress chilled me to the bone. I wasn't anxious about what would happen after leaving, but about the remaining days and nights in his house, under his roof.

Ten days left – the countdown had begun. I kept to my morning ritual. Wait until Cedric was gone, then have my black coffee and a cigarillo in the living room, where the morning light slanted in at a nice angle. One day I didn't wait for him to leave, and I could tell it annoyed him. I heard him getting ready, but I held my mug of hot coffee in my hands and took a puff, looking around the room. Everything was where Cedric wanted it to be – not a book or knick-knack out of place. The well-dusted photo frames in their spots, placed just so, neither too far to the right or left. Yet, something looked different, not quite right.

I got up and peered around at the shelves. The framed photos! I could see my reflection, but not the photos. Cedric had removed every photo of the two of us. The room suddenly darkened, and my spirits too. Why leave the empty frames there? Then I noticed new photos of his mother, his daughters, and his grandparents. My very image was to disappear from this house, swallowed up by his family. Except the nude photos in his office, of course – my body as an object was fine, and they were hung where his mother, daughters and grandparents wouldn't come across them. Or at least I hoped they never would.

I shuddered with disgust and hatred for him. The familiar noise of his grooming in the bathroom irritated me, the splooch of hair gel, the whir and zap of nose hair clippers, his humming as he moved into the bedroom to get dressed. I knew he was selecting his Hermes tie, dusting his shoulders, then flicking the pants to fall just so. I swallowed hard and wiped the grimace from my face. I couldn't let him see how I hated him.

He came out wearing a flawless blue suit, crisp white shirt, and gold cufflinks a Middle Eastern client had given him. The perfect corrupt banker.

"You're already up?" he said. "That fucking stinks! Can't you smoke outside? And what the fuck are you pouting about now?"

"Nothing, but did you really have to leave those empty frames and add photos of your family? You could have waited for me to leave. It's like I died."

"You're going to make a scene for that? Already, this early in the morning? What the hell is wrong with you? Go see your shrink, Chloe, you're a fucking mental case."

His flushed face and violent reaction threw me off guard. I got up, as I didn't want a confrontation, but he stepped in front of me, blocking me from going into the kitchen. Close enough to smell his familiar clean-and-cologned smell. I pushed him back, saying I wanted to go get dressed, but he wouldn't move out of my way. He grabbed my cigarillo and ground it into the ashtray, cursing.

"Why are you so mad?" I said. "All I did was ask about the photos!"

"Photos! Always photos!"

I knew he was mad because I was defying him, not because of the photos. I'd found the courage to stand up for myself by asking an honest question.

Cedric had never hit me, probably because it would show on my face, and I could go to a neighbor and show the evidence. Unless he leashed me to the radiator, of course, until I healed. What an awful thought! But he looked crazy, as if he badly wanted to hit me. Instead of that, he spun me around and grabbed my arms, and shoved my face down against the photo frames, one by one. My nose pressed hard against the glass; I couldn't move. I didn't dare; I was too terrified. I thoughts he was capable of killing me right then. Then he pulled me up and crushed me against the bookshelf. It was all happening so fast I didn't have the time or the wits to scream. And then slammed me against the shelves, again and again, the books and gewgaws and even the photos of his family flying out and hitting the ground. Some shattered.

He used me like a punching ball. It was as if he couldn't stop; he'd lost control of himself. He'd never raised a hand against me but now he hit me all over, especially my head. I was unaware of the pain, but I registered the thumping sounds of his fist and of my body smacking against the shelf, against the wall. Then he shoved me to the ground on my back, ripped open my bathrobe and tore down my underwear. Pulled down his pants, got his dick out and to my horror, it was erect, and he raped me. He raped me, just like that. I was in a state of shock by then and couldn't even struggle. The pain was beginning to rush through all my nerves now, but my legs felt limp, heavy, against the hardwood floor. I thought later about the random nature of it – had the gardener or the housekeeper been there, I would have been spared his violence. He came inside me, got up, and pulled up his pants.

He trotted into the bedroom and changed his clothes, patted his hair back into shape, made himself a coffee and drank it in one gulp as I lay still on the floor. I could feel shards of glass in my back, and warm blood underneath the sharp stinging.

"Have a good day," he said with a sneer as he went out.

I heard the gate close at the end of the driveway, heard the motor purring down the street. He left me lying on the floor. He knew me too well for my own good – he knew I'd be too ashamed to call the police or get help or even tell anyone. The thought whispered in my mind, "Out of shame, or pride?"

I shifted my body back and forth to turn over, got to my knees, ouch, right on more glass, warily got to my feet, then shuffled to the bathroom and looked in the mirror. Not a pretty sight. There was a cut on my cheek, bumps and red spots and bruises all over. Lots of cuts on my back, my knees, the backs of my legs, and I hoped there were no shards embedded in the skin because who would help me remove them? I wailed inside, "Why can't I ask someone to help me get them out? What is wrong with me?" I hated myself; I hated him and the whole world.

The bruises on my face worried me the most, as I needed to go out and get things done. It would take days, maybe weeks, for them to disappear. I stood up straight and stared myself down in the mirror. The sight hardened me – battle scars can do that to a person. A glimmer of hope returned. I took a shower in tepid water, washing away Cedric's cologne and bodily fluids for a good ten minutes. Washing him off. I poured antiseptic soap all over myself and stood under the showerhead for another five minutes. Then I gingerly patted my aching, smarting body, finding new pain spots every few inches. I bandaged myself, rubbed ointments on my bruises and dressed in loose clothes. I combed out handfuls of hair from my head, shocked at seeing the wastebasket fill up – it seemed like enough to make a wig!

I then surveyed the crime scene. Wearily, I swept up the broken glass and mopped up the blood, my blood, from the floor. Straightened the books and put back the gewgaws. Did he think his violence proved he still had control over me? To show him it didn't, I put everything back in a different order, a disorder he would itch to correct.

I felt more determined than ever. I limped to the kitchen for an ice pack for my face, then I lay down on the couch, thinking about our first lovers' weekend in Madrid, when he insisted I watch the bullfights with him. The connection between that event and our life together was all too clear. I was the strong but long-suffering bull, and Cedric was the matador in his Suit of Light. Despite my pain, my mind kept ticking away, my thoughts crystal clear. This would save me, and I knew what I had to do. I decided to learn more about the art of bullfighting.

After resting a while, I dabbed some Arnica on my bruises in front of the mirror. My face was so swollen it was hardly recognizable. How had he dared? I felt another explosion of anger filling me and to let it out, I screamed. That hurt too much though, and I started laughing, which hurt too. So I went back to the couch, and looked up "bullfighting" on Google, and spent the rest of the day with my ice packs and ointments and my computer, watching videos, studying the tactics, learning the rules. No insult to the matadors of this world, but the similarities between Cedric and them were undeniable: their behavior, actions, strategies and personalities.

My research confirmed I had experienced the opening and the first two acts: the Paseo, the Tercio de Varas, and the Tercio de Banderillas. And that I was smack in the middle of the ultimate act, the Tercio de Muerte, the "putting to death." The last moment before the animal receives its fatal blow. Cedric had planned it all. He'd missed nothing in five years, never suspecting that one day I would see the connection between this barbaric tradition and the relationship he'd forced upon me. I was so absorbed, I didn't notice how late it was getting, but when I realized Cedric would be home anytime, I grabbed some bottles of water and hid myself away in my room, wishing it had a lock on the door. Just as I lay down, I heard his car in the driveway, then the hinge of the front gate. I counted his steps as he came in the house, until they reached my door.

"Chloe, are you there?" Of course I'm here, you bastard. How could I go out looking like this? Fucker. Fucker. Fucker, look at what you've done to me.

"Can I come in?" He didn't wait for my answer. I watched the door handle slowly turn, and I watched him come in. I said nothing, just stared. I wanted to be sure that the man standing there was the one who'd beaten my face that morning. No doubt, it was him, Cedric. The Matador.

"You don't look too well. Did you put ice on that? It'll go away quickly. In a few days we won't see a thing."

He looked around the room, at all the boxes, and at my computer on the bed.

"Can I ask why you're so interested in bullfighting all of a sudden?"

Always with the spying! He knew everything: what I did on my computer, in the house, on my cell phone. A 24-hour warden. I didn't answer him, but turned to my side, hoping he'd leave me alone. He closed the door behind him, and only then did I cry. My battered body needed rest, and I needed my strength for the final act. I'd survived his beating. I would survive these last days in his house. I fell asleep.

The name came to me in a dream. *Lidia*. What the bullfight is called by its fans. And it's a beautiful first name. One I would have liked for myself. Lidia, the world of bullfighting. The world's permanent combat. Lidia, my muse. The combat has to come to an end, eventually. Lidia, Lidia, such a soft, lilting first name. I could hear it deep inside my brain. Lidia, Lidia... wake up...

The next day my mother called me several times, until I finally answered. She wanted to see me, all of a sudden. I told her I didn't have time to go see her, but that we could talk on the phone. I was too ashamed to tell her what happened or let her see me with my broken face. Again, I wondered what the fuck was wrong with me. I could have ended the whole mess by showing my parents my face that day. They would know it was Cedric; they would have to consider what my life had become. I don't know how my father would have reacted to that knowledge, maybe by accusing me of pushing my husband to the end of his rope, and maybe my mother would have drawn me into her arms. Maybe. I'll never know.

"What's so important, Mom? Go ahead and tell me over the phone."

"Cedric came over to tell us how you've been acting. Sleeping with 15-year-old boys and stripping for the houseguests! I didn't raise you like that!"

"And you believed him? How could you? He's a liar! Listen to me – once I finally get away from this monster, you'll beg for my forgiveness. I have nothing else to say to you. Not to you, or Dad. You can go to hell."

I hung up on her. If I couldn't swallow my pride and open up to them, I had to accept the consequences. I could do nothing about the lies he'd told my parents and probably to everyone we knew. But one day the world would know all about Cedric Moreau.

And then I got another phone call.

"It's Mr. Girod. I'm calling because your husband has been harassing me since early this morning. He seems to be unaware of Swiss law. When you bought the house, he withdrew his pension funds for the down payment, to qualify for the mortgage. By law, you are due half of those funds. Mr. Moreau is shocked because he didn't know. You read the email I sent? The divorce papers are attached, so you can go through them. I don't technically have the right to call you about this, because I'm acting on behalf of you both, but having never experienced this level of provocation and vulgarity from a client, I felt it necessary to warn you to be on your guard – your husband may come home in a very bad mood this evening."

"I never received your email. Cedric must have gone into my account and deleted it – he has access to all my accounts, even my bank account. And my internet search history, I found out recently. I won't say anything else, because this line might not be safe. I know he spies on me, and who knows if our conversation is being recorded."

Good news and bad news. I wouldn't be destitute, with my part of the proceeds from the sale of our house, and half of Cedric's pension funds. But yes, he would be in an extremely bad mood when he got home. I didn't know whether I should run away or challenge him or call a locksmith immediately.

I remembered my dream. The bull's death scene came to my mind. Such a cruel execution. Cedric was probably imagining the same scene at that moment, over in his office. I considered my options, and decided to pretend I didn't know he was watching me, pretend the cape had blinded me to the truth. Wondering if it were hard for a normal human being to imagine such a strategy, I went over the death scene again in my head in slow motion. The matador's movements were Cedric's. The bull was weakened by the barbs in his sides and back, covered in blood, but he kept his gaze locked on his adversary. Had he understood where the danger was coming from? The cape or the man?

I called Christelle. She and her husband had offered to help me with my move, as they probably felt ashamed about refusing to guarantee the apartment for me. I had paid for a rental van and arranged for them to pick it up, then come to the house.

"I'm calling about my move, and to make sure you're still ready to help. It's only five days away. I wanted to see what time you can come by with the van. Everything's ready, and I think it'll only take us an hour or so."

"No problem, sweetie. We'll be there. We're ready to support you any way we can. I'll check with Doug about the time and call you back."

Something was off with her voice, and her "sweetie" sounded fake. I became wary. Were they somehow in league with Cedric now? Had he gotten to them? Were they organizing my murder? I rolled my eyes, and tried to shake it off, but at this point, I felt I couldn't trust anyone. Cedric was capable of turning the entire world against me with his lies. He'd manipulated everyone, including me, in his fight to dominate me, but I was no longer his dupe. This time, I was going to win.

I wandered into black thoughts. I'm the one knocking him to the ground, covered in blood, and pushing his nostrils into the dust until he chokes. His breathing is labored. His breath smells bitter. The baking sun beats down on his spent body while flies land on his crusting blood. Solemn and standing proudly upright, I say to him, "It's your turn to suffer the slow death you've inflicted on others."

The afternoon passed, the evening came on, and still Cedric didn't come home. I had waffled so long in indecision that I had done nothing to protect myself. I was at once filled with anxiety and in a complete mental and bodily stupor. I was far from being healed. The bruises had turned from purple to blue to greenish yellow, but my face was still red and puffy, and I ached all over. By midnight, I was exhausted, but I couldn't close my eyes, too afraid to wake up with a knife at my throat. His emotional abuse had rarely kept me from sleeping, but now that he'd beaten me, and after what the lawyer said, I was terrified.

Finally, the sky lightened, the sun rose, and still, no sign of him. I made my coffee, lit my cigarillo, and slumped on the couch, my eyes heavy with fatigue. At 9:10, my phone buzzed. A text from Cedric. I sighed. Maybe I'd been hoping he was in a car accident, dead or in a coma or in a ditch. After reading his message, I fervently wished that were reality.

"You're nothing but a fat slut. I'm ruined because of you. Think hard about what you're going to do. You can choose not to accept my pension funds. MY funds. It's your choice, but be very careful - if you make the wrong decision, it will be all your fault."

Someone who didn't know him might not take his threat seriously, but I did. Cedric wanted me to give up the money that was lawfully mine? I called Sylvie right away and asked her advice.

"Are you insane? You can't give him anything. Hasn't he done enough? Besides, you've got the law behind your back, Chloe. Believe me, he can't do anything to you. He's just trying to mess with you. Fight him, and he'll give up. Be confident! You deserve every penny."

She was right. I deserved it after the hell he'd put me through, and the law was the law. He couldn't change that. I resolved to hold out no matter what. There were only a few days left, so what more could he do? Hadn't he already destroyed me? He wouldn't dare do more, no, he wouldn't do it. He wasn't a killer, was he? I hesitated – what good was money if I was dead? Maybe I should make the "right" decision and turn it down. And Sylvie didn't know Cedric had crossed the line into violence, or maybe she'd have changed her advice. The pros and cons were whirling around my mind when the house phone rang. I picked up, and to my dismay, Didine started screaming at me.

"What the hell do you want, Chloe? You trying to kill my son? Stop hurting him, you hear me? I knew you were evil even before he told me. Take your money and get the hell away from him. Thank God you can't have children. You would've tainted their blood! You're a monster and you can go back to hell where you came from!"

Ouch. I held the phone away from my ear. I felt sorry for the poor woman, regardless of her insults. She didn't know they all applied to her son, not to me, but to Cedric, her sick fuck of a son who beat up on women. I hung up on her for lack of a better reply, then went out to the garden for solace.

"So? Did you make the right decision?"

I clambered up from the reclining chair. I must have dozed off, because I hadn't heard Cedric arrive. Instinctively, I got behind the chair, putting it between us, then screwed up my courage, having made my decision then and there, on impulse.

"Listen, Cedric. The law is the law. Marriage contract, divorce contract. Between the two there are some rules. Our lawyer is simply applying Swiss marriage law. I'm sorry, but I'm not going to say no to the pension funds. It wouldn't be right, not after what you did to me."

His eyes narrowed and he nodded slowly. "We'll see about that."

His threat seemed vague, which could be good or bad. And he was very calm – that was definitely not good. No flash of anger, only a disdainful look before turning to leave. Confusing. Did he already have something in mind, or was he going to plan something now? Maybe he'd give up and move on with his life. I was too tired to think about it right then, so I turned over onto my stomach, and fell back to sleep.

I woke up about an hour later, shivering. The sun had set, and Cedric had turned on the lamps in the garden. I shifted, wanting to get up, but when I tried to move, I felt a strong resistance. My hands were tied behind my back. My feet were tied to the deck chair. He'd managed to tie me up while I was asleep, and now he could do anything he wanted. He wouldn't hesitate to fist me, sodomize me, or even get his friends involved for some kind of human sacrifice. I struggled, panic rising, then I heard his voice. I froze.

"Chloe, my love, my sweetheart," he cooed. "You're so beautiful when you sleep, and you were sleeping so soundly I didn't want to wake you. You must be so tired, poor thing, that you didn't even move when I slipped the ropes around your wrists and ankles. If you continue like this, your health will suffer. But I'm here, so don't worry about anything. Yes, don't worry, you'll get your money – my money – once you've earned it."

"Please, let me go, Cedric. What are you doing? Don't you think you've hurt me enough? I won't tell anyone, but please let me go."

"You didn't think I'd let you go without a little punishment for ruining my life, did you? I wanted to retire at 60, and buy myself a Porsche, maybe a little boat. But thanks to a mentally disturbed little girl, I'm going to end up behind a desk until I'm an old man, while my clients live it up in their beach houses along the Riviera. You. Fucking. Dirty. Whore. You're gonna get what you deserve. Your ass is mine, remember?"

I twisted my head around to look at him. He was holding a huge dildo. Frighteningly huge. I went rigid with fear, knowing it was going to hurt like hell. I took the deepest breath of my life, hoping to relax my anus, hoping to be able to shout. But he'd darted to my head and was already stuffing a kitchen towel into my mouth. I bit down hard on the cotton, trying to get his finger. Then Cedric handed the dildo to someone, smiling an evil grin at me. Someone else was there, a stranger he'd paid, I guessed. Cedric knelt down and squeezed my head in his hands. He wanted to watch me suffer. He kept his eyes on mine the entire time, telling the stranger exactly what to do. The person obeyed. The dildo did its work, ripping me apart. But that wasn't enough for him. The stranger, evidently some pervert like my husband, took his turn. Without a condom, he penetrated me, and that's when I passed out.

When I awoke, my mind was fuzzy, and it took me a moment to get things sorted, limb by limb. My entire body hurt, every inch of it, from my scalp where the man had pulled my head back by the hair, to the raw skin forming a bracelet around my ankles. My ass burned like it was on fire. I was lying in Cedric's bed, and I saw he had dressed me in a T-shirt and underwear. I smelled like perfumed soap. I came to my senses, and the images rushed in. I managed to get out of bed and into the bathroom before vomiting. There was a towel on the floor, red with blood, lots of it. Was it my blood? After I'd passed out from the pain, what else did they do to me? My memory blanked, but then I remembered the last seconds of consciousness, when that stranger had sodomized me without any protection. Where did all that blood come from? I ran a hand over my bottom, gently. My anus was completely raw, like an open wound. My ass was weeping blood. I tried to clean it and shrieked. Cedric must have heard, for he suddenly appeared at the bathroom door. I pulled up my underwear and hid myself between the bathtub and the toilet.

"I'm not going to hurt you," he said, approaching me. "Did you sleep well? We showered you and I put you to bed like the Prince Charming that I am. Are you okay? I see you're still bleeding. Come here, I'll take care of it."

He was the cause of "it," but just like he always acted so tenderly to me after an argument, he did the same now, after his heinous act of violence. His lightning-fast switch from outsized violence to outsized empathy. I'd been taken in so many times. He knew the right words and the perfect comforting tone to use. That day I was absolutely helpless to reject him. I had no choice but to let my torturer take care of me. He got what he needed from the medicine cabinet and treated my anus.

"See? You won't even need to see a doctor. I hope you understand now. I won't let you go, not ever. You'll pay for what you've done until the day you die. But don't worry, I'm not going to kill you. That would be too easy. Perpetual misery is much worse than death, don't you think? You'll live, and you'll pay, and keep paying. You shouldn't have fucked with me, Chloe."

With those words, he left me alone in the bathroom and went off to work. I could hardly move for the pain, but I crept to my room and lowered myself to the bed, maneuvering carefully to lay on my stomach. If only I had a lock on the door so he couldn't touch me again or come near me. If only I could call someone to come get me, to save me. His words "perpetual misery" shook me to the depths. I had only three days to go. Would I make it? After the abuse I'd endured, he wouldn't be able to touch me again for a while, so I might last the three days I had to remain under his roof. I prayed, then went back to sleep until the phone rang. I hoped it wasn't Didine again.

It was the realtor this time, with bad news. There would be a few days' delay before I could move in because the workers couldn't finish until July 12th. Five days extra?

"What do you mean? You promised me I could move in on the 7th. Listen, you don't understand what a horrible situation you're putting me in."

But there was nothing the realtor could do about it. I had to find a solution. Cedric wouldn't put up with it; he'd throw me out on the street or lock me to the radiator until moving day. I called Christelle to let her know of the change of plans, and screwed up my courage to ask if I could stay with her from the 7th to the 12th. She hemmed and hawed. I could tell she felt awkward about it, and I was about to tell her to forget about it, when she said she'd have to ask Doug.

She couldn't leave me at Cedric's! She had no idea what I was really going through, but she must have suspected a little, for fuck's sake.

Five extra days. It was as bad as five years. I'd served my time: exactly five years and five months. Adding five more days to my sentence seemed immeasurably long.

I broke the news to Cedric over the phone. He grunted, then said he didn't care, that I'd better be out on the 7th. I was no longer useful to him in my pitiful state.

"I'm leaving for Israel tomorrow and coming back on the 9th. You won't be there. Your boxes will be stacked out in the studio. I don't want to find anything in the guest room. You're forbidden from ever again entering the house. And be there at exactly 9 a.m. on the 12th to pick up your stuff."

The next day, I waited for him to leave on his business trip before I ventured out from my cave. It was Thursday, the housekeeper's day to clean. When she arrived, I asked her to help me move my boxes into the workshop. Lifting the first one made me cry out in pain, which startled her. She looked at me, and I could tell she took in my condition at one glance. The gingerly way I moved, the bruises I had unsuccessfully tried to hide with makeup. And because I blushed with shame, she refrained from commenting, and good soul as she was, she wouldn't let me move a single box. She went in and out, shaking her head every time she passed Cedric's office door, her lips shut tight. When it was done, she cleaned the house, and just before leaving, she asked me if I would be okay. I shrugged and told her I wasn't okay, and that I was moving out, which I'm sure she knew by now, especially after helping me move my boxes. I thanked her and wished her good luck, then slipped some money into her hand. I was going to advise her to find a new employer, but something told me she was already planning to do that.

Christelle and Doug came to get me on the 7th in the late morning. When they arrived, I warned them not to hug me. I couldn't hide my physical pain from them, although I wasn't about to give any details of why I winced with every movement. They didn't ask me anything. I was just so happy, despite my pain, so relieved to be leaving him, truly leaving him. I looked around one last time to make sure everything was ready, so I could return on the 12th and get my boxes out of there quickly. Doug opened the car door for me, and I crawled into the back seat. The car started up and as we rolled away, my head was spinning. I gazed at the house, his house now. The next time I saw it would be the last time I'd ever have to see Cedric's face again. I sure hoped so, anyway.

Christelle and Doug settled me into their calm, quiet guest room. I needed to rest, so I closed the door, and without even meaning to, I slept through the entire day, until a delicious odor wafted into the room and woke me up. It was nearly dark outside. I joined my friends on the balcony, where they had laid the table, and Christelle handed me a glass of rosé with a smile.

"You had quite a nap there!" Doug said as he came in from the kitchen with a platter of steaks.

"It was divine," I said, laughing. "Doug, can I steal one of your cigarettes?"

"Of course. But isn't it dangerous? I thought you couldn't smoke anymore because of your ischemia."

"Never say 'never.' I've been smoking cigarillos for years, but they kill my throat. I'd love a cigarette for once. Nothing will happen. I've experienced worse."

I swallowed a mouthful of wine and drew deeply on the Menthol Vogue. It felt like the most glorious moment of my entire life. This sudden entry into normalcy was a shock, though, and I realized it was because I was no longer used to enjoying myself. And all this – the crackling of the meat grilling on the barbecue, the scent of basil on the garden-fresh tomatoes, the light conversation and laughter – it seemed like a dream. Christelle noticed the glisten of tears in my eyes, and she patted me on the shoulder. They didn't say one word about Cedric, they didn't look at me with pity, they made me feel perfectly at ease. I smiled and relaxed. We were about to sit down at a meal together without having to sleep with one another afterwards. My brain broke into a thousand pieces at that thought, and I sobbed and laughed at the same time. I raised my glass to them and got out one word, "Freedom!"

Back in bed later, my anxieties resurfaced, and I understood it would take more than one evening like this to adjust to a normal life. I thanked God I'd at least made a start, though, and decided I'd best focus on one small step at a time. For now, that meant simply keeping it together mentally during this holding period. I still had to face Cedric one more time before I could begin the real healing.

We were late on the 12th. Cedric called me at 9:01 to ask where I was. I knew it was too much to hope he would be at work, because of course he wanted to be on hand for the removal, for one last chance to needle me.

I set my jaw and replied, "We'll be there in ten minutes."

"As usual, you show no respect for anyone. Get the fuck here, now. I have things to do."

But when we arrived, he came out smiling, like we'd been invited to have breakfast with him. "So, today's the big day! Come on in." He practically frisked around us, giving Christelle and me air kisses, and clapping Doug on the shoulder.

"I'm guessing this won't take long since Chloe's taking so little with her. Everything is stacked in the workshop."

He followed us around, making comments and trying to "help," as when he started rolling out an old bicycle from the garage. I shook my head at him.

"What, you're not taking the bike I gave you? Guess I'll give it to Sarah then, so we can go biking together."

I wanted to tell him to keep that cheap, extremely heavy beach bike he got on sale. It had never been practical for this hilly area, and trying to keep up with him on his expensive, sleek road bike had been a real slog. He could sell it and add the amount to his Porsche fund, I thought, and my indifference said just as much.

It took 45 minutes to load up the van and say goodbye. Only 45 minutes to leave Cedric, after five and a half years together. A tear rolled down my cheek, which Cedric noticed with a look of triumph and contempt. He didn't know it was from relief, not sadness. I wasn't going to miss that man or that house or that life I never fit into, a life I'd grown to hate. As we drove away, Cedric stood there watching, stony-faced, until he faded into a shadow. I turned my head away before he completely disappeared. Deep inside, I had a feeling he wasn't completely out of my life yet.

It took even less time to move my boxes and few pieces of furniture into my new apartment. The first thing I did was to sit on my low sofa, the one I'd brought from New York, and bounce on it a few times, smiling because I finally had my space, mine alone, to launch myself from. I would find balance, write myself out of that horrible story, and type "The End" with a flourish. That is, once I figured out how much it had really affected me. I hated what had happened to me, that I had let happen I admit, I hated it, but now it was over, I could learn to embrace it as a springboard for all that could happen after. My future was an open book, empty pages waiting to be filled.

The first thing Christelle did was put a couple bottles of rosé in the fridge. For the rest of the day, she and Doug helped me unpack and arrange my belongings. I'd already imagined how I would set up the space with my furniture. Everything was clear except the life I would lead. That would take some planning, and this wasn't the time to start working out my plan. July 12th was too momentous a day for me to get so serious, and it was a beautiful warm day too, so as the sun was about to set, I decided it was time to celebrate. All my possessions were in order, from the clothes color-coded in the closet to the Ikea cutlery neat in the kitchen drawers. The empty boxes were stacked in the van. I cleaned three glasses, put them on a platter with a bottle of wine and went out on the balcony.

Christelle and Doug were admiring the scenery. From here on the 5th floor, nothing blocked our view of the mountains, Lake Geneva and the flourishing green gardens of early summer surrounding the small homes on all three sides of my building. As Doug uncorked the bottle and filled the glasses, I took several deep breaths, feeling my neck and shoulders relax. I handed out the wine and we sat down and lifted our glasses.

"To your new start, Chloe!"

"Hear, hear!"

We drank a sip of cool, fruity wine and I thanked them both.

"And thanks so much for all your help and your kindness today and the last few days. I couldn't have done it alone. This is a great place for a new start. I'm going to be okay here."

We ordered pizzas later and finished both bottles of wine. They left sometime after midnight. I turned off the music and bounced on my sofa again, looking around at my new home. All my old things had found a new place. I could finally see them again. Like me, they'd been lost in the shuffle for years, pushed into a box or a dark corner in Cedric's house, but now, we had a new space where we could breathe and shine.

I opened my eyes the next morning around eleven and looked around the studio. It was all still there, it was real. I grinned, but then my smile faded. I suddenly felt a little bewildered as to what to do next. A list would help – remember, small steps. So I got up and pottered around the kitchen, made a list while drinking my coffee, leisurely got cleaned up and dressed, all the while enjoying the fact I had no Cedric to deal with.

THIS IS BULLSHIT, NOT A LOVE STORY

I rearranged my furniture to create a bigger work space, then set up my computer on my desk. The building had free WIFI, so after a long and deep discussion with a technician, I was online, ready to connect with the world again. I needed to make sure Cedric hadn't digitally followed me, so I sent an email to Christelle, including some bits of fake news about my therapy. I had warned her that Cedric hacked my computer and probably still had access to it.

She called me later, freaked out. "You're right! He just sent me a message, and mentioned what you wrote about, almost exactly. I really believe you about him now. I'm so sorry not to have seen it or trusted you enough to believe all of it before, and that I wasn't there for you."

After we hung up, I wondered if I could ever truly escape his grasp on me. Was the earth big enough to keep him away? It was obvious the ten measly miles separating us weren't enough. Would this prison last forever? What a fucking nightmare.

But I could do something about my Mac being spied on, so I leapt into action. I brought it to a computer nerd I knew, who confirmed I wasn't simply being paranoid. A few days later, I picked it up.

"I've cleaned it completely," he said. "There was malware in your system. I've encrypted everything that can be encrypted, installed firewalls, blocked remote access, and I did a few other things besides. Believe me, no one will be able to hack your computer now. But bring it to me every few months, and I'll give it a thorough check."

I was relieved. Once Cedric realized he was no longer in control, he'd move on. Despite this reassuring thought, I was still worried. He might still be watching me day and night. I searched every inch of the studio for microphones and cameras, and even checked the hallways of my building as surreptitiously as I could. I found nothing. But he could have hired someone to spy on me. I checked the windows and roofs of nearby buildings and saw nothing suspicious, no sign of men with binoculars. Could he have put a microphone in the soles of my shoes to learn where my steps were leading me? I couldn't find any. Did his infra-rouge eyes follow my shadow everywhere? His hearing was so good, could he hear me talking to myself? I grabbed the sides of my head – I had to stop these spinning thoughts.

But proof of his spying kept coming, and I couldn't dismiss my suspicions, which preyed on my mind and spoiled my newfound sense of well-being. For example, he somehow knew friends of mine from Paris came to visit me two weeks after my move. He called them on their return to France, saying, "So...you paid a little visit to the lovely Chloe? Seems you kept the building up with your parties!" Unless he'd been parked outside the building, I don't see how he could have known this. Was he some kind of detective all of a sudden? I could just picture him in his car, eating a ham sandwich as he waited for his mark. Maybe he was paying off the concierge? Another mystery I had no control over.

One thing I did have power over was to get rid of anything that reminded me of him. I sold clothes, shoes, perfumes – any item he had given me. I thinned out my wardrobe until there was nothing left to remind me of him. I threw all of my underwear away – they gave me waves of sickening memories every time I put them on. Shopping for new ones, and new jeans, the kind I liked best, and comfortable shoes, gave me a burst of pride. One step further. I sold all his gifts of jewelry to an Armenian diamond dealer, except my wedding ring. I threw that into the lake. It deserved to be forgotten out there deep in the mud. It wasn't worth a dime. It wasn't even pretty, and it irritated my finger. When I loved him, that had not bothered me; it was just another little sacrifice I could make for the sake of our "perfect" relationship, but for the entire last year with him, I'd fiddled with it constantly. A sign of my discontent.

I held a little ceremony before tossing the ring into the water. I took it off my finger, then slipped on a topaz ring I wore before I met Cedric. Before Cedric: B.C. I threw it as far as I could, and with a huge sigh, I said aloud, "Everything is going to change now. I am going to recover all that is beautiful, pure, and innocent." I repeated it again and again, hoping to make it come true, like it did for Dorothy.

That night in bed, I promised myself I would respect myself again, and never fall into the hands of a man like that again. After all, my own family abandoned me because of that heartless villain. But should I consider myself a victim? Wasn't it a sin to bear false witness, to have lied to myself when I knew the truth? Should I feel guilty? Help me, God.

After a good cry, I started thinking more clearly. To move forward, I needed to understand Cedric's specific pathology. What mental illness was he hiding? He had more than enough abnormal behaviors to warrant psychiatric treatment.

I had an appointment with Dr. Thyssen the following day, so at the end of our session, I asked her what was wrong with Cedric.

"I only met him once, after he sent me that letter I showed you," she responded. "He's the type of person who would never go see a therapist. He's not interested in his own weaknesses. He prefers ferreting out the weaknesses of others and exploiting them, to make them suffer."

She seemed to mull something over for a moment, then she said, "I think you should do some research on narcissistic perverts. I won't say more, as we can talk about it later. See you next week, Chloe."

Narcissistic pervert. Finally, a diagnosis. Words to describe him, to understand him. I followed her advice and typed "narcissistic pervert" on Google, and what I read startled me – the scientific description of a narcissistic pervert matched Cedric Moreau to the letter. My husband, the matador stripped of his brilliant suit. All his tricks and talent at dealing out pain, drawing out death for as long as he could, to keep the excitement up, the tension taut. Cedric the narcissistic pervert turned everything good to his favor and made everything bad my fault. And how capricious he was! All those times he screamed, shouted, flew into a rage at nothing...then followed it up with caresses, compliments and praise. He believed he was invincible, just like one of those matadors fighting in some arena in the Spanish countryside.

I'd never met anyone like him, so I was fooled, not recognizing that he did nothing but lie, that he had no deep feelings, that he was incapable of truly loving, that his fine words were forgotten once they left his mouth. Now I finally understood his nature, but how would I get away from him for good? How to prove to others who he really was, without seeming crazy myself? How to keep it from him that I'd finally discovered what he really was? Like matadors, narcissistic perverts can deftly deliver a fatal blow, and they will do it carefully to save their own precious skin. Would it end with my death? His death? I was no longer living under his roof, but I couldn't avoid the threat hanging over me.

Don't think about revenge, Cedric. Be careful, the bull knows you now and is watchful. Aim well if you must, because you might miss.

Months passed and still he crowded my thoughts, keeping me from becoming a normal woman. I closed myself up in a shell, sweet and bitter at the same time; that was the name of my perfume. No one could bring me a happiness cure. I was on my own and starting from zero, no, not even zero, more like negative 100. I was testing my strength. I needed to establish new connections. I wasn't a complete stranger to Geneva, and some people knew me as coming from a respected family, but I avoided anyone who only knew me as Cedric's wife. Not a great association.

He didn't waste any time ruining my reputation, either. The gossip came to my ears.

"The doctors said it would be better for her to spend a few months in a psychiatric ward."

"Her father disowned her."

"She's the one who lured him into her shocking, perverted world. It was all her – he wanted nothing to do with all that."

"Anyway, she'll never be happy."

"He gave her that apartment. She took more than half a million from him in the divorce."

"She'll be back on drugs now that he's no longer in her life. She'll never find anyone better for her than Cedric was. He took such good care of her!"

People passed along all his lies, then moved on to the next juicy topic. I tried to ignore it and focus on building my life, adapting and finding new meaning to it. A period of transition set in, marked by moments of hopefulness and buoyancy, but mostly periodic depression and loneliness. Then came the anger, at him, at myself. Anger at his cruelty, anger at my inability, for five whole years, to fight him or stick up for myself. Anger at knowing he'd quickly moved on without the slightest scar, while I was still in complete disarray. And the disgust! I was disgusted with myself, tortured by the images that kept me up night after night.

Eventually, I preferred being alone all the time. No one invading my space, no one looking at me with questioning eyes. Especially, no one wanting to enter my body while I slept. My body had been used as an object for so long, it had to re-build itself, find its simple human shape and connect its hormones and emotions and natural processes. I'd been shaken in every way, and I didn't want anything touching my skin while I lay sleeping. For a long time, I couldn't even imagine giving my body to another man. I didn't look at men, and they seemed to pick up on my abhorrence, because they didn't approach me. Eventually, I realized that if I ever made love again, it would be slow and careful, without a single violating gesture. Just a caress, only a caress. Two bodies nestled, comfortable and comforting, and not a single word. Too many words had killed me. I didn't need a man to tell me lies, saying he loved me, but simply to take me into his arms.

I recovered my looks thanks to my freedom and the rest it brought with it. I was eating better, meditating, exercising, and the damage inflicted during that sad time nearly vanished. Relief from the terrible stress improved my skin tone, my face softened, and my eyes, instead of being red and glowering from so much violence, grew as bright as they used to be, before Cedric. Whenever I caught myself saying "B.C." it always made me smile. It was a harmless bit of revenge, and if I could joke about it, he truly was becoming part of the past.

Over the course of more months, I stopped dwelling on my marriage, stopped looking around constantly whenever I left my apartment, and I started walking with my head high.

Sometimes, late at night or on a dull, rainy day, this promise of an exciting future troubled me. I doubted it was actually happening, or that I deserved this newfound freedom. My very life troubled me. When these black moods settled on me for too long, I went to see my therapist, where I cried, trying not to feel ashamed. And one day, I finally shared what I'd experienced during those last few months with Cedric. The words spilled out, overflowed, along with my tears and emotions. I told her all the things he did, all, and then I reached back, and recounted all he'd made me do over the years. Getting out all those horrors helped me start re-building my world. This time, I really was at a new beginning, and I vowed not to repeat the same stupid mistakes.

I would talk to my monster late at night, in my deep thoughts, saying these words:

THIS IS BULLSHIT, NOT A LOVE STORY

You can't touch me. You don't haunt me anymore. You no longer wake me up at two in the morning. You have no more power over me. You might have ruined me for life, but you did not kill me.

I was learning to love myself, finally, and my soul and I were speaking to each other again.

Lidia:
The Art of the Bullfight

The last act of the Lidia, the corrida de toros in its entirety. Finally, the putting to death. The matador holds his red cape unfurled in his left hand, and his sword in his right hand. To kill the beast, he can mesmerize it with his skill and wait for it to stop moving, then leap at it and sever the aorta, or he can force the fight by tapping his foot, waving his cape and waiting for the bull to charge, or the two adversaries can confront each other in the center of the arena – so many ways, but the thrill is in the mastery of the bull.

I'm a narcissistic pervert.

I'll always be a young matador, always on the lookout for another bull to fight. Ah, yes, here comes a bull that's never seen a fight. Oh, my beautiful Lidia, my corrida, my bullfight, please, don't ever change!

I'm a narcissistic pervert. Concrete walls, steel door forever locked, I'm locking you into your deep darkness. I remove you from all that's good, without hurting you. I'm taking you straight to hell, to a place where absolute perversion is really nothing but slight madness. You'll live there in permanent paranoia, and I pride myself on this, as I'm the one who's made you this way. Double locked, key thrown away, you can save yourself only by pure miracle. I'll be at you from all sides, and never leave you time or opportunity to escape the arena and find your freedom!

I'm not sick! Read these words carefully: I'm not sick. I'm a monster, the worst human being God ever created. Fuck you, anorexia, fuck you, schizophrenia, fuck you, borderline personality disorder – and all those other fancy mental illnesses that line the pockets of the psychiatrists. You're all idiots. I'm the only one who knows the perfection of my vices. I'll hide inside my Suit of Light, and you'll never find me; in fact, I won't deny it – I like my game of hide and seek. You can take your emotions and shove 'em. If a tear rolls down my cheek, it's only to soften you up, and if I sigh and act sad, it's to lure you in. If I whisper "I love you" in your ear, it's because I want to fuck you. Preferably from behind, because then I don't have to see your face. My own pleasure is paramount, and you're simply the object that gets me there. Sexual perversion? No, that vice falls to you. You're the twisted bitch; I'm the saint, and all Holy Men dream of fucking whores – everyone knows that. That's why I'll marry you. I'll make my way on my own terms, no hurdles, no detours and no remorse, and I'll leave the dead in my wake.

The Matador never dies.

About the Author

Meet author Nicole Kranz, free-spirited citizen of the globe, indefatigable traveler and self-made woman. Born in Brazil, she grew up in Switzerland, then lived in Rio, New York, Paris and many other places before settling down in Lisbon. Nicole speaks five languages and makes use of them in her work as a journalist, communications specialist and life coach. Writing fiction novels is her primary pursuit, however, and in the four books she has written so far, Kranz painstakingly portrays the truth of this world we live in – its raw beauty, its depravity, but also its glory.

Read more at www.nicolekranz.com.

www.ingramcontent.com/pod-product-compliance
Lightning Source LLC
Chambersburg PA
CBHW022041240626
47154CB00007B/2517